ALSO BY KATE MCMURRAY

Whitman Street Cat Café Series
Like Cats and Dogs
What the Cat Dragged in
Chasing Your Tail

CHASING YOUR TAIL

Kate McMurray

sourcebooks
casablanca

For all the pet parents.

Published by Sourcebooks Casablanca, an imprint of Sourcebooks
P.O. Box 4410, Naperville, Illinois 60567-4410
(630) 961-3900
sourcebooks.com

Cataloging in Publication Data is on file with the Library of Congress.

Printed and bound in Canada.
MPB 10 9 8 7 6 5 4 3 2 1

CHAPTER 1

LINDSAY SOMERS SHOULD HAVE KNOWN she was about to be betrayed.

Lauren Fitch, one of her closest friends of almost ten years, sat across from her at Pop, their favorite bar, and said, "Okay, please don't hate me."

Lindsay narrowed her eyes. "What did you do?"

"So you know how I've been wanting to hire a pastry chef for the café?" Lauren was the manager of a Brooklyn-based cat café, not coincidentally just up Whitman Street from Pop.

"You didn't," said Lindsay.

"We interviewed five candidates and ate copiously of the sample stuff they made us. And the best candidate not only made delicious pastries for humans to eat, but also baked cat treats that went over so well that the cats followed him around for the rest of the interview as if they were trying to get their next fix."

"Just say it."

"Diane made the final decision, not me. In my defense."

"It's Brad. I can already tell it's Brad. Just say, 'Hi, Lindsay, we hired your ex-boyfriend to work at the cat café.'"

"Hi, Lindsay, we hired your ex-boyfriend to work at the cat café."

Lindsay groaned and pressed her forehead to the table. "Of course you did."

"He was the best candidate by a mile."

Lindsay groaned again and picked up her head. "I'm sure he was. Which begs the question of why he was auditioning to work at a cat café. No offense."

Lauren grinned. "None taken. He said he'd only ever worked under other people. He wanted creative control over the menu, and I was happy to give it to him."

"You do know that he cheated on me."

"Yes, and I hope he rots in hell for it, but that doesn't affect his baking. The frosting on his cupcakes is... Oh, there are no words. Like eating whipped magic."

Lindsay knew she was scrunching up her face, but she couldn't help it. Brad was still a sore spot. Sure, the man could bake—and he could heat up the sheets, too—but that didn't make him any less of an immature douchebag. And now he'd be working at the cat café? Just having him in the same city was bad enough, but knowing he'd be in a location where Lindsay would be likely to run into him... How could Lauren have done such a thing?

Evan walked into the bar with his boyfriend, Will, and they slid into seats at the table. He looked back and forth between Lindsay and Lauren and narrowed his eyes before realization came over his face.

"You told her!" said Evan.

"I'm not speaking to Lauren anymore," said Lindsay, crossing her arms in a way she hoped would come off as theatrical. She *was* mad, but she was trying not to let on how much this bothered her.

"Ah, handling the news with the grace and aplomb we expected of you," said Evan.

"What's going on?" asked Will.

"Brad Marks, the new pastry chef at the café, used to date Lindsay," said Evan with a smirk. "Their relationship did not end on good terms, and now Lindsay and Brad are sworn enemies."

"I don't know if Brad knows that," said Lauren. "He asked how you were."

"What did you tell him?"

"That you were doing well. That you're writing about food."

"Oh, great." This was such a nightmare. "So now he knows I write about food instead of making it."

"I mean, he could google you to get that information," said Lauren, glancing at Evan and looking alarmed. "I didn't know it was a state secret."

"It's just so humiliating. I went to culinary school with him. And now he knows I couldn't cut it as a chef."

"I couldn't either," said Will, who worked as a cookbook editor. "But we still work in the industry. We're just showing off our expertise in different ways."

"And you write for one of the most-read food websites in New York," said Evan.

That was true, although writing restaurant reviews for two cents a word was no way to get rich. She'd been supplementing her income with other freelance writing, but the truth was, she loved writing about food. Her culinary degree gave her an expertise few other food writers had, and she loved being able to apply that expertise to finding new ways to talk about food. Anyone could write a review of a steak house by talking about how good the food tasted, but Lindsay liked to take in the atmosphere and think critically about how the dishes were put together. Hell, she loved food, loved cooking, loved making elaborate meals for her friends. She hadn't done much of that lately because she'd been working so much to make ends meet. She sighed and picked up her phone, pretending to read her email while her friends teased her.

She mentally shoved Brad aside while conversation around her drifted toward something else. She focused on her phone while Evan told some story about something that happened at work that she half listened to. She knew she was being rude, but she had to recalibrate and try not to think too hard about what Brad working for Lauren would mean. Then an interesting email snagged her attention. It was from her editor at the food website. "Oh my god."

"What?" asked Lauren.

"You will never guess what's opening in the old Star Café space." The Star Café was a coffee shop that had been across the street from the Whitman Street Cat Café. It closed a couple of years ago when a real estate developer bought the building. Since then, the first floor of the building had been occupied from such a long series of failed businesses that everyone on the block was starting to think the space was cursed. There'd been a shop owned by a national chain clothing store that had gone out of business, a fast-food taco place, a stationery store, and even a retail store for a cellular phone company, and none of them had lasted more than three months.

Evan leaned forward. "It's a restaurant, right? It looks like a restaurant. I walked by there on my way here."

"Not just any restaurant. This one is owned by one of the singers from the Bayside Boys."

"Ooh, which one?"

"Little Joey Maguire."

Evan laughed. "I had such a crush on him when I was twelve. Joey was the dreamiest."

Will elbowed him.

"Which one is Joey?" asked Lauren. "The one with curly hair or the one with the tattoos?"

"Curly hair," said Evan and Lindsay in unison.

"I know you were going through your disaffected tween stage when the Bayside Boys were popular," said Evan, "but they were *everywhere* in the early aughts. Surely you know their names. And Joey's had a decent solo career. Remember that song 'Love like a River'?"

Lauren shrugged. "Sure."

"You don't. Philistine."

"Anyway," said Lindsay. "This email from my boss says he's from Georgia originally, so he's 'going back to his roots' and invested in this restaurant that is supposed to be refined soul food, whatever that means."

"Fried chicken, but make it fashion," Evan suggested.

"Anyway, they want me to review it next week."

"You *have* to let me come with you," said Evan. "Will Joey be there? Can I meet him? Do you think he would sign a napkin? Or my body? Oh my god, I would die."

"I'm sitting right here," said Will.

"Yes, but sweetie, it's Joey Maguire. I mean, if you had an opportunity to meet someone from your celebrity cheat list, I would let you."

"Joey Maguire's on your celebrity cheat list?" asked Lindsay.

"Of course. And you have nothing to worry about, Will. He's in a very dramatic relationship with that blond actress with weird eyebrows from that CW show you like. But I can at least try to get a selfie with him. After he signs something on me."

Will narrowed his eyes. "Nothing below the belt."

Evan laughed and kissed Will on the cheek. "I'll be an angel, I swear." He turned back to Lindsay. "I can come, right?"

"Oh, all right." Lindsay was pretty excited about the—unlikely—possibility of meeting Joey Maguire, too. He'd starred in a lot of her teenage fantasies as well. Usually, these celebrity restaurateurs were pretty hands off, but maybe he'd show up for the opening week. "I'll make a reservation for all of us," she added.

"Oh, that will be fun!" said Lauren. "A night out, good company, judging food."

It *would* be fun, but Lindsay was clearly still mad because she said, "I love you, Lauren, but you still hired my ex-boyfriend."

"He's only going to be working in the morning. The odds of you ever running into him are really small. And he makes cookies for the cats! None of the other chefs offered that."

Lindsay sighed. Lauren was right; Lindsay rarely ever stopped by the café before midafternoon, so the odds of her running into Brad were low. But not impossible. What if they ran into each other? What would she say when she saw him? What if... She took a deep breath and told herself that Brad's little intrusion into her life would be fine. Right?

———————

"So let me get this straight. You're making pastries. For cats."

Brad understood how silly it sounded. He stared at his friend Aaron and said, "Yes."

"You were a sous-chef at Milk Bar. You got a ton of press for your work at that chocolate place. Your doughnuts were featured on a Food Network show. And you're leaving all that behind to make pastries for cats."

Brad signaled to the bartender that he wanted a refill on his beer. "I am also making pastries for humans, and the café is giving me complete creative control, which I've never had before."

That really had been his motivation. He hadn't realized when he'd applied for the job that the Lauren who managed the café was the same Lauren who'd been close friends with his ex, Lindsay. Lauren had gotten married, so he hadn't recognized the last name in the job ad. But when he'd arrived with his samples, he'd recognized her. They'd only met a handful of times while he and Lindsay were dating, but that whole period of his life was seared into his brain. It was a series of happy memories he didn't want to remember.

Lauren had outlined the parameters of the job: their bread and butter was pastries for the morning coffee crowd, but she wanted some special things for people who came into the café to sit during the day. The cat treats had been his idea. A culinary school buddy worked at a bakery for pets in Park Slope and had given him some recipes that he'd tweaked based on what he'd researched about what cats needed nutritionally and what was poisonous. The chicken-flavored cookies had tasted pretty weird to Brad, but the cats had loved them, and Lauren had loved the idea of offering them to the café's customers.

And, okay, he *had* asked after Lindsay. Once he realized who Lauren was, he wondered if fate had brought him to this cat café. He was embarrassed by the fact that he still thought about Lindsay a lot, even though they'd broken up almost five years ago. He'd been in two other relationships since then. But Lindsay had always been the one he remembered most. She was the one who got away.

"Weird coincidence," Brad said. "The manager at the café is good friends with Lindsay."

"Your Lindsay?"

"Well, she's not my anything, but yeah."

Aaron frowned. "Lindsay doesn't work at the café, does she? Because if this just an elaborate plot to win her back, I'm going to pour my beer on you."

"No, no. It's just a coincidence. The manager said Lindsay's writing for *Eat Out New York* now, which I already knew."

"Wow, really? I read that site, although I never look at the bylines. They actually have pretty decent recipes. Probably nothing for cats, though."

"You're not getting over that anytime soon, are you?"

"I'll let it drop when you let go of Lindsay. She's not coming back, dude."

"Did I say I want her back?"

Aaron shrugged.

"So, yeah, I'm working at a cat café. What's going on with you?"

Aaron grinned. "I'm developing a new show." Aaron worked as a producer at the Food Channel. "It's a half-hour competition show. Three chefs have to work against the clock to make a dish with one wackadoo featured ingredient. We're planning on cuttlefish for the pilot."

"That doesn't seem that weird. *I've* cooked cuttlefish."

"We're kind of leading the viewer into it. Start off with a few episodes with ingredients chefs work with but home cooks generally don't. Cuttlefish, sea urchin, bone marrow. Then we can bring in some ingredients that are only really used in specific cuisines. Gochujang, maybe. Durian. Rocky Mountain oysters. The stinkiest cheese I can find in Chelsea Market. And I saw an episode of the Japanese *Iron Chef* where the chairman's ingredient was fish eyeballs. Wouldn't that be a twist?"

"I'm an adventurous eater, but I don't want to eat fish eyeballs."

"They're a delicacy!"

"Have you eaten them?"

"Once. The texture is *very* weird. And I couldn't get over the fact that I was eating an eyeball."

"See?" Brad shivered involuntarily imagining it.

"We also might do some episodes where we withhold an ingredient. Like, everyone has to make risotto, but you can't use rice."

"That's just mean."

"I had a cauliflower risotto at a restaurant last week that was delicious." Aaron made a chef's kiss motion. "Cauliflower doesn't taste like anything so it sops up sauce like a sponge."

Brad laughed and sipped his beer.

"You could do the show," said Aaron.

"Hardly."

"There's a dessert round. Or we could do a special all-pastry episode. But even if not, you're a good savory chef, too."

"Sure, but I don't want to be on TV." Cameras made Brad nervous. When he'd still been working at the chocolate restaurant, he'd been asked to do a short on-camera interview for a feature story on a local morning show, and it was like all the words he knew had fallen out of his head. He'd said "well, so" about a hundred times. He worried he'd go on Aaron's show and forget what salt was.

"Just think about it. You'd be great. And you won't have to talk very much, if that's what you're worried about."

"I'll think about it. *If* the focus is on pastry."

Brad liked the world of pastry a lot more than he liked savory cooking. No one would ever ask him to use cuttlefish or fish eyeballs in a cupcake. The stinky cheese was giving him ideas, though.

And, see, this was why he wanted creative control. If he wanted to see what happened if he put Brie or Gorgonzola or Limburger in cake frosting, he should be able try it. But since he was making cookies for cats, too, he'd need access to all kinds of weird ingredients he never worked with—fish, liver, beef stock.

More than anything, he liked the challenge. Breakfast pastries like muffins and danishes were no problem. He could make a batch of scones in his sleep. It was everything else that came with this job that had piqued Brad's interest. Aaron just couldn't appreciate what a weird opportunity this was.

And, well, if he got to see Lindsay again, that was a bonus. He knew full well that she hated his guts, but he wanted to show her he was not the man she thought he was, that he'd grown up in the time they'd been apart. Would she come by the café when he was working? Would she even speak to him? He wasn't sure, but it was worth a shot.

He would have taken the job even if his ex's friend wasn't involved, but he couldn't help but think that he'd been handed an opportunity. That this was exactly where he was supposed to be at this point in his life.

He'd never been with anyone he clicked with so well, that he could talk to about anything, that understood his job and why he loved it so much. And, well, she'd lingered in his head, in his heart, long after she'd walked out of his life. If the universe was putting him in Lindsay's orbit, then he intended to do what he could to show her what she'd walked out on.

"Well," said Aaron. "Let's toast to new adventures."

"I suspect both of us are about to experience a lot of those." Brad clinked his glass against Aaron's.

CHAPTER 2

THE TIME TO MAKE THE doughnuts was five in the morning, but Brad was used to a baker's schedule. His new boss, Lauren, clearly wasn't; she yawned as she let him into the café on his first day of work.

"I'm getting you your own key," she mumbled. "Just as soon as I have coffee."

She led him through the café. The main door opened into a vestibule with another heavy glass door, a safeguard against cats trying to escape, although Lauren had told Brad during his interview that they'd never had an instance of that. That second door led to the main café area, where there were a counter, a glass display case for pastries, and the requisite coffee and espresso machines on the back wall. A huge menu hung over the counter. One corner had a display of T-shirts with the cat café's logo and punny phrases like, "Spent a purr-fect day at the Whitman Street Cat Café!" and "Cats are paw-some!" A couple of café tables sat near the counter for those who just wanted coffee and not to sit with the cats, a necessity created by a few other coffee shops closing in the neighborhood recently.

Behind that, there were two doors. One led to what Lauren called the cat room, a sumptuous space with big sofas and several more café tables and chairs. The café kept fifteen to twenty cats there at any given time, and customers could lounge there and hang out with those cats. Lauren had told Brad during the interview that the café was mostly a pretense for the space to operate like a shelter, finding forever homes for the café's feline residents. The café periodically hosted adoption events and then rotated in cats from local shelters.

Lauren had also explained that the other door off the counter area was new. A wall had been added to the cat room to create a hallway that led between the café counter and the kitchen. This space had been an Italian restaurant before it was a cat café, she told Brad, and the full restaurant kitchen in the very back was now Brad's to use how he saw fit.

The hall between the café counter and the kitchen was very narrow, only really wide enough for an average-size man to walk through. Its purpose was to provide a cat-free area to bring food from the back to the counter in the front.

This was going to be a very interesting place to work.

Brad had looked at the kitchen during his interview but hadn't felt like he could make recommendations before he had the job. He looked a little more closely now. The kitchen had been cleaned to a shine, the stainless-steel appliances sparkling in the lights as Lauren flipped the switches near the door.

The kitchen was really designed for savory cooking, but there were four ovens, and that was a good start. Lauren led him to the pantry, which was stocked with all the ingredients he'd requested after she'd hired him. In his bag, Brad had a notebook with recipes he'd been developing in the week since he'd been hired, all things he'd tested at home.

"I'll leave you to it," said Lauren. "I'm gonna go see if I have enough mental power to make the coffee maker work. If I'm successful, do you want a cup?"

"Sure."

"You'd think after eight months with an infant who wakes up at all hours of the night that I'd be used to being awake at five, but you'd be wrong."

"This time of the morning is tough if you're not used to it."

Lauren nodded and left.

Brad got down to business. The café was still bringing in bagels from a bagel shop a few blocks away, but everything else was up to him. He figured he'd start with the human food. His first order of business was muffins, of which he planned to make four kinds: blueberry, chocolate chip, carrot, and lemon poppyseed. He figured he could change those up depending on what was popular.

His idea for the midday crew was to provide a few types of bread that could be used for premade sandwiches. So once the muffins were baking, he planned to start sandwich rolls, and while that dough was chilling, he'd make a brioche.

Lauren brought him a cup of coffee in a mug stamped with the café's logo while he was getting the second batch of muffins ready to slide into an oven.

"It already smells amazing in here," she said, cradling her own cup. "This was such a good idea."

Brad laughed. "Once all the human food is baking, I'll get

started on the cat treats. I tried a few on my friend's cat. The tuna treats were a huge hit."

"You know, if you need a cat in your home to taste test those treats, I've got a few candidates."

"I don't need a cat." He really didn't. He wasn't home much, for one thing. Plus, and not that this even mattered, he could hear his father's voice asking what sort of straight man had cats. Weren't the cupcakes girlie enough? He swallowed a sigh.

"You say you don't need a cat, but... Come with me."

They had to go back down the narrow hall to the counter in order to enter the cat room. They were greeted by mews and indifference. A chubby, striped cat trotted over and sniffed Brad's pants. She gave a little *brrrup* and rubbed against Brad's leg, her tail snaking around Brad's calf.

"That's Sadie," said Lauren, pointing to the cat at Brad's feet. "She's the office manager here. She's a permanent cat at the café. I sometimes let her up front after hours. Don't tell the health department."

Brad chuckled.

"The rest of these cats are up for adoption. Look at this fellow over here." She ran her hand over a cat who was sitting on a table. The cat was the color of apricot jam. He leaned into Lauren's hand as she pet him. "This guy is named Hamilton."

"That's a mouthful of a name for a cat."

"Paige gave all of the cats in our most recent batch of new residents the names of American historical figures. Her reasoning for this guy was that Alexander Hamilton had auburn hair."

The cats were cute and all, and Brad even *liked* cats. He

wouldn't have bothered applying if he didn't. He just didn't want one in his apartment. He reached over and let Hamilton sniff and then rub against his fingers. "I really don't need a cat."

"Give it time."

"I should get back to the kitchen."

Lauren followed Brad back there. After he checked on everything in the ovens, he said, "We can try the new treats on the cats today."

Lauren grinned. "I custom-ordered some bags to package the treats in. They're over here." She put her coffee cup down and went to the pantry, where she pulled out a box and opened the lid. Inside were brown paper bags with plastic windows, like cookies often came in at the store, and the cat café's logo printed on top. The bags were cute and the perfect thing to hold his baked cat treats.

"Very cool," Brad said.

"Right? I'm so excited about this."

He laughed, appreciating her enthusiasm.

An hour and a half later, Lauren helped him carry trays of baked goods to the display case. The bagels arrived as he was heading back to get another tray of muffins. Once everything for the breakfast rush was in place, he stood back to admire his work.

"Beautiful," said Lauren.

A tall woman walked into the store. Lauren introduced her as Monique, one of the baristas. Brad shook her hand and then said, "Let me know if you get any customer feedback. I can adapt and change out the menu if you think some other items would be more popular."

"Sure," said Monique. "It smells like magic in here."

To Brad, Lauren said, "You met the owner, Diane, at the interview, and she was polite then, but she was reluctant to sign off on having our own baker on-site. We've got that kitchen back there, so why not use it? And I think if we're making our own pastries, that has the potential to expand our customer base, especially during the morning rush. If we're offering one-of-a-kind cat treats that we sell exclusively? I think it'll be a boon."

"I'm happy to help."

"And feel free to experiment. I'm sure your blueberry muffins are delicious, but you can get a blueberry muffin just about anywhere in Brooklyn. If you need any other ingredients, just let me know and I'll see what I can do. Or I can give you some petty cash if you want to hit the farmers market at Cadman Plaza. That's only a few blocks from here."

"Cool. It might be good to do a couple of seasonal items, depending on what's available."

"My thought exactly."

Brad went back to the kitchen a few minutes later, a new wave of excitement rolling through him. Lauren really was giving him almost complete creative control. It was something he'd wanted nearly his entire career. As fun as making other people's food was, he loved creating new recipes. His brain constantly hummed with ideas. What if he put this thing with that thing? How would that cake taste if he added cardamom? What fruits would taste best together in a tart?

His last job had been at a chocolate-themed restaurant, where even the entrées had chocolate in them, and he'd been responsible for the dessert menu. But the executive chef there was a control freak. He'd let Brad design a couple of desserts but had offered opinions freely, constantly asked Brad to tweak the menu, and insisted a number of items Brad was not that excited about were served every night.

Brad thought about his conversation with Aaron as he took the sandwich rolls out of the oven. Yeah, he was about to make treats for cats. But it was the most exciting, creative work he'd ever done, and Lauren was letting him run with the planned menu. In a lot of ways, this was the best job he'd had. And he'd only been at it a few hours.

The new restaurant was called Pepper. Lindsay couldn't figure out what that had to do with anything, beyond that the decor felt like the inside of a pepper shaker. Everything was shades of black and gray with occasional pops of color. The chairs in the main dining room were upholstered in the color of pink peppercorns, for example. Vintage salt and pepper shakers were positioned on shelves around the space, and most of the art on the walls was still-life paintings that featured salt and/or pepper shakers and mills prominently.

"This is already trying very hard," said Lindsay's friend Paige right after they were seated.

Lindsay had invited Lauren, Paige, and Evan for a night without their significant others. She'd been hoping for a night of good food, but she felt the odds of that were declining the longer they sat in the restaurant. The waitstaff still had that new-restaurant smell on them, and service was a little slow and confused. A waiter brought them all menus after they'd been sitting for about five minutes—the leather cover had an imprint of a pepper grinder on it, of course—and Lindsay looked it over.

She didn't know what pepper had to do with soul food, but the menu was heavy on soul-food staples: fried chicken, collard greens, okra, mac and cheese. Except everything was pretentious. Chicken breaded in the chef's unique twelve-spice blend, for example, or the "five-cheese cavatappi," which sure sounded like mac and cheese to Lindsay. She didn't mind a twist on an old staple, but taking food that should be a little rough around the edges and served in restaurants with plastic tablecloths was probably not the way to go.

The best soul food Lindsay had ever had come from a place in Brooklyn run by a family from Georgia that served heaping portions on paper plates. The food was tasty, affordable, and made by a pair of sisters who clearly loved what they did. Best fried chicken in Brooklyn, as far as Lindsay was concerned. *That* was soul food. This was…something else.

Her friends looked equally baffled.

"Okay, here's how I want to do this," said Lindsay. "Everyone order something different so we can each try everything."

"I want to try the chicken and waffles," said Evan. "But I have some concerns."

They had all agreed what they'd order by the time the waitress came back. They all ordered cocktails, too. Lindsay had ordered something called Peachtree Punch that tasted suspiciously like vodka and Kool-Aid. Who the heck had designed this restaurant? It was somehow cheap and pretentious at the same time.

"So how is everyone?" Paige asked when they'd settled into their cocktails. "Did you all behave while Josh and I were on vacation?"

"Lauren didn't," said Evan.

Lauren slapped Evan's arm.

"What happened?" asked Paige.

"She hired Brad," said Lindsay.

Paige laughed. "Oh, I already knew that. She texted me when it happened."

"And I'll have you know, I did agonize over this hiring decision," said Lauren. "Diane took the final decision out of my hands, but Brad really was the best candidate. And I'm happy to have the extra help at the café, especially while Paige was out of town. Well, running the café at all was hard with Paige out of town. Last week was rough. But now Caleb is home with the baby and I am having a night out with my friends and I am going to enjoy it, dammit, because I deserve it." She took a sip of her cocktail. "Hoo, boy. That's a lot of rum."

"The bartender has a strong pour," said Evan. "And Joey Maguire isn't even here, is he?"

"Doesn't look like it," said Lindsay. She'd spotted his name in very tiny print on the menu, like even he was already on the way to disowning this place. Likely Maguire was just an investor and didn't have much say in the menu.

When their food arrived twenty minutes later, it at least looked good. Everyone started digging in, but by the looks on her friends' faces, everyone was noticing the same things she was.

"I don't think any of the twelve spices was salt," Evan said as he held a fried chicken leg. "Or an actual spice."

Lindsay ate a forkful of the five-cheese cavatappi. In theory, it was hard to go wrong with cheese and pasta, and yet it was dry and kind of flavorless. Was one of the cheeses the cardboard box this came out of?

Everyone around the table agreed. For a restaurant called Pepper, all the food was pretty bland.

"I mean, it's not the worst meal I've ever had," said Lauren, reaching for the salt shaker on the table.

"Oh, I know mine!" said Evan. "My friend Lester threw a dinner party one year where he let his boyfriend do all the cooking, and everything came out charred. That was an experience."

"Never order from Mr. Szechuan on Tuesdays," said Lauren. "That's the regular chef's night off."

"It's called Mr. Szechuan? Really?" said Lindsay.

"What? It's really good! Best Chinese food on Whitman Street. Except on Tuesdays."

"I got food poisoning from that sushi place on Flatbush, near where Evan lives," said Lindsay, playing along. "So that was not great."

"Ooh, yeah," said Evan. "I walked by that place recently. The health department gave them a C."

"I didn't know restaurants could get Cs. I've only ever seen As and Bs," said Lauren. "The café has an A, by the way."

"Oh, the sushi place deserved that C," said Lindsay. "I couldn't eat sushi for like three months after that. And it's a shame because I love sushi, and that place is convenient."

"All this talk of bad meals is kind of making this meal even worse," said Lauren.

Everyone sampled from everyone else's dishes and agreed the food was bland, the okra was slimy, the corn muffins were too sweet, and the "maple butter sauce" that came with Evan's chicken and waffles seemed like butter melted into pancake syrup—the cheap kind from the grocery store, not real maple syrup.

Lindsay didn't want the restaurant staff to know she was a critic, so she tapped out notes on her phone as discreetly as possible. The review would be scathing, but this place deserved it.

She didn't relish giving negative reviews. She loved eating a great meal and finding ways to celebrate it in her writing. She loved coming up with the perfect words to describe how something tasted, so her readers could taste it along with her. She wanted to lure customers to these restaurants, because she wanted good restaurants to stay open. But this was not good. Everything here said *amateur* to Lindsay.

"This space is cursed, for sure," Lauren said as she looked at the dessert menu. "Why is everything so extra? Is the devilish surprise in the devil's food cake something spicy?"

"Based on dinner," said Evan, "probably not."

CHAPTER 3

.

LINDSAY WOKE UP THE DAY after her review of Pepper went live to a phone full of notifications.

It took her a minute to figure out what was happening, but it seemed that the review was starting to go viral.

She couldn't immediately figure out why. She'd written negative restaurant reviews before. She'd written jokey reviews of high-profile restaurants. Her takedown of a popular steak house in Williamsburg was a perennial favorite, for example, but it hadn't gotten much traction outside of foodie communities. Just a year ago, a celebrity chef had opened a new restaurant in Park Slope that Lindsay had panned because everything she'd ordered had been dry and overcooked. That restaurant had since closed because Lindsay had been correct, but if more than a hundred people read that review, Lindsay would have died of shock.

Maybe it was just who happened to log into the internet on any given day. Still, somehow, Lindsay's article was getting a ton of buzz on social media.

Joey Maguire has put his name on a remarkable restaurant in

Brooklyn, Lindsay had written. *It is remarkable mostly because the restaurant is called Pepper, and yet it serves food that contains none. There didn't seem to be much salt, either. This is Cooking 101, is it not? Or maybe it's some kind of hipster irony to go with the rapidly gentrifying neighborhood around it. Because it certainly wasn't good food.*

She'd then spent the next eight hundred words tearing into the restaurant for being bland and uninspired and kind of silly.

And people were eating it up.

A thrill went through Lindsay. Criticizing steak houses many considered New York institutions was one thing. Lindsay wrote for an online magazine that didn't have much of an audience outside of the New York metropolitan area. Making fun of a restaurant owned by a celebrity with a huge fan base apparently had a more national appeal.

She showered and got dressed, and when she looked at her phone again, it was still blowing up. Not all of it was positive. Joey Maguire fans were starting to come after her. Maguire himself had been out of the public eye for a little bit as his solo career floundered, but fifteen years ago, he and the Bayside Boys had been everywhere, their songs in constant rotation on radios, and he still had passionate fans. A lot of the negative comments were angry, misspelled nonsense, but a few people told her to go to hell or worse. Lindsay wasn't very bothered by the comments, even the ugly ones, because the vast majority of the buzz was positive, congratulating her for landing so many punches against a restaurant that a lot of other critics had agreed was not great.

Then her boss called.

For the first time, Lindsay worried suddenly that she might be in trouble. What the public thought was one thing, but what the corporate owners of *Eat Out New York* thought was something else. The review had gone through two editors before it was posted and no one objected, but if Joey Maguire or someone else associated with the restaurant had called to complain to the higher-ups, Lindsay's job could be in jeopardy. She'd never held herself back in her writing, but maybe she should have here. There was no shortage of food writers in New York willing to be more politic who would happily take Lindsay's job. She answered her phone reluctantly, but started cooking up a defense as she did.

"The good news," said Dawn, the editor in chief of *Eat Out New York*, "is that Joey Maguire called me himself and has a good sense of humor about it. He said that their reservations are through the roof, although I think that's probably because people want to see this mess for themselves. In the meantime, he wanted to issue an official comment that he's making some changes at the restaurant."

"That's wild."

"You probably did him a favor."

"Well, that's a relief. I worried for a second that you were calling to fire me."

"Nope. This was great for both you and the website. Page views are hitting some kind of new record. Congratulations, Lindsay. You've gone viral."

Lindsay worked from home, so now that she was dressed and ready for the day, she didn't really have anywhere to go. She sat down at her desk with her notes from an interview she'd conducted with a Brooklyn-based chef who was fresh off his win on a popular competition reality show. She turned off her phone so that she could focus on finishing the story. Once she sent it in, she turned her phone back on. Three seconds after it powered on, it rang.

After Lindsay answered, the caller said, "I'm Erica Sanchez. I'm a features editor at the *New York Forum*."

"Hi," Lindsay said, wondering what this was about. The *Forum* was one of the last weekly newspapers still standing in New York. They kept their print edition afloat by building a huge audience for their website, where, in addition to running a digital version of the paper, they had several blogs about pop culture, food, fashion, and politics.

"I saw your review of Pepper this morning," said Erica. "But I've actually been following you for a little while. That review you wrote last year about that Florent in Midtown?"

"Still the best filet mignon I've ever had. You could cut it with a fork, it was so tender."

"Yeah, that was a great review. Very visceral. I could almost taste the steak as I read."

"Thank you, I appreciate that."

"I'll cut to the chase. The *Forum* has been on the hunt for a new food editor after Frank left us a few weeks ago."

Lindsay's heart pounded. Frank McElroy was a legend in the food world, one of the best-known restaurant reviewers and food writers in the country. He was also in his seventies and had just retired.

"Are you interested? Responsibilities would include writing reviews and other food-related articles as well as assigning articles to some of our other food writers and interns. Some other things, too. But what do you say?"

This would be a huge step up for her. All because she'd made fun of a restaurant owned by a celebrity. But still, this was the kind of break she'd been hoping for the last few years as she'd transitioned away from being a line cook after culinary school to being a food writer. Dawn had been a great boss, but this was too good an opportunity to pass up.

"I'm very interested," said Lindsay.

"Wonderful! Let's meet to talk about it. Are you free for lunch today?"

A few hours later, Lindsay had been officially offered the job as food editor at the *New York Forum*. In exchange for a salary and benefits, something she hadn't had in a few years, she had to show up in the office a few days a week, but this job was everything she'd been wanting. Someone was going to pay her a good salary to write about food, and she would manage a small group of writers.

As she walked to the subway from her lunch with Erica Sanchez, she called Lauren. After explaining what happened, she said, "We're getting drinks tonight. Bring the baby if you have to. I'm celebrating."

Lauren laughed. "I think I can get Caleb to watch Hannah. What is a husband for if not to watch the baby when your friend got amazing news? And I want to celebrate, too."

"Why?"

"Okay, don't hate me. But Brad is doing a great job. We've sold out of his pastries every day since he started here, and we're starting to sell his cat treats, too. We totally sold out of those yesterday."

"I still can't get over that he's making cat treats."

"I know you hate him, but he's a great baker."

"Right. We'll be discussing that later."

"And also scum on an old bathtub."

Lauren laughed, but Lindsay wasn't kidding. Brad was the villain of her story.

They made plans to get drinks at Pop with the regular crew that night, and Lindsay got off the phone and ran down the steps to the subway. She was not going to let Brad ruin her amazing day.

―――――――

"Was that Lindsay?" Brad asked when Lauren got off the phone.

One of the regular baristas had called in sick, so he was helping out at the counter after all of his baking was done for the day. He didn't mind and actually quite liked talking to customers. They were in the midafternoon slump at the café, the weekday dead time after lunch but before the evening crowd, so Brad had been busying himself rearranging his pastries in the display case. He'd made cupcakes today that he'd decorated with frosting to look like cat faces, and those had proven to be quite popular.

"It was Lindsay," said Lauren ruefully. "She's still mad, by the way."

"I figured. I feel like maybe I should call her. Clear the air."

"Yeah. I mean, she hates your guts, so I don't see her coming to the cat café as long as you're employed here, so you're probably safe, but just for everyone's peace of mind, it can't hurt to reach out."

Brad sighed. "I have never met a more stubborn woman. She's not going to forgive and forget."

"Oh, I'm aware," said Lauren. "You know why she hates you, right?"

"She thinks I cheated on her. I didn't, by the way, but she dug in her heels and didn't believe me. I can't even deny that what she saw didn't look great, but she just…left. Wouldn't let me try to make amends. Maybe that's what she needed to do, but I also like to think I've grown as a man since then."

"I mean, you seem fine. Although I'm easy. Those cupcakes are amazing. And also, I'm not trying to date you. And she's my friend, so of course I also think you're no better than a piece of gum stuck to a subway platform." She shrugged.

"Fair." Brad picked up a cleaning cloth and wiped down the outside of the display case. He'd been surprised at how nice Lauren was being, but he also appreciated her professional distance, such as it was. This was a chatty workplace, but Lauren never talked about Lindsay unless Brad asked, which he wasn't generally inclined to do. Except, for some reason, talking to Lauren about Lindsay now felt like a lifeline.

"I hope you know, I didn't hire you because of Lindsay. Or despite her. I did it because you were the best pastry chef we interviewed."

"Thanks. I appreciate that."

"Anyway, apparently the review she wrote went viral."

"What review?"

"You have your phone on you?"

"Yeah."

Lauren raised an eyebrow.

Brad pulled out his phone. He'd had it on silent while he was working in the main part of the café, but it was quickly becoming clear that Lauren was pretty loose about that kind of thing if there weren't many customers around. He had a handful of text messages from various friends, most of them referencing Lindsay. One contained a link to a story in *Eat Out New York*, so he clicked on it.

He leaned against the espresso machine and read the article. Lindsay really laid into that new restaurant across the street. Brad knew the chef by reputation only; a buddy of his from culinary school had worked alongside him slinging burgers at some middle-of-the-road tavern in the theater district. Rumor had it this guy was a hack, so it wasn't much of a surprise that the restaurant boasted bland food and sugary cocktails.

The review was clever, too. Lots of wordplay, but also a clear knowledge of food. Lindsay had known her way around the kitchen; that was apparent when they were at culinary school together. She was a great chef. It had always saddened Brad that she'd opted to become a food writer instead. But maybe writing about food was her calling. He barked out a laugh at a particularly funny line. She was good at this. And if this made her happy, then that was great.

Maybe it was arrogant, but he'd sometimes wondered if what had happened between them had made her want to leave the kitchen. But that still wouldn't have been his fault. Would it? And maybe that idea was completely off base if she was turning in articles like this.

"This is a great review," he said to Lauren. "She really let this place have it."

"I was there with her at dinner. The food was just as bad as she says."

"The hipster irony line is good." Brad pocketed his phone. "So Lindsay's still mad at me, eh?"

"Yep." But rather than elaborate, Lauren made a face.

"What?"

"I shouldn't say anything. I mean, I want it to be clear, I'm on Lindsay's side. Sisters before misters."

"Of course. I would expect nothing less."

"But, like, I think it says something that she's still mad at you. Are you mad at her?"

"No, not at all. I'd love to see her again."

Lauren looked at him thoughtfully.

"If I could take back what happened to end our relationship, I would," he said. "Biggest regret of my life."

"All right. I will make a note of that."

Brad laughed. He understood that obviously Lauren's friend came first, but he hadn't been joking when he'd said he'd love to see Lindsay again. He'd been wanting a chance to explain himself for years. He'd thought for a long time that if he could just tell her what really happened, she'd see reason and come back to him.

He didn't hold out much hope that Lindsay would forgive and forget—she really was the most stubborn woman he'd ever met—but maybe they could at least be friends again.

Although when had he become this sappy guy? Well, probably around the time he'd figured out how to make cat faces out of frosting.

Paige came in then to relieve Brad from the counter so he could go home. Once she was set up at the register, he walked through the cat room to get to his locker in the staff lounge in back. That apricot-colored cat eyed him as he walked by, so Brad stopped to pet his head. The cat leaned into Brad's hand and started to purr. This cat had very soft fur and was being very sweet, but there was no way Brad was adopting a cat.

"You can take him home," said Lauren, suddenly behind him.

"I'm just saying hi. I still don't want a cat." No matter how cute he was. The cat purred louder. "I don't even know if my landlord allows cats."

"Most do in this city. I can be very persuasive. Or the cats can be."

"I'm sure."

"Just you wait." She turned to the cat, who was sitting on the table, looking quite smug. "Turn on the charm, Hamilton. Brad will be putty in your hands."

As if he understood, Hamilton looked at Brad with wide eyes. Like a puppy-dog look. Or a kitty-cat look, he supposed. He lifted a paw and tapped Brad's hand.

"Sorry, buddy," said Brad. "I don't have space in my life for a cat. Don't you like this nice place here? You've got lots of friends and...couches to lounge on...and kibble and toys whenever you want them."

Hamilton just stared at Brad with that sad, pleading expression.

"No, really. I'm never home and my apartment isn't that big. I'm not the human you want."

"Uh-huh," said Lauren, sounding like she knew something Brad didn't.

CHAPTER 4

THE *NEW YORK FORUM*'S OFFICES had recently relocated to a larger space, one that took up an entire floor of an office tower in Chelsea. Executive offices lined the perimeter, each with a window, and then the center of the office was an open area with tables and chairs dotted throughout. The regular staff didn't have assigned desks, and most only worked in the office a few days per week. So when Lindsay showed up to work in the office, usually on days when she had assignment meetings, she just claimed a space and worked there on her brand-new, company-issued laptop. It was exciting, albeit a little distracting, to sit in a fairly high-traffic area; it reminded Lindsay of an old-fashioned newsroom where reporters bustled around and chatted with one another about the big events of the day.

It was a great gig. Lindsay loved her job already. Not only was she managing a team and coming up with story ideas, but the bright, colorful office had its own coffee shop and snack bar, and her work space was cheerful and comfortable. Her new coworkers all seemed really great. Erica encouraged her to think outside the box and be creative when pitching stories, and the *Forum* had a much bigger budget than *Eat Out New York*, which opened up some new possibilities. Lindsay had a lot of breathing room here, which felt safer than the constant cycle of pitching and scraping for freelance assignments. Given the decline in print newspapers, she was a little surprised to find the offices so nice and well outfitted. Hopefully this spoke well for her future job security.

On her fifth day working in the office, Erica walked over and said, "I've got an assignment for you."

"For me?"

"Yeah. Buzzy new bakeshop in Brooklyn. I think you're the best writer for the job. You game?"

"Uh, for baked goods? Yes. Anytime."

"Cool. It's not exactly a bakeshop, though. It's a cat café."

Oh no. Lindsay's stomach flopped. She held her breath to keep from commenting because she wanted to be a professional, but she already knew where this was going, and all her walls were going up.

"Apparently," Erica went on, "they've got this hunky new baker working there who is the talk of the neighborhood. My friend Lucy said she was there the other day and met him in person. He's superhot, he makes the best pastries on Whitman Street, and he also makes treats for the cats. Hard to beat that, eh?"

Lindsay didn't know what to do with her face. She nodded slowly as she tried to think of a way out of this assignment without seeming petulant in front of her new boss.

"No? Are cats not your beat?"

"Oh, no. Cats are totally my beat. I have a cat. But, see, my friend Lauren is the manager at that café."

"Perfect! You've got an in!"

"You don't think my review would be biased? That it's not a conflict of interest?"

"I'm not asking you to do a review. I want you to do a profile on this pastry chef. Find out what made him start baking at a cat café and see if he's got any cat-friendly recipes he'd be willing to share in the magazine."

Lindsay nodded. She'd been working here less than two weeks. She wasn't in a position to refuse to cover a story for her boss. She supposed she could have admitted that she used to date this hunky chef, but she didn't feel like she could say that, either. It would make her look dramatic. Wouldn't it?

So she'd have to suck it up and take the story. And she'd have to confront Brad.

But she could be objective. Right?

"All right. I'll call my friend and set it up." She hoped she sounded sufficiently excited about the story.

When Erica went back to her office, Lindsay grabbed her cell phone and went to an empty conference room to call Lauren.

After Lindsay explained the assignment, Lauren said, "This is perfect."

"What? Perfect? What are you talking about?"

"It's great publicity for the café, first of all. Somewhere Paige is having a tiny orgasm because we're able to line this up. An article in the *Forum* will for sure bring in a lot more customers."

Lindsay laughed because that was likely true. One of Paige's main jobs was to bring new people to the café. She mostly did this with events, but she loved good publicity.

"Second, I feel like maybe you and Brad should have a conversation. I'm not saying you have to like him, but I am saying it might make everything easier if you reached some kind of truce."

"Is he there right now?"

"No, he went home for the day. He's usually only here in the mornings, actually. So you should come by, say, tomorrow morning. After the rush. Around eleven, let's say."

"You really think I should talk to him?"

"You're still allowed to hate him. But he's very good at this job, and the customers love him. And, oh my god, he made these cinnamon rolls the other day? So good. Melted in my mouth. I've had dreams about them ever since."

"He's already bribed you with baked goods, hasn't he? Don't do this to me, Lauren. This is going to be hard enough. I need you on my team."

"And I am now and forever Team Lindsay. I'm not gonna fire him, because he's very good for business, but if you need me to kick him in the nuts or something, I'm your woman."

"Okay." Lindsay sighed. She was going to have to face him sooner or later. "Fine. I'll come by in the morning."

"Doesn't have to be at eleven. He usually clocks out around one."

"Understood."

"Good. Cool. I'll save you a cupcake."

Brad decided to hang out in the cat room when he finished baking for the day. He had a book he figured he'd read while he waited for Lindsay to show up, but he was too wound up to read it. A little gray cat with black stripes and a white face hopped up on the table and sniffed the book before lying on it. Then Sadie walked over and tapped his leg with her paw, so he leaned down to pet her.

"You cats are demanding sometimes." Brad eyed the little gray cat, suspecting that sitting on the book was a way to capture his attention.

Sadie did not seem offended, but instead started purring and rubbing against his leg. So now, apparently, it was a contest between these two cats to out-cute each other. The gray cat gave him the cute-kitty eyes and rested her chin on her paw as she gazed up at him. Sadie purred louder. The gray cat lifted her paw as if to say, *Hey, over here.* Sadie flopped onto her side and then showed Brad her belly. Unable to choose, Brad gave both cats little scritches on their heads and then shooed the gray cat off his book so he could go back to pretending to read. The gray cat huffed off, but Sadie kept rubbing on his leg.

Brad sighed and closed his eyes for a moment.

That last time he'd seen Lindsay had been by coincidence at a restaurant opening. He was there because he was friendly with the executive chef, and she was there because she was covering it for *Eat Out New York.* They'd had part of a civil conversation before it dissolved into acrimony.

He of course knew why she was mad. She'd seen him with Phoebe, another friend of theirs from culinary school. Phoebe had been pursuing Brad hard, although Brad hadn't been interested. She'd come on to him one night, Lindsay had walked into the room, and then the relationships between all three of them had imploded. Lindsay had assumed the worst and wouldn't listen to Brad's explanations—he suspected she'd deleted most of his texts and voicemails without reading or listening to them—and that was the end of that.

And while Brad had spent months wishing Lindsay would just talk to him so he could explain, part of him also felt that if she'd been so quick to assume the worst of him, then she'd never known him at all. If she was too stubborn to see the truth, their relationship was doomed anyway.

But, man, what a good run they'd had. Lindsay was gorgeous and funny, and they could talk about food for hours. He loved her dry sense of humor, her creativity, and the way she cared about her friends. They'd had a lot of fun together, both in and out of bed, for just over a year. He hadn't had his life together enough in those days to be contemplating the long term—he'd wanted to wait until he had an established career before making any decisions—but he'd been happy. He'd thought she was happy, too.

She appeared at the door to the cat room looking much as she had the last time he'd seen her. Her dark hair was tied up in a ponytail, and she wore jeans with a button-down shirt and a purple scarf draped around her shoulders. She wasn't wearing her glasses, but he knew they must be nearby. She looked like a journalist. A sexy journalist. He felt hooked right to her, the same way he had been when they first met. His heart pounded as he watched her look around the room and make eye contact with him.

Their whole relationship played out in an instant, images

of them talking or cooking or making love flashing through his mind.

"Hi," he said, pushing that aside. He closed the book he wasn't reading and sat up in his chair to give her his full attention.

The last remaining customer in the room packed up and left. Lindsay waited until she was gone to sit across the table from Brad and say, "Hello."

"Long time, no see."

He smiled. She seemed tense, her whole body compact like a compressed spring.

She eyed him warily. "I assume Lauren told you why I'm here."

"To write a profile on me for the *Forum* on account of my movie-star good looks and my ability to make magic with pastry."

Her face twisted to suppress the smile that leaked out anyway. "I wouldn't go that far," she said.

He shrugged, trying to seem cool, but he felt gratified by that smile.

"I'm surprised, after the gig at Milk Bar, that you'd deign to make cupcakes for the teeming masses at a coffee shop in Brooklyn."

"Is this an interview question?"

Lindsay got a notepad out of her bag. "If you like."

"Don't get me wrong, I loved working at Milk Bar, but I was making someone else's recipes there. It was great as a learning opportunity, but I've been wanting to design my own menu since I graduated from culinary school. This is an opportunity to do that without me having to create my own shop. Lauren is giving me complete creative control. Plus the cat treats are kind of a fun challenge."

He could tell that his cheerful tone—and the canned answer he'd been mentally rehearsing all morning—was bothering her. He knew she wanted to hate him, and he was making that hard for her.

She scribbled something on her pad of paper.

"I'm not your enemy," he whispered.

"Aren't you?"

He grunted. "We can keep this professional if that's what you'd prefer."

She sighed. "This was a mistake. I'll get one of my freelancers to do the interview."

"Do you really hate me so much that you can't even have a simple conversation about my job with me?"

Lindsay looked chagrined.

But Brad was irritated now. He didn't deserve this level of enmity. He'd tried to make things up to her dozens of times, and she'd never even heard him out. He hadn't cheated on her, and she hadn't seen what she thought she had, but she'd never let him explain himself. She'd made some decision about what had happened between them and wasn't willing to back down from it. "You are the most stubborn woman I have ever met," he said.

"Stubborn? *I'm* stubborn?"

"You also hold a grudge longer than anyone I know. We had a good thing going for a while, and it fell apart, and I'm sorry that happened. But it was five years ago. We're both older and wiser now, or at least I am. I'm not asking you for anything more than to sit here without griping while we do this interview for your magazine. I'm surprised that's not what you want."

Lindsay bristled. He'd offended her. Good.

She sat there staring at the table for a long moment. Brad thought she'd calm down and get back to the interview, but instead she shoved her stuff back in her bag and stood up. "I can't do this right now."

"So you're just going to leave?"

"We'll reschedule. Or I'll send another writer. I'm finding this too overwhelming."

Brad didn't think Lindsay knew how telling that admission was. "Come on. I'm sorry. I'll behave."

Lindsay shook her head.

Brad grabbed a stray napkin and the pen Lindsay had left on the table. He scrawled his phone number and then handed her the pen and the napkin. "Text me when you're ready to talk. I promise to limit anything I say to cats and baked goods. But that's my number. It's the same number I've had since before culinary school, but I assume you deleted it from your phone the same day you ritualistically burned all the photos of me after we broke up."

Lindsay snatched the napkin out of his hand. "You don't have to do that."

"Do what? Give you my number?"

"No. I meant make a joke."

"I'm just trying to lighten the mood. And you have to admit, if you could shoot daggers from your eyes into my chest, you would have done it by now."

She frowned at him and then hefted her bag over her shoulder. "Well, we got this reunion over with. I'll text you when I'm ready to set up another interview. But now I–I have to go."

He stood, but once he was on his feet, he had no idea what to do. "Linds, it doesn't have to be like this."

"It doesn't?"

"I didn't cheat on you."

Her eyebrows shot up to her hairline. "I don't know about you, but where I come from, kissing another woman is cheating. Not sure how you square that circle."

"If I could just explain—"

"That's not necessary. I don't plan to date you again."

"Sure, okay. Then let's keep this professional."

She raised a hand and then dropped it again. "I just… I wasn't ready. This was…a kink to work out. I'll text you."

Then she was gone.

Brad sat back down. He knew why she didn't want to talk to him. Her old trust issues mixing with walking in on him kissing another woman were a recipe for disaster. But somehow he hadn't anticipated that she'd still be this bitter.

Hamilton, the orange cat that had taken a shine to Brad, jumped up on the table and then rubbed his head against Brad's chin. Brad reached out to pet him, and Hamilton immediately started to purr.

"Are you trying to make me feel better?"

As Hamilton paced back and forth on the table, his tail went straight up in the air and tickled Brad's chin.

Brad pulled a cat cookie out of his pocket and offered it to

Hamilton, who ate it greedily. Then the cat looked up at him expectantly.

"You're like an addict who got a hit but wants more. But you don't get to have more."

Hamilton butted Brad's chin with his head again. Brad sighed and pulled another cookie out of his pocket. "Okay, but this is all I have."

Hamilton stole the cookie from Brad's hand and dropped it on the table. Then he gobbled it up.

"Don't think this means anything," Brad told the cat. "You're very nice, but you're not moving in with me."

Hamilton made a *brrup* sound that sure sounded like, "We'll see."

CHAPTER 5

LINDSAY SET UP A SECOND interview at the cat café two days later but wasn't feeling any less tense about it.

But she reasoned she could go in prepared. She'd written a list of questions she would have asked any chef she interviewed, and she told herself she'd stick to the script, get it done, and then get out.

Brad looked perfectly nice. Well, no, he looked better than nice. His brown hair was cropped short these days, and he looked like he was in good shape. He had on a Milk Bar T-shirt that stretched over his chest, and he was clean-shaven to reveal the dimple in his cheek, and he looked great. Stupid, handsome Brad.

Of course, it wasn't just that he was handsome. It was that Lindsay had once known this man intimately, in all senses of the word. They'd once shared their hopes and dreams with each other, and they'd shared beds, and she knew so much about Brad already. She'd once known his family, his friends, his hobbies, his favorite ice cream flavor. It had been five years and he was basically a stranger now, except he wasn't, because he looked so very *Brad* as he sat at that table with a paper coffee cup cradled in his hands.

It wasn't that she'd been angry when they'd made that first attempt at an interview. Well, she *was*, but mostly at herself for being so very much not over him. She'd seen him and *felt* things, felt it all come back to her immediately. It was like getting hit in the chest with a baseball bat, and she hated that he made her feel all that so intensely. He hadn't even done anything. He'd just been sitting there being perfectly nice. That had infuriated her as much as anything. She wanted him to be an asshole. She wanted him to remind her why she'd left him. Instead, he'd just sat there and was polite. That jerk.

She swallowed and walked forward.

She sat across from him and got out her notebook, where she'd written her questions. Then she got out her phone. "Mind if I record?"

"Not at all."

"To be clear, I'm going to try to keep this on script. No personal stuff. We're here to talk about food."

"Sure. Let's get right into it. Rip off the Band-Aid."

She hit the Record button and looked at her notes. "So, you took the job because you wanted creative freedom. What new recipes have you tried here?"

He launched into a discussion of the breakfast pastries he'd been making for the café, including seasonal muffins and Danishes. According to Brad, the zucchini spice muffins had been particularly popular. Lindsay was hit with a wave of memory then, of them standing around a table as one of their culinary professors explained the two dozen spices she'd put in little dishes and invited each student to smell and taste each one. It was a lesson in being able to tell the difference between turmeric and cumin and saffron and anything else, and how each spice would affect a dish. Brad had stood next to her, tasting things and saying things like, "This would be good with citrus" or "This would pair well with vanilla in a cake," and Lindsay had been in awe of his ability to create in that way.

Culinary school had woken up Lindsay's palate. She'd grown up on her mom's meat-and-potatoes cooking, which was fine but bland. If her mom had ever cooked with anything more exciting then oregano, Lindsay didn't know about it. Being introduced to herbs and spices from around the world had been something of a revelation. She hadn't thought she liked spicy food, but it turned out she did as long as it was flavorful and not just tongue-scorching. She'd learned about foreign cuisines and was particularly fond of Asian flavors, like Thai, Korean, and Vietnamese. And, because he'd been at her side for a lot of it, so many of those spice-related memories made her think of Brad.

And those zucchini spice muffins sounded delicious.

She wrote some notes and then asked, "What inspired you to try making cat treats?"

"You remember Bobby Benton from culinary school?"

Lindsay remembered Bobby as kind of a pretty boy from Brad's pastry classes. "Sure."

"He works at a pet bakery in Park Slope. They bake treats for cats and dogs in-house, and they also make dog birthday cakes, if you can believe it."

"Is that a thing? Dog birthday parties?"

"Yeah. They're very popular. But dogs are more omnivorous than cats. If you made a cat cake, it would be all meat-flavored. Although cats are so dainty, I don't know if I see one going to town on a cake."

Lindsay laughed despite herself. "You and I have not known the same cats." She didn't want to find him funny, so she tried to shake it off. He'd always made her laugh, but she didn't want to be reminded of the good times. "So you make meat cookies for cats?"

"Yeah, pretty much. So far, the tuna and chicken ones have been big hits, but I want to try lamb and beef next."

Lindsay noted that and tried not to revel too much in how silly the idea of meat cookies for cats was.

But this was going okay so far. She was sticking to the script. She could get through this.

"How do you like working at a cat café? Any of the cats stolen your heart yet?"

As if on cue, an orange cat hopped up on the table. He sized up Lindsay before walking closer to Brad.

"This one's named Hamilton," said Brad, petting the cat. "There's also a Franklin, a Jefferson, and a Washington."

"I sense a theme."

"Apparently the real Alexander Hamilton was a ginger."

"So the name fits."

"This cat seems to think he's my friend."

"I don't see you disputing that."

Indeed, Brad was still petting the cat, and Hamilton was purring so hard it was making the table rumble a little. Brad seemed to notice he was doing it and jerked his hand away. "Anyway, yeah, it's pretty fun here. Lauren is a great boss."

"Yeah, I figured she would be."

"There's kind of an everyone-is-family vibe among the staff, but she's also stern when she needs to be. Everyone comes in on time and does their job and seems to have fun doing it."

"Yeah. I've always gotten that impression, too. Although Lauren and Paige had some drama last year."

Brad balked. "Sweet, hardworking Paige? Really? Not that I know her well, but I find that hard to imagine."

Lindsay didn't want to get into a conversation about personal stuff, even if it wasn't *her* personal stuff, so she just waved her hand. "It was a personal thing, not work-related."

"Is it because Paige is engaged to Lauren's brother?"

"In part. See, it really is a family here."

Brad laughed. "I guess so!"

Lindsay had forgotten how fond she was of his laugh. It had a booming quality that tended to soar over everything else in the room.

She decided to plow forward. "So, do you just bake, or do you work up front, too? Because my boss said you've gained something of a reputation."

"What kind of reputation?"

"As the hot baker. I asked around a little and heard a rumor that you are singularly responsible for more women, and a few men, stopping by here for their morning coffee now."

Brad's eyebrows shot up. "Are you kidding?"

"Unfortunately, no."

"I've been filling in when people call in sick, if that's what you mean. Otherwise, I just stick to the kitchen. They're really saying that about me?"

Lindsay enjoyed that Brad looked a little uncomfortable. "My boss's angle for this story was a profile on the hunky baker who makes treats for cats. Some people go crazy for that sort of thing."

Brad shifted in his seat. "Um. Did you know this space used to be an Italian restaurant?"

"Yeah, Lauren has mentioned that." Lindsay swallowed a giggle and glanced at her notes. "What's the kitchen like?"

"It's nice. Very clean. Clearly calibrated for a restaurant and not a bakery. Depending on how profits go this quarter, Lauren might let me make some upgrades, but it's adequate. I can show you."

The bubble popped. Being in a kitchen with Brad was too much like the past. Lindsay had almost forgotten how sad and frustrated he made her feel. All the magic seeped out of the moment.

"No, that's okay. I'll take your word for it."

She was also running out of questions, so her escape was imminent. The issue was that the last question was a little more personal, intended to help the reader get to know the chef. Erica had wanted her to ask if he was single, so that they could either dangle an eligible bachelor in front of the audience or wrap up the story with a "Sorry, ladies..." Lindsay hated that kind of thing in an interview with a chef and usually just said something inane like, "Do you draw inspiration from your family?" She crossed out the question she had written and said instead, "What was the best meal you've ever eaten?"

"Is that a standard question?"

"I'm thinking about making it one. I think you can tell a lot about a chef by that."

Brad leaned back and thought for a moment. "Atlanta," he said. "That trip we made to that food and wine festival shortly before graduation. You remember that?"

Lindsay did, because of course she did. And that trip had been about two weeks before they broke up. "Yes."

"That place where we ate after going down the wrong Peachtree Street, the one that looked like the inside of a shed. Remember that?"

Lindsay did. They'd gotten a restaurant recommendation from someone they met at the festival, and they made a wrong turn because for some reason, almost every street in downtown Atlanta was called Peachtree. By the time they realized their mistake, they were far off course and also very hungry, so they decided to eat at the next restaurant they walked by that looked halfway decent. Coincidentally, they'd wandered into the restaurant owned by a former *Top Chef* winner who made elevated southern cuisine— genuine southern food, not whatever they sold at Pepper. It was a rich meal, and everything had been delicious.

"That *was* a great meal," said Lindsay.

"Sometimes, when you're really hungry, a peanut-butter-and-jelly sandwich tastes like ambrosia, and I would have eaten you if it had taken us any longer to find a place to eat, but that food was amazing. So was the company. That was my favorite meal." He gave her a meaningful look.

Lindsay sighed. She'd been happy then, totally head over

heels in love with Brad, and had envisioned a future for herself in which she and Brad traveled the world and ate meals like that. They'd talked about doing just that when they'd been in Atlanta together. And then it all blew up in her face. She *missed* him, more than she thought. Or maybe more than she'd let herself feel. And him sitting here reminiscing and smiling and being very much himself was a reminder both of how great he'd been and how much he'd hurt her.

But she swallowed and said, "Why do you have to be so sweet about it?"

Brad crossed his arms. "I'm telling the truth."

Lindsay frowned at her phone and considered ending the recording and fleeing before this conversation got too personal.

"Uh, any other pearls of wisdom?" she asked instead.

He nodded. "Well, I don't know if I have much in the way of wisdom, but I'll add that a job like this is really fun for me, and I hope it's fun for the customers. And Paige would be very sad if I didn't urge you to include the café's hours in your article. I'll emphasize also that my current menu includes staples like muffins and several kinds of bread. I make grab-and-go sandwiches for the lunch rush. So, like, you can get a blueberry muffin or a ham-and-cheese sandwich. But a lot of the menu is seasonal, so it may vary by week or even by day, depending on what's available."

Lindsay wrote a few more notes and closed her notebook. "Okay," she said, turning off the recording. "I think I've got what I need."

"Really? That's it?"

"I told you I wanted to stick to food."

"And cats."

"Yeah, and cats. I think I've got that part covered. Lauren's going to talk you into adopting that orange one."

"She's already started trying. I'm too wily for her."

Lindsay shook her head. "She'll get you eventually. This is how I ended up with a cat."

"Yeah?"

"Yeah. Little tuxedo named Fred. As in Astaire. He's handsome."

Brad laughed. "Yeah, that checks out."

It bothered Lindsay that Brad knew her as well as she knew him. So he'd know that she liked old movies and associated tuxedos with Old Hollywood. She hooked a thumb toward the door, ready to get out of there. "Well, I guess I'll just be—"

"So you're not going to talk to me about anything personal at all. You're just going to come in here and do your job and leave."

"Yes. I told you that's what would happen."

"Is that all I am to you now? A stranger for an interview?"

Lindsay really did not want to have this conversation. Why couldn't she just have lived the rest of her life without running into him again?

"That's all you *can* mean to me."

"I'm not a bad guy."

But Lindsay shook her head, needing to put a stop to this. "I can't let you break my heart again."

———

Brad knew few things for certain. He had about a dozen recipes rattling around in his head that he could make at the drop of a hat. He knew the science behind why different kinds of flour worked better in different baked goods. He knew the New York City subway system like the back of his hand. And he knew part of him was still and always would be in love with Lindsay Somers.

He stared at her now, surprised she was willing to admit that much. He knew she'd been hurt. He knew that what she'd walked into on the day they broke up had not been great. But he'd been hurt, too, and he'd missed her every day since she left.

"Come on, Linds," he said. "You *know* me. Or you did once. I'm not your enemy."

"What happened with us happened five years ago," she said, though he saw her nostrils flare and knew he had her attention.

"Just tell me one thing. Why didn't you give me a second chance?"

Lindsay grunted, stood, and shouldered her bag. She snatched her phone off the table and pocketed it. She looked around, probably noting that it was just them and the cats in the room. "Because Phoebe Drake had her tongue in your throat."

"She came on to me."

"You still kissed her."

"Not willingly. She ambushed me. You walked in at the worst possible moment."

"Because I caught you."

"I never liked Phoebe in that way. I didn't want her to kiss me. She just did it."

"You had to know she was interested. The two of you flirted

all the time. You *really* expect me to believe there was nothing between you?"

"Yes, because it's true. It also happened five years ago. Even if all the bad things you assume about me are true, which they aren't, it's old news. Are you still that angry about it?"

Lindsay frowned. "I'm not talking about this here."

"Will you talk about it somewhere else? Like my place?"

He hadn't meant to be quite that personal. He should have suggested a neutral location, not his apartment. But instead, the invitation hung in the air for a long moment. Lindsay stared at him, her lips pressed together.

She moved suddenly, jerking her whole body toward the door. "No. I have to go."

Brad knew he probably wouldn't have another chance like this, so he had to put everything out there. "Phoebe meant nothing to me. The worst part about that night is that you walked in and of course saw something awful and then you left me. The three of us were friends, and then fucking Phoebe ended it all with one stupid kiss. But I didn't want her. I wanted you."

"Friends? You thought all three of us were *friends*?"

"Weren't we?"

"You and I weren't friends, Brad. We were a couple. But if it was all a lark for you, then I won't waste any more of either of our time."

"It wasn't a lark. God, Linds, can't you just sit and listen to me instead of constantly assuming the worst?"

"No. Turns out I'm still mad. And I have to go. Expect the story in next week's issue of the *Forum*."

She stormed out.

After staring at the door for a good, long moment, Brad realized he was standing. He hadn't remembered standing up. He dropped back into his chair. Hamilton dutifully hopped into his lap. Brad petted him.

As Hamilton started to purr, Brad concentrated on the feel of soft fur under his hand and the gentle vibrating against his leg. Okay, he could see how having a cat might be an asset. This was helping him calm down.

Paige walked into the cat room. "Did she at least finish the interview this time before you pissed her off?"

"Yes, but what makes you think *I* pissed her off?"

Paige shrugged. "She looked pretty mad when she stormed out of the café. Lauren tried to give her a latte, but Lindsay turned it down."

"She's so stubborn."

"I know."

"She thinks I was cheating on her with one of our friends. I was not, for the record. But she has her own interpretation of what happened imprinted on her brain and will not let go of it or listen to me."

Paige sat in the chair Lindsay had just vacated. "Yeah, that sounds in character."

"What is it they say about the definition of insanity? Doing the same thing again and again but expecting different results? Well, I must be insane, because I want her back. I want her to give me another chance."

Paige gave him an appraising look. "Really?"

"Seeing her again made it all come back. I never wanted to break up. She's the one who ended things."

Paige nodded. "I lucked into my fiancé, but I am otherwise pretty stupid about romance. But did you not just complain about her being stubborn?"

"I always found that equal parts frustrating and arousing."

Paige giggled. "You two are probably made for each other, then. Although, for the record, I am on Lindsay's team. She says you're scum. So officially, I hate you."

Brad sighed. "Fair enough. But you also only have her side of things. And anyway, it happened years ago. I can barely remember the name of the woman I dated last year. How is Lindsay still so mad?"

"Well, the running theory among her friends is that she's still hung up on you, but don't tell her I told you that."

"You guys seem awfully eager to help me. I'm confused by it."

Paige laughed. "Again, I'm on Lindsay's side. I just think she's quick to anger because she still has feelings for you and doesn't know what to do with them. To be clear, if she says she wants no part of you, then that's it. But if I were to tell you that we've got a cat adoption event scheduled here in two weeks, and I'd like you to make some desserts for it, and I think I can persuade Lindsay to come, what would you say?"

"She won't come if I'm here."

"She might. She's come to every other adoption event. Mostly for the free booze, granted, but also to support her friends."

"I can make some bite-size things. Mini-cupcakes, mini-quiches, that kind of thing."

"I'll work on Lindsay. But the rest is up to you. And if she doesn't want to talk to you, there's nothing more I can do."

"I'll take that under advisement."

CHAPTER 6

LINDSAY WAS STILL SEETHING WHEN she got to Pop the next night. Everyone was there—her friends and their significant others—crammed into a table in the back. Lauren and her husband, Caleb, had brought their eight-month-old, who was happily gurgling away in her stroller at one end of the table. Paige sat next to her fiancé, Josh. Evan had brought his boyfriend, Will. And here was Lindsay, alone.

She blamed Brad for that, too.

As Lindsay sat, Will said, "I saw that review of Pepper. That was something else."

"Yeah, I'm famous now. I got a shiny new job as the food editor at the *New York Forum*."

Will gaped at her. "Are you kidding?"

"No, it's true. I've been there for two whole weeks now."

"Oh my god! That's amazing." Will looked around the table. "This is old news to all of you, isn't it? This is what happens when I miss the weekly drink night."

Evan laughed. "It's fine, honey."

"You don't review cookbooks, do you?"

Lindsay smiled despite her foul mood. Will edited cookbooks and seemed to be constantly looking for ways to promote them. He mentioned now that he was working on a celebrity cookbook. The author was a popular actress from a primetime drama, the daughter of a chef, and had a bunch of innovative family recipes she wanted to share with the public. Lindsay took this to mean she wanted to cash in.

Will got up to use the restroom, so Lindsay asked Evan, "How's that going?"

"Fine," said Evan.

That didn't sound like a ringing endorsement. "Just fine?"

He shrugged. "I like him. We're having fun. Do I think he's the one? Remains to be seen."

"You're not still—"

"Hung up on Pablo? No, no. That ship has sailed. I'm taking everyone's advice. I found another fish in the sea."

"Right," said Lindsay. It came out sounding more sarcastic than she intended.

Evan's back was clearly up. "You're one to talk." His tone was salty.

She let out a breath. "What are you talking about?"

"Like you're not still hung up on a certain ex-boyfriend."

"Who, Brad?"

"Yeah, Brad. Lauren said you stormed out of your first interview with him. That sounds like something a mature adult would do."

"You guys don't get it. Brad is different. And he and I actually dated."

Lauren and Paige glanced at each other, clearly uncomfortable with the harshness in Lindsay's tone. So, okay, maybe she was being unfair. Pablo was an acquaintance of theirs from the neighborhood; currently, he worked at Stories, the bookstore two doors down from the cat café. Evan had harbored a crush on him for years, but hadn't been able to summon the courage to ask him out before Pablo found a boyfriend. Now Pablo and this guy were in a committed relationship and Evan was with Will, and although Lauren was not convinced Evan had moved on, that situation was nothing like the one between Lindsay and Brad. Still, she could tell she'd pissed Evan off.

Lindsay swallowed and said, "I'm sorry, Evan. But—"

"Ixnay on the Ablo-pay," said Evan. "Will is coming back."

A moment later, Will slid back into the booth. He seemed to sense the tension at the table and said, "Did something happen?"

Probably as a cover, Evan said, "I made the mistake of bringing up Brad."

"I'm new," said Josh. "So explain this to me. What the hell happened with Brad?"

Lindsay sighed. "Well, we met in culinary school and hit it off right away, and we were pretty hot and heavy. We dated seriously the whole last year of school."

And, god, it had been amazing. Lindsay hated to think about it now because the memory of losing something so great was too painful, but back in those days, they'd been all over each other all the time. They'd had sex in one of the kitchens at school after hours one night. And one time in a pantry. And all over both of their apartments. But it wasn't just sex with them. They enjoyed each other's company and liked to cook together and liked to talk over slowly sipped cups of coffee or tea in the evenings. They'd been in love. Lindsay had been happy.

She could admit that Brad was both hot and charming. He'd cleaned up some now, but back in culinary school, he'd worn his brown hair a little longer so that it hung rakishly over his eyes— he held it back with bandannas in the kitchen—and he shaved less often. Despite baking decadent desserts for a living, he ate very healthy otherwise, and he'd always had a lean, athletic body.

He was hot and funny and easy to talk to. He was so easy to talk to that Lindsay had told him things she'd never told anyone. So he knew that her divorced parents had done a number on her, that her father hadn't known the definition of the word *faithful*, that watching her parents' marriage dissolve at a formative age had left Lindsay with trust issues. And what had Brad done? He'd kissed Phoebe. Lindsay had put her trust in a man for the first time in her life, and he'd betrayed her.

"Okay. And?" asked Josh.

Lindsay sighed. "I walked in on him kissing another woman one evening."

"Ah," said Josh. "I can see why that would be a strike against him."

"Not just another woman, but this friend of his who had been trying to get in his pants for weeks."

"I'm not defending him," said Lauren, "but he says it was a misunderstanding."

"Hard to misunderstand his tongue inside another woman's mouth."

"Fair," said Lauren.

"How long ago was this?" Josh asked. "And how did I not know you went to culinary school?"

"We graduated five years ago." Lindsay smiled, despite still feeling riled up. "I worked as a line cook for a year and hated it, so I decided to write about food instead."

"Interesting," said Josh. "So this means you can cook, right? Why don't we have dinner at your place more often instead of smushing ourselves into this tiny bar?"

"Because my apartment is even smaller than this bar," said Lindsay, "but if you play your cards right, I'll cook for you soon."

"Come to our place," said Paige. "We'll have a dinner party. We've got plenty of space and a very nice kitchen that we hardly ever use." Josh was a lawyer who had, until about six months ago, worked at a big corporate Manhattan law firm. He worked for the Brooklyn DA now, which had been a pay cut, but he still did well enough for him and Paige to afford a two-bedroom apartment in one of the fancy new high-rise buildings in downtown Brooklyn. Lindsay remained in awe and not a little bit jealous, since food writing only paid for a studio on the fringes of a good neighborhood.

Lindsay nodded. "Good plan. I've been wanting to get my hands on your kitchen for a while."

"I can be your sous-chef," said Paige. "I'm not terrible at the cooking."

"I can verify that," said Josh.

Hannah started to fuss, so Lauren picked her up and started to rock her a little. Caleb plucked a bottle from the diaper bag and handed it to her. It was like watching a well-choreographed ballet: smooth and practiced.

"I get that a bar is not the best place for a baby," said Lauren as Hannah started to settle down.

"It's Brooklyn," said Evan, as if this were an explanation.

"The babysitter had other plans tonight," said Caleb.

"If you're bringing your baby to a bar, you guys are really peak Brooklyn parents now," said Evan. "If you join a message board and start complaining about how the neighborhood is going downhill because the stroller store became a juice bar, I'm going to have to disown you."

Lauren leaned down and kissed Hannah's head. "If that ever happens, I will have deserved it."

There was a beat of silence while everyone drank their cocktails. Then Evan asked, "So what are you going to do about Brad?"

"Nothing," said Lindsay. "I did the interview. It's over."

"He works at the café. You don't think you'll run into him again?"

Lindsay shrugged. "He works in the morning. It's easy enough to avoid him. And if I run into him? I'll...be civil."

"No," said Evan.

"No?"

Evan sighed. "I've known you a long time, Linds. In the five years since you graduated from culinary school, you've dated a handful of guys. You were even with that guy Clark for almost a year."

Lindsay sighed, sensing where this was going.

"I liked Clark," said Paige. "What happened to him?"

"He moved to California," said Lindsay. Clark had been a voice actor who was tired of narrating commercials and moved to LA because he had a shot at doing voice work for cartoons. She kept seeing his name pop up in things, so he'd clearly found success there. He was currently starring, if that was the right word for it, in a popular sci-fi spin-off cartoon. He played an alien who was good at fighting with a sword. Lindsay was happy for him. See? She wasn't bitter about all of her exes.

"Right," said Evan. "He moved to California like two years ago. He was a nice guy; you seemed to like him. But we never hear about Clark anymore. Do you know who we do hear about? Brad. Anytime he does anything, you mention it."

"I hate him."

"I think you *love* him. That's why this is chapping your hide so much. You're still in love with Brad, he broke your heart, and you'll never stop thinking about him. You know what I think you should do?"

"Avoid him for the rest of time?" Lindsay asked hopefully.

"Jump his bones. Get it out of your system."

"Does that work outside of TV shows?" asked Lauren. "Sleeping with him will surely just complicate matters."

"I'm not sleeping with him," said Lindsay.

"What's the over-under on Lindsay sleeping with Brad?" Evan asked the table.

"I'll put ten dollars on that," said Paige.

"I hate you guys," said Lindsay.

Evan laughed. "I'm not saying forgive him. He's scum if he

cheated on you. And I mean that gross green scum that tends to accumulate at Dog Beach in Prospect Park."

"Ugh, that place is always gross," said Will. "I won't let my dog play there."

"Exactly," said Evan. "But what I am saying is that it seems like you have some unfinished business with Brad, and maybe you should finish it. That's all."

Lindsay did not want to admit Evan might be right, but she couldn't deny that seeing Brad again had done something to her. She hadn't been able to get him out of her head all week. She was still angry, but underneath all that, she missed him. They'd had something special back in their culinary school days, but it had always felt precarious.

In those days, Lindsay had been less jaded and more optimistic. She'd been twenty-five when she graduated from culinary school, looking forward to a career making great food. At the time, Brad hadn't quite had his life together yet. He'd been living in an apartment share with three other guys from school, in a tiny, crowded bedroom that had been taken over by his bed. Lindsay hated staying there and preferred bringing him back to her place, a nice two bedroom she shared with a friend from undergrad.

Brad enjoyed going out at night, trying new cocktails, getting stupid drunk with his friends, and eating at whatever hole-in-the-wall was still open when the bars closed. Every now and then that was fun. She fondly remembered one night on the Lower East Side when they'd dance until their feet hurt at a little club under a burrito restaurant and then sobered up by eating pastrami sandwiches at Katz's Deli. But Brad's partying used to make

Lindsay anxious and jealous. The girls at the clubs loved rubbing up on him, and he never turned them away. Although he always came home to Lindsay.

That was part of what had made her blow up when she caught up with Phoebe. Women came on to him all the time. He never seemed interested in discouraging them. In fact, he usually flirted back. At the time, Lindsay had thought he was either with her or he wasn't.

Apparently he wasn't. He'd known all of her secrets. And he'd kissed Phoebe anyway.

She signaled the waitress for a drink refill.

———————

"Welcome to the set," Aaron said as he led Brad through a door and onto a sound stage.

The sound stage was divided into two areas: on one side, there were four stations that looked like kitchen islands, each complete with a stove, oven, sink, and maybe three square feet of counter space. That was almost nothing as far as prep space went, but it was room enough for a cutting board and a few bowls. The other side of the stage contained a massive pantry that looked stocked full of anything a chef could want: rice and various grains in large plastic containers with brightly colored labels, mountains of fresh produce, several loaves of bread, a whole shelf of condiments, and a dozen other things.

"Spoiler," said Aaron. "Today's secret ingredient is halibut."

"That doesn't seem that weird."

"We decided that if every episode was wacky, then no one

would talk about the really weird ingredients. Plus halibut is a good challenge. It's a versatile fish that can nonetheless go horribly wrong if you don't cook it correctly."

"Sure." Brad thought the set looked pretty cool and it might be fun to cook here, but he wasn't sure if he could cook halibut in a way that would stand out. Good thing he wasn't a contestant.

Aaron crossed the room to a huge refrigerator and took a couple of beers from it.

"You can just do that?" Brad asked as Aaron handed him a beer.

"Being in charge has some privileges." Aaron pulled a key-chain bottle opener from his pocket and flipped the top off Brad's beer.

They sat together at the judge's table. The chairs were nice, with cushy seats and ergonomic backs. "I didn't expect such good chairs," Brad said as he adjusted to be comfortable.

"Filming each episode takes a couple of hours. The judges sit and watch the whole thing. Since the judges are usually VIPs, we wanted them to be comfortable."

"Cool." Brad looked around the room, trying to imagine what it would be like to be a judge on the show.

"So, wacky question. Why is Lindsay Somers interviewing you in the *New York Forum*?"

Brad grimaced and sipped his beer. "You read it?"

"Yeah, we subscribe. You're the hunky chef who makes treats for cats."

Brad groaned. "Yeah, that's what I hear." He glanced at Aaron.

"Lindsay works at the *Forum* now. If it makes you feel better, the interview was awkward."

"She still hates you?"

"She still hates me."

"That doesn't come across in the interview. Did you read it?"

"No, I couldn't bring myself to."

Aaron nodded. "It was a fine interview. Bland, even. Ladies and gentlemen of New York, there's a handsome pastry chef who works at the Whitman Street Cat Café making treats for humans and cats. He's charming, and his favorite meal was at some restaurant in Atlanta. That was really all the interview said."

"That doesn't sound too terrible."

"You don't mind being a piece of meat for women to fawn after when they come to the café to…do whatever people do there. Eat cupcakes and pet cats?"

"I mean, I feel weird about it, but it seems like good publicity." Brad sighed. "Lindsay bothers me more. The actual interview was… antagonistic. She's being stubborn and won't listen to me."

Aaron tilted his head and sipped his beer, as if he were thinking. "I know what will get your mind off it. A buddy of mine is the new mixologist at a cocktail bar in the Village, and I have an open invite to drink all night at happy-hour prices. You game?"

The thought of spending a night out suddenly filled Brad with dread. He'd been up since 3:30 a.m. and had spent most of the day training his new assistants how to bake most of his recipes so that they could take over for him a couple of days a week. He'd been working seven days a week for a month now. He was *tired*.

"I'm beat, man."

"Aw, come on. This bar is classy, not like the places we used to hang out. Nice decor, bespoke cocktails, fancy ingredients."

"It sound great, but do you know how early I have to get up to make muffins and danishes for the morning rush?"

Aaron nodded. "All right. I'll let you have that."

They chatted about food and people they knew. Brad appreciated the tour of the studio, but he happily got on the subway to go back to his place in Brooklyn.

He was renting an apartment in Prospect Heights, the third floor of a narrow three-story row house. It was a big space—long, albeit narrow—but hadn't been updated since the nineties, so Brad had gotten a pretty good deal on it. The kitchen was small but functional, just enough space to let him play around with new recipes. This was his first place without roommates, and he was happy with his two bedrooms, one of which he was using as an office.

Not that he was ever home, which was why he did not need a cat. He didn't see himself as a cat person. It didn't matter how cute Hamilton was or how much of a shine that cat had taken to Brad. And, okay, since Brad usually opened, he always looked in on the cats, and Hamilton always beelined right for him. And, sure, sometimes Brad talked to Hamilton about whatever was on his mind, and Hamilton always sat there staring at Brad like whatever he said was fascinating. And, fine, unburdening himself to a cat was surprisingly cathartic.

He'd thought about getting a dog, but his long hours were an even bigger problem with a dog. Lauren had told him that she and her husband hired a dog walker to take their dog out when they were both working. Brad had seen that poor woman a few times, walking between three and five dogs at a time down Whitman Street. So that was a possible solution. And maybe Brad was protesting too much about adopting a cat. But he just didn't see the point of adopting a pet when he was never home.

He dropped onto the sofa in his mostly bare living room. He'd only been in the apartment about six months and was still deciding what to put on the walls. His old posters were sitting in a box in the bedroom, and he'd put some Post-its up that said things like "Rolling Stones" and "Matisse print" where he thought his various artworks should go. He'd get there. Not to mention, he'd finally had enough of working for his eccentric boss at the chocolate restaurant and had decided to leave, and he'd been anxious enough about finding a new job that he hadn't wanted to jinx his ability to stay in this place by decorating.

He flipped on the TV and saw he'd left it on the Food Channel. He laughed and watched a few minutes of the last show Aaron had worked on, a show called *Flash Fry* about chefs who had to make complete meals in thirty minutes. Then fatigue from the day finally set in, and he started to doze.

As he always did when he was half-asleep and no longer able to ward her off, he thought of Lindsay. There had to be some way to at least have a conversation with her. Maybe he could make her see that he'd grown up enough for her to merit giving him a second chance. Maybe he could track down Phoebe and get her to explain to Lindsay that the kiss in the kitchen that night really had been nothing. Maybe he'd just charm her socks off this time, make himself irresistible, and talk her into going on a date with him. It could be just like old times. He imagined her texting him flirty things, his phone lighting up with words and images from Lindsay.

Then he realized his phone actually was chiming and he wasn't just imagining it.

The text was from Paige. You're still in for the adoption event cupcakes etc., yes?

Yes, he responded.

Cool. Lindsay dropped by the café bc she knew you wouldn't be here. But I think I talked her into coming.

Brad laughed. He wasn't sure what it said about him and Lindsay that her friends, despite their protestations, seemed to be rooting for him, but he was grateful. He texted Paige a thumbs-up emoji.

Now he just had to figure out how to get Lindsay to talk to him.

CHAPTER 7

SINCE NO ONE WAS ACCEPTING "Brad will be there" as an acceptable excuse to miss the café's quarterly adoption party, Lindsay reluctantly walked into the cat café.

She attended these parties if she was available as a way to support her friends who worked for the café. Paige hired a bartender to sling drinks, and usually they got catered food from local businesses, but as soon as Paige entered the cat room, she saw that it was Brad carrying around trays of snacks. A table was set up on one side of the room, and as Lindsay walked in, Brad laid a tray of mini-cupcakes there.

He was stupid cute when he was in work mode. He wore a plain white chef's jacket and nicely fitted dark jeans rolled up at the cuffs to show off his ankles and brown boat shoes. No city boy should have worn boat shoes, and yet Lindsay still thought his ankles were, well, attractive and masculine, which felt like a stupid thing to think about ankles.

He grinned at a few of the women who walked over to take a cupcake before walking over to talk to Lauren. Lindsay wasn't anxious to have him know she was here yet, so she walked to the bar on the other side of the room and ordered a martini. When she turned around again, he was leaving the room. *Phew.*

Evan approached. "You're not subtle."

"What?"

"I saw you come in and carefully dodge the direction of Brad's gaze like you were Bugs Bunny hiding from Elmer Fudd in a cartoon."

"I need a cocktail before I can talk to him."

"I'm surprised you came."

"I'm trying to support my friends. I mean, you, Lauren, and Paige are my three best friends in this whole godforsaken city. Lauren and Paige both work here, and you do enough freelance work for them that you might as well work here, too. If I didn't love my new job, I'd probably try to work here, too. Except, oh wait, now my ex-boyfriend does."

"Yeah, sorry about that. I've been trying to shoot lasers out of my eyes so that he'll catch on fire whenever I see him, but it's not working so far."

Lindsay laughed despite herself. "Keep trying."

"Of course. What are friends for?"

Brad reappeared with another tray, this time full of savory pastries. From where Lindsay stood, it looked like mini-quiches and some kind of triangular thing wrapped in phyllo, maybe mini-spanakopita.

Which, of course, reminded Lindsay of the day they made a huge spanakopita at culinary school. Brad had decided to make his own phyllo, and they'd had an argument about why that was stupid, with Lindsay arguing that they could just buy some premade dough. It would have been easier to work with, since rolling phyllo out to the correct thinness was kind of a trial, and it fell apart after that anyway. But Brad had persisted and successfully made phyllo from scratch.

He was talented. Lindsay hated that. She hated that he was handsome and charming and talented and the sort of guy every woman wanted, and she'd had him, and she'd let him go.

She sighed.

"Those little spinach pastry things are *delicious*," said Evan.

"Traitor."

"I can't help it. I got stuck in a client meeting and had to skip dinner, so I ate like five from the first batch when I got here."

Lindsay crossed her arms and wondered if Brad had made his own phyllo this time.

"Your profile of him for the *Forum* was surprisingly kind. I almost expected the accompanying photo to have devil horns drawn on it."

"I didn't want my boss to know I detest him. Also, it was good publicity for the café. And look at this turnout tonight. This is more crowded than these things usually are."

"Part of it is that the room is smaller, since Lauren built that little hallway to the kitchen."

"Sure, but there are, I don't know, maybe five or ten more people than usual."

Lindsay looked around. Lauren's husband, Caleb, was a veterinarian at the clinic next door. He wore a bright-blue T-shirt with the clinic's logo on it and seemed to be gamely answering the questions of a few prospective cat owners. Lauren and Paige were both circulating and talking to customers. Josh stood near the refreshments table, trying to make it not look like he was wolfing down mini-quiches. She and Evan sipped their drinks.

"Is Will coming?" Lindsay asked.

"No. One of his authors is doing a book talk at that indie bookstore in SoHo. He felt he had to be there, and also he's worried if he sets foot in the café that Lauren will make him adopt a cat. And, well, he's not wrong."

"True."

Evan sighed. "I like him a lot, but I don't know."

"He's not the One?"

Evan shrugged. "Will has no discernible flaws. He's cute. He has a steady job he's good at. He has passions and hobbies. The sex is…fine. But, I don't know. He doesn't exactly light me on fire."

"So break up."

"I'm trying this thing where I don't just dismiss guys out of hand for stupid reasons, because I don't want to be that guy who turns down a good thing because I don't like the flippy thing his hair does or whatever."

"That's fair." Lindsay didn't have much of a leg to stand on here because it wasn't like anyone she'd dated since Brad had lasted long. She was certain she'd dumped more than one guy because she didn't like his teeth or thought he had a weird laugh or something equally superficial.

"So I'm giving Will a shot. Plus, he's gotten us in to a couple of really amazing restaurants because the chefs are among his authors, and I've been very well fed recently."

"Well, that's something."

They sipped their cocktails in silence for a moment as Evan rocked on his heels. "Also, not for nothing, but if someone *does* light you on fire, it might be worth it to see what he has to say."

"Subtle." Because of course Evan was talking about Brad. Who still did completely light Lindsay on fire. He drew her eyes right to him as he smiled and handed people cupcakes. She already knew what going to bed with him was like, and it was awesome. But… She just couldn't get that image of him kissing Phoebe out of her mind.

"I'm just saying," said Evan.

"Why are you guys all taking his side?"

"I'm always on your side. But it might be worth it to get whatever is left between you out in the open so you can yell about it and then we can all move on with our lives and you don't spend the whole time at this party feeling awkward and avoiding him. Oh, by the way, here he comes."

Evan slid away at the same time Brad walked up to her and said, "Hi."

"Hello."

"I know you're here under duress, but I'm glad to see you."

Lindsay sighed. "Not under duress as such. I wanted to support my friends."

"But you probably would have rather stayed home than see me. Hell, I'm guessing you would have rather been stuck in a subway car without air-conditioning on a hot day than see me."

It was hard to know how to feel about Brad when he was looking all handsome, with his hair just so and his eyes sparkling.

But, Lindsay reasoned, she could be attracted to him while still hating him. Or her friends were right, and they could reach some kind of truce.

Because what had he even done to her recently besides be perfectly nice?

She grunted. "Maybe," she said. "Why did you even take this job? Lauren changed her last name, but you must have seen it was her when you came in for the interview."

"I did, and I was hoping you and I could let bygones be bygones if we ran into each other. Also, and I know this will come as a shock, but the world does not actually revolve around you, and this was a good opportunity for me."

He looked down suddenly, so Lindsay followed his gaze. The orange cat she'd seen during the interview was rubbing against Brad's leg.

"That cat thinks you're his friend."

Brad sighed. "I know."

"Did Lauren talk you into taking him home yet?"

"I work long hours. It can't be a good idea to keep a cat at home under those circumstances."

"Cats mostly sleep during the day."

"Don't take his side."

A woman walked over and knelt next to the cat. "And who's this little guy?"

The woman was cute in a blond and busty way. Lindsay had not been born yesterday, so she knew this woman was using the cat as a pretense to talk up Brad. That annoyed Lindsay for reasons she didn't want to examine too closely. She tried to school her face, because irrational jealous was never a good look. Although, even if Lindsay and Brad had no history, it was rude of this woman to just horn in on his attention.

"That's Hamilton," said Brad, oblivious.

"What a darling name!"

"I didn't pick it, but it is, rather. I thought it was silly at first, but now I think it suits him."

The woman stood up again and met Brad's gaze. "It's a long name for a cat."

Brad chuckled. "I thought so, too."

The woman leaned close and lightly brushed her fingers over Brad's arm, an unmistakably flirty gesture. Brad grinned at her. Lindsay seethed.

"I always wanted an orange cat," said the woman.

A strange expression came over Brad's face. "Oh, uh, this one's already spoken for."

"Of course he would be." The woman stood up. "Your food is delicious, by the way. My name's Maggie." She held out her hand.

Brad shook it. "Nice to meet you. I'm Brad. And this is my friend Lindsay."

His friend? White-hot jealousy sliced through Lindsay, because of course it did, because no matter how much she tried, she could never hate Brad. But surely she was not just his friend. And surely he wasn't just using her to make this woman go away.

The woman seemed to take it that way, though. "Nice to meet you, too. Apologies for interrupting your conversation."

Lindsay snorted, and then regretted it because Brad slid her a sidelong glance that told her he knew what her reaction had been about.

He cleared his throat. "There's another orange cat named Jefferson around here somewhere. He has a white belly. Absolutely adorable."

Maggie laughed. "Hamilton and Jefferson, of course! I saw *Hamilton* like everyone else did in this city. Are the names a reference to the musical?"

Brad tilted his head. "The cats are named after various Founding Fathers. There's a Washington and a Franklin and a few others around. A girl cat named Betsy and another named Martha."

"Sure, sure," said the woman. "Well, I'll go find Mr. Jefferson, then, won't I?"

When she was gone, Lindsay let out a breath.

"You want to talk about how you tried to kill that nice woman with your eyes?" Brad asked.

Nope, she was not ceding any emotional ground. "Oh, Brad, not sure if you noticed, but you just claimed that cat. He is *so* going home with you."

"Uh-huh. I see what you're doing there. But fine, I'll bite. I just wanted him to stay at the café."

"Nope, that's not how this works. I've been around long enough to know that Sadie is the only permanent resident. She knows it, too. That's why she's sitting on the couch over there looking smug."

Lindsay pointed and Brad followed her gaze. Sadie was sitting on the arm of the sofa with a satisfied cat look on her face, observing the scene like the other cats were suckers.

Brad frowned. "My apartment is not set up for a cat."

"You're just a litter box and a few cans of cat food short of being a cat owner, buddy."

Brad sighed and looked down at Hamilton, who looked blissful as he rubbed his face against Brad's leg.

"This is not what I signed on for."

Lindsay laughed again.

———————

Brad had been chatting amiably with Lindsay for five whole minutes. He wondered if she'd noticed.

She'd definitely noticed that another woman had come talk to him. The way Lindsay had tried to mentally murder Maggie had not escaped Brad's attention, nor had her dodge at his question. That was very interesting.

Lauren wandered over, and before Brad could say anything, Lindsay said, "Brad's adopting Hamilton."

"I knew it!" said Lauren. "I've got cardboard carriers in back if you—"

"I'm not…" But Brad knew a losing argument when he saw it. He sighed. "Not tonight. My apartment's not ready."

Lauren winked. "Sure. I'll just tell Monique not to let anyone adopt Hamilton."

When she was gone again, Lindsay surprised the hell out of Brad. "Maybe we should just bury the hatchet. Now that you work for Lauren, it's clear that I will be running into you regularly. I hate all the tension between us."

"So you *don't* hate me?"

"I mean, I do, but maybe we can find a way to be civil."

Now it was Brad's turn to laugh. "Look, I just want to talk to you in a place where we're not surrounded by a lot of other people. I need to stay until the end of the party to make sure everyone has enough to eat, and then I have to clean out the kitchen, but do you want to stick around and then come home with me?"

Lindsay's eyes practically popped right out of her head, she looked so surprised.

"Not for sex!" said Brad. "Just to talk. No hanky-panky, I promise. You can help me make a list of all the stuff I need to buy for Hamilton and then show me where to put it. You have a cat, right?"

She pressed her lips together and looked around the room. The longer she stayed silent, the more convinced Brad became that she'd say no. But then she dropped her arms and said, "Fine. But no touching. Just talking."

Brad held up his hands. "No touching."

"Okay. Fine. Okay."

"Good." Brad glanced at his watch. "I've got something in the kitchen I have to check on. Don't leave, okay?"

"I said okay!"

And Brad smiled, because he knew he had her now.

Well, he didn't *have* her, he reasoned as he walked back to the kitchen. She was still angry. But he reasoned that if they were ever going to make up, they'd have to talk. This felt like progress.

When he returned to the kitchen, the last batch of cupcakes had cooled enough to frost. He grabbed a piping bag and got to work, letting the repetitive motion of swirling frosting over each cupcake soothe him.

Lauren walked into the kitchen. "Those mini-cupcakes went fast."

"I can bring the next batch out in about five minutes," said Brad, not looking up from what he was doing.

Lauren picked up a plastic tub of sprinkles into which Brad had mixed tiny cat-shaped candies he'd found at a party store. She started dusting the finished cupcakes with the sprinkle-candy mix.

"Thanks," Brad said.

"You okay?"

"Yeah, fine. Better than fine. I got Lindsay to agree to talk to me."

"Progress!"

Brad laughed. "Yeah, I guess. I mean, yes, it's progress. But I can already tell it's going to be a big fight."

Lauren nodded. "What are you hoping will happen?"

Brad wasn't willing to hope for too much, so he said, "A truce?"

"All right. Best of luck, then." Lauren put the sprinkles down. "Four cats got adopted tonight. Five if you count Hamilton. You're going to need a litter box, litter, some dishes, probably a place mat, and food."

"You have recommendations for all that?"

"As a matter of fact I do!" Lauren grinned. "If you talk to my husband, he can give you a flyer with vet-approved recommendations for what we're calling the cat starter kit."

"I can't believe you talked me into adopting a cat."

"It's my superpower. And besides, that cat clearly chose you. That's usually how this goes."

"Sure."

"Aw, buck up. You've made the decision to bring a small, furry friend home. You live alone, right? He'll keep you company if Lindsay doesn't."

"Yeah, I don't think she's going to keep me company. I'm pretty sure she still hates me."

He finished frosting, and Lauren dropped sprinkles on the last of the cupcakes. "Beautiful. And I don't think she hates you."

"Jury's still out on that. I guess I'll find out shortly."

CHAPTER 8

"WHERE ARE YOU LIVING THESE days?" Brad asked as he and Lindsay walked out of the café together.

He felt wiped out now that he'd finished work for the day. The cats had been tucked in, the kitchen was clean, and it had been a long-ass day. He was thinking better of his plan to bring Lindsay home, but he didn't want to let this opportunity pass by. If he waited any longer, she would have likely make some excuse or disappear into the dark night never to be seen again.

"Prospect Heights," she said.

"Me too. Where?"

"Underhill. Near Eastern Parkway."

"Okay. I'm on Washington, closer to Atlantic."

"Not far, then." Lindsay rolled her shoulders. "Are we really doing this?"

"Yes. Going to my place. I'm getting a car." Brad held up his phone to show he had a ride-share app pulled up. "But no touching."

Lindsay was quiet on the short car ride to Brad's apartment. When they arrived, Brad led her upstairs.

"You have roommates?" Lindsay asked as he unlocked the door.

"Nope."

"That's something."

Brad let her in and then led her to the living room, which involved cutting through the kitchen.

Lindsay looked around. "This is a lot of space. Could use some art, though. And that kitchen is kind of an eyesore."

"You don't have to be critical of everything. You know as well as I do what apartments cost in this city. When I was looking, it was basically down to this place or a place half this size but with newer appliances. That was a pretty easy decision."

"Sure, okay." She sighed. "Evan lives one block over. And you've been right here the whole time."

"Less than a year, but yeah." He gestured toward the sofa, hoping Lindsay would sit.

She did, and then she folded her hands in her lap. "So talk."

He stood in the middle of his living room trying to decide how to approach this. He decided and took a deep breath. "I have two ground rules for this discussion."

She rolled her eyes. "Fine. What?"

"One, we're honest. And two, we listen."

She crossed her arms. "Okay." She nodded once, clearly understanding what he meant.

Good.

So, okay, they were doing this. Right now was Brad's one shot to get out everything he wanted to say, and he had to do it right so Lindsay wouldn't storm out. He took another deep breath. "Let me get this out of the way. I did not cheat on you. I would never cheat on you. Phoebe came on to me in that kitchen, and then you walked in."

"Why should I believe you?"

Okay. That was how this was going to be. "When did I ever lie to you?"

That seemed to give Lindsay pause. She glared at him for a moment, then let out a breath. Her posture relaxed as some of the fight leaked out of her. "Fine. Tell me what happened."

"We were working in the kitchen, Phoebe and I were goofing around a little, and then out of nowhere she kissed me. I was so surprised, it took my brain a minute to catch up. And that's what you saw."

"You're too much of a flirt, you know. You lead people on."

"Not on purpose. I never meant to lead Phoebe on. I swear, I was never interested in her that way. I wish you could believe me."

Lindsay closed her eyes for a long moment. She leaned back on the couch. Brad realized he was pacing, so he stopped doing it.

"She probably knew I was coming," Lindsay said at length.

That surprised Brad so much, he had to sit down in the armchair near the sofa. "You mean she set me up?"

Lindsay let out a breath. "I mean, I don't know anything for certain. I just know that walking in on you and Phoebe was the worst moment of my life. You say you didn't want to kiss her. I'm just trying to come up with a reasonable explanation, I guess. I know she had a thing for you."

While Phoebe's crush was not news to Brad, it surprised him a little that Lindsay knew. Well, and also, he seemed to be winning her over. He was almost afraid to breathe lest this delicate moment slip away from him. "I was faithful to you."

She met his gaze and nodded. "But you can see how I might doubt that, right? Women were throwing themselves at you all the time."

"Did I ever return their affections?"

"How should I know?"

Brad sighed. He'd lost the moment. Arguing with Lindsay was sometimes like arguing with a brick wall. "Look, I don't know what happened. All I know is that I was with you, I wanted to be with you, and one day Phoebe approached me and mauled me and you walked in. You chose to believe the worst of me instead of letting me try to explain myself."

"You had a foot out the door."

Brad balked at that. He had no idea what she was talking about. "I didn't. What makes you say that? I was committed to you."

She shook her head. "We talked about traveling, or opening our own restaurant, or moving in together after we graduated, but whenever I brought up those plans, you acted like you couldn't plan more than five minutes into the future. So we made all these plans, but I always felt like I was the only one who was taking them seriously."

Had he really given her that impression? In those days, Brad had been a live-in-the-moment kind of guy. He figured he'd graduate and get a job somewhere, and he and Lindsay would still be together, and sure, they'd travel and work together, but he hadn't realized he'd needed a five-year plan. But that didn't mean he didn't want those things. "I was serious. I was also a little preoccupied with graduating. Was there some rush to make plans?"

"No, but nothing ever got past being hypothetical. You always put me off when I asked about it. Do you get how frustrating that is?"

"I was twenty-five! Who knows what they want out of life at that age? I wasn't ready to make that level of commitment about the future yet."

"Don't you get it?" Lindsay shouted. "I was in love with you! I had this whole life planned. You and me, we had plans! I thought you were on board with those plans. But whenever I brought it up, you changed the subject. You kept saying it was too soon to make any long-term decisions. What was I supposed to think?"

"I wasn't ready."

"I know! And that would have been okay, too. But you should have talked to me. If you'd said, 'I don't feel ready to make a commitment like that, let's do something else first,' I would have understood, but instead, you kept saying, 'Let's talk about it later.' Do you know how that made me feel? Like I wanted to plan a future with you, but you didn't want that with me."

"Of course I wanted a future with you. You were always part of the plan, such as it was. I just didn't feel like I needed to decide everything right then. There were too many variables."

"And fucking Phoebe. It sure didn't look like you wanted to take any of this seriously."

Ah, back around to that again. Brad's head spun. "Phoebe didn't do anything."

"Didn't she? She wormed her way between us. Everything fell apart after that."

"But I was never interested in her in that way. I never wanted to date her. She was just my friend."

"It doesn't matter. She set out to sabotage us, and you let her."

Brad was taken aback by that. He tried to remember the night everything blew up.

He'd been noodling in one of the school's test kitchens. He had an assignment to design a dessert menu for a New American restaurant, and he'd wanted to test out some twists on the old standards like cheesecake and brownie sundaes. Phoebe had walked in while he'd been working and struck up a conversation about fudge. Brad had only been half paying attention; he'd been focused on keeping an eye on the tray of brownies in the oven because he didn't know precisely how long they needed to bake.

He therefore didn't notice when Phoebe's tone turned flirtatious.

"I have to confess," she'd said. "I know you and Lindsay are seeing each other, but I've had feelings for you for a long time."

Brad didn't know how to process that. "Oh," was all he'd said. He pulled the brownies out and put them on the counter.

As he turned off the oven, Phoebe sauntered over. He turned to see what she was doing, and she put her hands on his shoulders and kissed him before he could react.

Which was of course when Lindsay walked into the kitchen.

Brad hadn't been interested in Phoebe that way. He really hadn't, and now it sounded like he was protesting too much. She was pretty, yes, but also kind of arrogant and annoying. She thought she was a better chef than she was, always talking about her own food in superlative terms while usually it was pretty middle of the road. Serving potatoes with filet mignon was not exactly an innovation.

But they'd been friends for a long time, and Brad had thought he needed friends in culinary school, because there were days when it felt like the faculty was trying to break all the students. One of the teachers that semester had been a pioneer in French cuisine, the sort of chef who regularly appeared on TV as an expert in his field. Brad had been starstruck. But the chef had been a cruel taskmaster, challenging the students to think outside the box while also mastering the fine points of French technique. Phoebe had been a shoulder to lean on when Brad had thought he'd never make it through the program.

Of course, Lindsay had been, too. The three of them hung out together a lot, but Lindsay was always who he went home with.

When Lindsay had walked in, Brad was maybe not doing enough to put off Phoebe, but when Lindsay stormed back out of the kitchen, he went after her, shouting, "It's not what you think."

Had he been putting out signals that whole time that he might be interested in Phoebe? He hadn't thought so.

"She was terrible to me," Lindsay said now.

"Weren't we all friends?"

"Sure, she made sure you would think that. She was constantly undermining me, especially when you were around. She kept saying my cooking was bland and my ideas were boring."

"None of that was true."

"Yeah, but you never said that at the time. You were so... I mean, you'd take her side sometimes when I tried to point this out to you."

"I did?"

Lindsay stared at him for a long time. "Wait, are you saying you didn't notice? Are you really that oblivious?"

"I used to tune Phoebe out sometimes. She talked a lot."

Lindsay's eyebrows shot up. "This is a friend, but you tuned her out sometimes?"

Brad sighed. "Phoebe was in that awful French technique class with me, the one with Claude Hubert. That class nearly killed me, and I needed someone to commiserate with. That's why I kept inviting her to hang out. She understood the unique pain of that class. I mean, that class pretty much drove me to pastry. And then inviting her to hang out was habit. And I thought you liked her."

"I did at first. She could be fun, and she always had the good gossip. But as soon as I realized she was interested in you, I pretty much just wanted to kick her in the teeth."

Brad nodded slowly. A lot of their last year at culinary school was coming into focus now. He hadn't picked up on the dynamic Lindsay was describing, but he believed her. He'd had an inkling that Phoebe had a crush on him, but he wasn't interested and had no intention of acting on it.

"And then she kissed you," said Lindsay.

"I promise I didn't initiate it."

"So you say. She'd been putting me down for weeks at that point, saying really nasty things, sometimes when you weren't there. I started really doubting my own cooking abilities."

"I wish you'd said something. I swear I didn't know. I'm sorry she put you through that."

Lindsay looked at her feet for a moment. "You know what you *did* know, though? You knew that I had a hard time trusting people. You knew how my father's infidelity made me feel. I told you I had a hard time with the way you flirt with everyone and how it made me feel insecure. You knew all of that, and yet you kissed Phoebe."

Brad could hear the emotion in her voice. "I did know that. I didn't want to kiss her. If I could undo it, I would."

"Why did you want to talk tonight? To absolve yourself of your sins?"

"No." Brad pressed his lips together for a moment, trying to gather his thoughts. "I wanted to explain myself in a way that you never let me before. Clear the air. I'm not saying we even have to be friends, but I wanted you to know I wasn't the villain you think I am."

"Is Phoebe?"

He shrugged. "I don't know. I actually haven't seen or talked to Phoebe since culinary school. Although I think we're Facebook friends, in case you decide to check and conclude I'm a liar."

"I won't. But she just… I mean, I didn't trust her for a second. And she got so nasty the closer we got to graduation that I thought she was trying to steal you, and I thought you might let yourself get stolen because she was pretty and you seemed to like her."

"I didn't."

"You keep saying that. But what was I supposed to think?"

"That I loved you? That I wouldn't cheat on you? That you could trust me?"

Lindsay shot him a dubious look. "It's not that easy. I let her get in my head. I started to doubt my own abilities, both to keep you and to do good things in the kitchen. And I get that it's my issue, but... You see where I was coming from?"

Brad sighed. "I wish we'd had the opportunity to talk about all this at the time."

"Well, maybe that was the problem. We only ever talked in the abstract." Lindsay looked at the blank wall opposite the couch.

"I *am* sorry. I don't know how I could have prevented Phoebe from kissing me or you from walking in on me, but you're right. We should have talked about this stuff before it became a crisis."

It seemed to Brad, though, that Phoebe was more an excuse than a cause. It was good to have a rational discussion about this stuff. Or at least one using inside voices. And, yes, they should have had a real talk about the future back in culinary school, and Brad should have been more mindful of the minefield created by Lindsay's issues with her father and how that made her unable to forgive cheating. But he never would have deliberately hurt her, and he wished she would see that.

It felt like they'd come to some sort of conclusion.

"So what happened after culinary school? Why didn't you get a restaurant job?" It probably wasn't the right question to ask, but he was curious about it.

She rubbed her forehead, looking a little irritated. "I worked as a line cook for about a year after school and hated every minute of it. I love to cook, but I hated working in that restaurant. Then this opportunity to review came up, so I jumped at it. It didn't have anything to do with Phoebe, if that's what you're asking."

Brad stayed quiet for a moment, thinking. Of course he'd kept tabs on Lindsay. He understood hating that first job; his hadn't been a bed of roses, either. But he guessed he had worried their breakup had somehow made food something she hated, too. He wouldn't have blamed her if it had. He was glad to hear she still loved to cook.

But, lord, Phoebe. He hadn't really thought of Phoebe in a long time, outside of her being the reason Lindsay dumped him. He hadn't known Phoebe and Lindsay hated each other.

"I really had no idea you felt that way about Phoebe."

"Because you weren't paying attention."

"No, I wasn't." He took a breath. That was true; he had been oblivious. "I was an idiot. But I'm paying attention now. And I want to keep talking. I want you to keep talking to me."

"Why should I?"

Something in her tone rubbed him the wrong way. She sounded snotty and angry. Hadn't he groveled enough? Did she not understand? "Because now you're not listening to *me*! You didn't then, either. You never gave me a chance. I *tried* to explain what happened, but instead of listening, you dumped me. You *always* believed the worst about me and used Phoebe as an excuse to leave me. You still don't seem to believe me now. You were the one who had one foot out the door the whole time, didn't you?"

"No more than you did!"

"I was in love with you, too. Maybe I didn't have our whole future planned out or anything, but I sure as hell didn't want to break up. Hell, if you said the word, I'd want you right here, right now. We were great together, Lindsay. I've missed you every damn day since you left."

The words rang in Lindsay's mind for a long time. Brad hadn't wanted to break up. He still wanted her.

Lindsay hadn't trusted him. For years, she'd assumed this was because her instincts were right—he'd kissed Phoebe, after all—but either way, deep down, she hadn't trusted him. But he hadn't trusted her enough to commit to the future. And that was no way to carry on a relationship.

"We didn't trust each other," she said.

"I guess not. I mean, yeah. That seems to be at the heart of it. Although it wasn't so much that I didn't trust you as much as I subconsciously thought you'd find some reason to leave me. And you did."

Lindsay nodded. She knew why she hadn't trusted Brad. Growing up with a single mom who put almost all of her energy into hating Lindsay's philandering dad would make anyone skeptical of relationships. The fact that Brad was always such a flirt didn't help much. Why did he have to be so goddamned charming? No wonder everyone was always falling in love with him.

This conversation left her feeling spent, like she'd just ugly cried at the end of a sad movie. She looked at Brad now, sitting and looking back at her like he expected her to say or do something. But what was there to say? Lindsay had trust issues; Brad had kissed another woman. He claimed he hadn't meant for it to happen, and she wanted to believe him. She still didn't trust him, not completely. So where did that leave them?

As if she'd asked the question aloud, Brad said, "I know your parents did a number on you. And not to be that not-all-men guy, but, well, not all men cheat. Not all men will let you down. I mean, look at your friends! Paige and Lauren are both with great guys, as far as I can tell. Were they wrong to trust their significant others?"

"No," Lindsay said quietly, knowing he was right. Lauren and Paige had actually given Lindsay some hope that romance was real. She just hadn't anticipated it happening with Brad. She'd thought that ship had sailed. But he'd just told her the ship was still waiting for her on the dock.

Brad moved over and sat on the sofa. "I wanted to talk because I thought maybe we could clear the air. I work for your friend now, and you must know how things are at the café with everyone being treated like family. So I figured you and I should find a way to put up with each other, because odds are good we're going to be in the same place every now and then. I don't know if we can be friends, but we can at least try not to murder each other in the cat room."

"That's not a terrible thought."

"Thanks." Brad grinned. "I have good ideas occasionally."

Lauren's head spun.

It was that smile that had hooked her the first time they'd met. They'd been paired together in a proteins class before Brad had switched to pastry. During a session on identifying which beef cuts came from which part of the cow, Brad had started cracking jokes and Lindsay had laughed.

"That sirloin thing is untrue," he'd said at one point. "I mean, they say Henry VIII loved the steak so much he knighted it Sir Loin, but that's not true. 'Sir' comes from the French, meaning 'over.' It's the top part of the loin."

"How nerdy of you to know that."

And then he'd grinned. There was something silly and self-satisfied in that smile, but it lit up his whole face and made something in her melt. She spent that whole semester with a stupid, overwhelming crush on him. When he finally asked her out at the end of the semester, she couldn't say no.

She'd never been happier.

He shot that grin at her now, and she wanted to kiss it off his face.

But that was not what they were here for.

Yet she could still feel the thrum in her body whenever he was near. He was gorgeous, no question. He looked a bit more reputable now, with shorter hair and a clean-shaven face. He had the sort of presence that filled a room. When they'd dated, Lindsay had found that warm and comforting, but now she found it a little intimidating. His eyes sparkled, his muscles stood out on his arms, and he even smelled good. If she *didn't* want him, she'd wonder about her own mental health.

And now he was being sweet and sensible and not like the villain she wanted him to be. She could walk away from a villain. She wasn't sure she could walk away from Brad.

"What are you thinking?" he asked.

"I hate that you're so...you, sometimes."

"What does that mean?"

"You're...you know. Handsome and charming."

He raised an eyebrow. "Oh, really?"

"Like you didn't already know that."

"You're beautiful but also quite prickly. But I guess you have some charms."

"Some charms?"

He threw his head back and laughed. "See? This is what I miss. We used to just sit around for hours, talking about food and making each other laugh. And I knew you were the One when you laughed at my dumb jokes."

Lindsay balked. The One?

He shrugged, as if to say, *you heard me.*

Lindsay lunged at him. Later, she'd wonder exactly what had made her do it, but something about him smiling and laughing and making her feel the way he used to robbed her of all reason and good sense. She kissed him hard. He put out his hands, probably in self-defense, and rested them on her waist.

Lindsay resigned herself to her fate. Something in her still cared about him, still wanted him, and even though she knew it was stupid and she'd regret it later, she went for it anyway.

She expected Brad to protest, but he went with it, letting her push him down on the sofa until they were both horizontal and she was straddling his waist. They each had a foot on the floor, and this position was not ideal, but she knew if she stopped, the bubble would pop.

He groaned and bucked his hips up against hers before thrusting his fingers into her hair and snaking his tongue into her mouth.

When one of his hands ran down the side of her face, down her neck, to cup her breast, she suddenly had second thoughts.

She pulled black slightly.

"My friends keep saying I should get you out of my system."

"Uh-huh. How do you propose to do that?"

"You don't think us having sex is a bad idea?"

He grinned again. "I think it's a *great* idea. Here, sit up."

She rolled until she was back sitting where she had been. Brad stood and offered his hand, so she took it.

Brad rolled his eyes. "Let's review. We seem to have reached some kind of understanding. Our prior relationship ended not because I cheated, which I did not do, but because we never quite trusted each other. Lesson learned. Can we be friends?"

Could they? Lindsay was not at all certain they could, but she said, "Sure."

"Cool. Now. You just jumped on me and then said you wanted to get me out of your system, which sure seems like an invitation to sex."

She'd made a wrong turn somewhere. She'd been willing to talk, but... Brad was right. She wanted to have sex, too. Her memories of what it was like to be with him were overwhelming. There'd been men before and men since, and yet these memories had never faded.

"I won't make you promise anything," said Brad. "You want to get your rocks off and leave, I'm game. You want to talk about more than that happening? I'm game for that, too."

She sighed. "I hate when you're reasonable."

"My bedroom is right here. The bed is far more comfortable and less lumpy than the couch."

This could be just sex. Lindsay was mostly worried she'd want more after.

She let Brad lead her into the bedroom. The first thing he did once they stood at the foot of the bed was let go of her hand and whip off his shirt.

Lindsay wanted this. Brad was into it, too. This was familiar. She reached over and ran her hands over Brad's bare chest. He definitely worked out more now than he had when they'd dated, and his chest was more defined than she remembered, but a lot of this was familiar, too. The breadth of his shoulders, the scar on his belly from a childhood injury, the sun tattoo on his pec. He'd gotten that tattoo when he was nineteen, she remembered, and it was a drunken mistake, but he liked the optimism it expressed. That was Brad, always looking on the bright side. He floated through life as if everything would work out.

Or he had when they'd dated, but that was five years ago. Had he changed since then? If so, how? Did they even still know each other the way they once had?

She didn't want to think about that just now. This was about the physical.

He dipped his head and kissed her. This was familiar, too. It all flooded back to her now. This is how he tasted. She'd always loved that he was an aggressive kisser, that he opened his mouth before his lips even touched hers. She loved the feel of his big hands on her body, how warm they were, how they molded against her shapes and curves. Her skin came alive where he touched her, even under layers of clothing.

His fingers slipped under her shirt. She arched her back as

his hands spread across the bare skin between her bra and the waistband of her jeans. Her heart rate accelerated in anticipation of where he might touch her next, and her breath caught in her throat. With practiced motion, he unhooked her bra and then slid his hands around to touch her front, and she bent up to meet his hands. It was like relief, in a way, to feel this again.

He knew just where to touch her, just how much pressure to exert, like he was reading her mind. She peeled off her shirt and bra and let Brad get an eyeful. He groaned and touched her again, then maneuvered her toward the bed.

His bedroom was small, really only with room enough for his big bed, a nightstand, and a dresser. His bed was made, but the bedding smelled like Brad. As he crawled onto the bed and hovered over her, she inhaled that scent again. He smelled sweet now, like cake frosting, but still had that undefinable Brad scent under that.

She reached for his fly. This she remembered, too. Brad had been a boxer-briefs type of guy and had nothing to be ashamed of underneath. His skin was hot where she touched him, and she was gratified when he let out a soft hiss. She undid the button on his jeans and let her fingers dance over the bulge there. He groaned. She smiled in satisfaction.

He pushed up and looked down at her with an eyebrow raised, like a dare. She returned the look. He grinned again and slid off her jeans and panties, dumping them and the ballet flats she'd been wearing on the floor. She watched him, touched his strong arms, felt heat flood her body. God, he was gorgeous. Maybe even more so now that he had a few more years on him. She started to ache with need between her legs.

She tried to convey that she wanted him to take off his pants without saying anything; she'd been able to do that with a look once upon a time.

He walked to the side of the bed—sauntered, really—his eyelids lowered but a smirk on his lips. He looked a little smug. Lindsay spread her legs. "You better hurry up. I might change my mind."

"Nah."

"You seem sure of yourself."

He shucked his pants and underwear. He was already hard. "You're naked. And now I am, too."

"Look at that."

He slid open the nightstand drawer and pulled out a condom, which he rolled on.

"So that's it? We just get right to it?" she asked.

"I'm just getting prepared so that when I have you wet and begging for it, I don't have to stop what I'm doing."

Lindsay went flush everywhere. It took all of her composure to raise an eyebrow. "You say things."

"I intend to put my money where my mouth is."

He crawled onto the bed again. He kissed her, and as he did so, he ran a hand down her body, cupping her breast on the way. He tweaked her nipples. Electrical currents radiated through her body, as if Brad's fingers were made of lightning. She swallowed a moan, not yet willing to let him know how turned on she was, but it escaped anyway. She threw her head back and surrendered to it instead, seeing the futility in holding back. He kissed her again, and she could feel his smile against her lips. She hadn't wanted him to know how good he was, but decided she should just roll with it. Feel this. Feel *him* against her, smug smile and all.

She tried not to think about all the other people they'd both been with in the last five years—especially all of the women he'd been with, as irrational as that was. Instead, she focused on the way his fingers danced over her body. She ran her hands over his chest and his back, over the curve of his ass. His skin was smooth and a little sweaty under her hands. His body was strong, with rounded muscles, more like a runner than a baker. She trailed her fingers along his spine and he hissed again, jerked a little in her arms, and she knew she was getting to him, too. This time she was the one who smiled smugly.

Then his fingers dipped between her legs.

"Already ready for me?"

"Not quite. I think you should try to earn it."

There was that goddamned grin. Then he moved, kissing his way down her chest. He sucked a nipple into his mouth. He kissed her belly button. Then he kissed her between her legs.

She melted. All the way, all the rest of her defenses just evaporated.

She moaned as he lapped at her, his expert tongue exciting her, making her body come alive. Everything in her wanted to buck against him, to urge him to press harder, to just make her feel *everything*, but not yet; she needed this to last. She moaned as he got his fingers into the mix. And, oh, there it was, just the right amount of magic, and everything in her was hot and tingly and racing toward the cliff. Her heart sped up. Her limbs turned to jelly. She thrust her fingers into his hair and tried to pull him closer, tried to get closer to that cliff.

Lindsay was on the teetering edge but not quite getting there, and she was going to go out of her mind if she didn't come soon.

"Brad," she said.

"Mm-hmm."

"I need you."

He lifted his head and raised an eyebrow. "What do you need me to do?"

"I need you inside me. Right now."

"With pleasure."

And before she even really knew what was happening, he moved with lighting quickness and was on top of her. He kissed her hard, and she could taste herself, but she didn't mind it.

"You want me?" he asked, the blunt head of his cock poking at the entrance to her body.

"God, so much." She canted her hips up to meet him, hoping to encourage him.

"This is the moment I was talking about, by the way. I'm ready for it."

"Good. Shut up."

He thrust forward.

She moaned as he sank inside her. Didn't even hesitate, just went right for it, the way he did everything. Damn, that was good. He filled her exactly the way she needed him to. She kissed him, put her arms around him, and thrust up against him. He started to slide in and out, build up a rhythm, and he slid a hand between them to rub his thumb against her clit. This was... This was everything, the perfect amount of pressure, exactly what she needed, and she was going to explode if he kept doing it. He rocked into her and grunted with the effort. She could see the strain on his face as he tried to postpone his orgasm.

A thousand memories hit her suddenly. Lazy lovemaking on weekend mornings. Quick, stolen moments in kitchens. Hot and fast in the shower. Slow and tender in the evening. The two of them fitting together the way two people were meant to. Over and over again, and it was never boring, always exciting, always exactly like this, the kind of sex that made Lindsay think her whole heart would explode.

The orgasm clobbered her, stole her breath, made the world go white. She arched off the bed and cried out. He cursed above her, grasped at her shoulders, and then she felt him shudder.

She wrapped her arms around him and held him as he came, something she'd done plenty of times when they were together, almost like a habit.

CHAPTER 9

"YOU REMEMBER THAT WEIRD CRUISE we took?" asked Brad.

Lindsay laughed. He took that to mean she did.

She was draped over him on his bed, still naked. He ran his fingers along her arm, and she sighed happily.

"I remember," she said.

Aaron had gotten a job as a bartender on a booze cruise. Brad had always been game to try new things, so when Aaron offered him tickets to the cruise, he liked the idea. The ship had a casino room that was only open during the time when the ship tooled around in international waters. It quickly became clear that this was the reason most of the people had boarded the ship. As neither Lindsay nor Brad had much interest in gambling, they mostly hung out at the bar with Aaron. Then Aaron said that the trip back to Manhattan had a view worth seeing, so Brad had led Lindsay up to the main deck.

Hardly anyone was up there. And Aaron had been right; the view of the skyline as the ship headed back toward Manhattan was breathtaking. Brad and Lindsay had sat alone on the deck of the ship gazing out at the skyline, letting the magic of the city waft over them.

"This is so weird but also kind of fun," Lindsay had said as they looked at the lights flickering on the tall buildings.

"I know."

"The crowd here is a little unsavory. Or at least very drunk."

Brad had laughed. "I believe it is largely what the locals call 'bridge and tunnel.'"

"I haven't lived in the city very long, so I can hardly make fun of them."

"You've been here, what, five years? Six? That's enough."

"It's a great city, isn't it?"

Brad looked out at the skyline. Something swelled in his chest, his breath stolen by the sheer magnitude of the buildings rising out of the land, right up to the edge of the water. "Yeah. It's pretty amazing."

The woman he was with was pretty amazing, too. He put his arm around her and kissed the top of her head. "I love you, you know."

"I know. I love you, too."

The words were a new part of their vocabulary. They'd only just expressed them a couple of weeks before the cruise. Brad liked how they tasted in his mouth, though. He wanted to say it all the time.

Even now, all those years later, he still cared about her. He wanted her back in his life. It wasn't love, exactly, not anymore. Too much time had passed. They needed to get to know each other all over again. Probably they were doing all this backward, though, considering they'd just slept together.

"What's Aaron up to these days?" Lindsay asked.

"He works at the Food Channel. Are you still in touch with anyone from school?"

"Sure." Lindsay yawned and snuggled closer to Brad. "Tom Roston works for Daniel Boulud."

"That checks out. He was obsessive about French technique."

Lindsay laughed. "The bane of your existence."

"That class was brutal. I learned a ton, but I've never had a teacher who was more anal about knife cuts. 'All those bits of celery for the mirepoix must be identical in size!'" He affected a French accent to imitate his teacher.

Lindsay giggled. "Well, anyway, Mandy opened her own brick-oven pizza place in New Jersey. Yvette moved to California and is making small plates at a winery in Napa." She rattled off a few other names.

Brad did the same, listing the half-dozen people he still talked to regularly, a few of whom were working at some of the city's top restaurants. And he had Milk Bar under his belt; it was a bakeshop at the top of many of the city's Best Dessert lists.

He did not mention that he'd heard through the grapevine that Phoebe was working at Serendipity. Phoebe didn't matter. Mentioning her would just upset Lindsay. Besides, he felt like they'd reached some sort of...well, maybe not truce, but an understanding at least. And she was here. No need to bring up the past again.

Brad took her hand in his, played with her fingers. They were long and graceful, her nails manicured and covered in pink polish but chipped in a few places. That seemed very Lindsay also.

They'd dated a little over a year. Enough time for Brad to have started thinking about the future but not really deciding anything. He hadn't thought Lindsay had really been in that place back then, either. They were twenty-five, on the verge of starting new careers, neither in a position to settle down or make a big commitment. Sure, they'd talked about the future in the abstract, fantasizing about opening a restaurant together, but Brad had thought it was hypothetical. A lot of their classmates had come to New York to study at one of the best culinary schools in the country and then gone off to find jobs in other cities, or in their hometowns, or wherever they could find jobs. It wasn't outrageous to think he or Lindsay might have to move to find employment. It seemed silly to make plans.

But maybe he should have thought harder, because wow, he'd missed this. He'd missed her in a way he was aware of but didn't fully realize until she was back in his arms again. This felt right in a way nothing had since she'd left him.

But he didn't want to say anything that would scare her off.

"And what about you? I googled you in preparation for my story," Lindsay said. "Your résumé is impressive."

He moved his shoulders, shrugging as much as he could while lying on his back. "I got lucky." And it genuinely felt that way. His culinary career was a lot of *right place at the right time.*

"You're talented."

He half shrugged again. "I had good teachers. Although my first job was baking cupcakes at that little bakery near school. Not the manliest of jobs."

Lindsay laughed. "I guess not. Is baking supposed to be manly?"

"Not if you ask my father. You may recall he was only so-so on letting me go to culinary school. I can make a mean frosting rose, but this was, like, the last indignity."

"I do remember that. I only met your father that one time, but I remember his attitudes on gender being old-school."

"That's like saying ghost chilis are a little spicy. His attitudes about gender are less progressive than some cavemen. You know what he said when I told him about the job at the cat café?"

"Oh, no."

"After he called me a homo—his word—he asked when I would be undergoing gender reassignment surgery. See, it remains his great shame that I'm not... I don't even know. Hammering up drywall or in the NFL getting a concussion."

"You know that's all nonsense, right? Everything about you is great the way it is."

He gave her a little squeeze. He appreciated the compliment and took it to heart, especially coming from Lindsay. "Thanks. I know that most of the time. Talking to him always makes me feel like garbage, though."

"Baking requires difficult skills. A lot of them I don't even have. I bet you can make one of those fancy cakes like on TV without breaking a sweat. I can bake a decent cupcake, but the frosting always looks deranged."

"It takes some practice."

"Don't sell yourself short. And you know a lot about, I dunno, how to make carrot cake without the moisture from the carrots making it gummy. And how to make meat cookies cats will eat. Even your dad has to admit that meat cookies are pretty butch."

He laughed. He hated talking about the garbage with his father, but letting some of it out now had been a relief in a way. He knew, intellectually, that nothing his father said mattered, that he didn't need to live up to whatever standard for manliness his father wanted to impose. Brad was comfortable with who he was most of the time. It had taken some work to get here, though, and back during his first post-school job, getting the perfect swirl on top of a cupcake had felt like a failure, somehow.

He savored holding Lindsay and the soft feel of her skin under his fingertips and pushed the rest of it away. He didn't want to wallow in his darker emotions when Lindsay was here.

He sighed. Just lying in bed with her chatting was satisfying in a way. He was a little afraid to ask her to spend the night, because he figured she'd freak and say no or start a discussion with him about where this was going, and he didn't want to talk anymore. He just wanted to hold on to this moment for as long as it lasted.

As Brad started to drift off to sleep, Lindsay wondered if she should stay or go. It felt unfair to just sneak out without saying anything, so she lay there for a moment to see if Brad might wake back up. When he started to snore, she realized he probably wanted her to spend the night.

Lindsay's stomach rolled over. This was all wrong. She hadn't come here intending to sleep with Brad. It had happened, and it was good, but that was all that this could be. She wasn't getting back together with him. They hadn't worked the first time, and there was no reason to think they could now.

Before she'd dated him, he'd had a reputation as kind of a ladies' man. He was good-looking and charming and flirted with everyone, even after he and Lindsay were in a committed relationship. He'd always insisted the flirting was innocent. It probably was. That hadn't made Lindsay less jealous.

That moment when she'd seen Phoebe kissing him had seared itself on her mind. Lindsay had been hurt by that, which wasn't exactly a state secret. Hearing Brad's side had mostly convinced her that he hadn't meant anything by what happened. But it had still happened. Phoebe had set them both up, probably with the aim of getting Lindsay to dump Brad so she could have him to herself. And, bottom line, Brad hadn't said no. He hadn't pushed Phoebe away or told her to back off. He'd *kissed* her.

But that was all water under the bridge. It was in the past. The problem for Lindsay now was that getting over Brad had been one of the hardest things she'd ever done—and she knew, deep down, she hadn't been completely successful. No matter how handsome and charming and affectionate Brad was, no matter how many times he said the right thing or asked for them to get back together, she could not put herself through that again.

She sat up, which made Brad wake up.

"Huh?"

"I'm going home," she said, swinging her legs out of bed.

"No, come on. Just go to sleep."

"I want to walk home before it gets much later."

"You can spend the night. I want you to spend the night. I'll make you pain perdu in the morning."

Leave it to the pastry chef to say "French toast" in the fancy way. And tempting as it was, she knew staying for breakfast would lead to spending more time together, and this had to be a one and done. "No, I need to get home. I–I need some time to think." She nearly smacked her forehead. That was giving him too much.

Brad flopped onto his back and threw an arm over his eyes. "You're freaking out."

She sighed. He'd asked her for honesty, right? "Well, yeah. This is not what I came here for."

"I will point out again that you came on to me."

She pulled on her panties and bra. His gaze kept raking over her body, so he was a little distracted. But she sighed. "If your plan is to make me fall in love with you again, it won't work. I can't. I'm not putting myself through that again."

His eyebrows shot up. "Is that what you think I'm doing?"

"I don't know what you're doing."

"I sincerely only wanted to talk tonight. Great sex was a bonus. You're hot, and I like you a lot despite the fact that you are the most stubborn, cynical woman I have ever met. I had no ulterior motive here. Don't put one on me."

"You want to get back together, though."

"The thought crossed my mind."

Lindsay shook her head.

"Do you disagree that the sex was good?"

Lindsay grunted and pulled on her jeans. "Sex was never the problem with us."

Brad got out of bed, seemingly unaware that he was naked. He crossed the room just as she was pulling on her shirt. "I'm not asking you for anything," he said, "except to maybe stop avoiding me."

"I'm not avoiding you."

"You are 100 percent avoiding me. Monique at the café told me you were a regular, but you haven't come by at all since I started working there, except for the interviews and tonight."

She slid her feet into her shoes. "What's your point?"

"You don't want to get back together, fine. I respect that. But even you have to admit we have fun together sometimes, and for a few minutes there, you actually seemed to like me, so maybe you could turn down your ire a couple of notches and trust that we can be in the same space every now and then without stabbing each other."

"Or fucking each other."

He had the balls to grin at that. "Or that."

"Don't look so smug."

He walked past her out of the bedroom. She glanced at the street-facing windows, which all had heavy curtains hanging from them. Lindsay could picture Brad walking around this space naked all the time. She hated that she found the image so exciting.

He slipped into the bathroom for a moment, then emerged wearing a robe. He grabbed her handbag from where she'd left it near the sofa and handed it to her.

"Go ahead and think about things," he said. "I'm here if you want to talk."

Ugh. Why was he so stupid perfect? She heard in his tone that he was being genuine. It wasn't so much that she wanted to go as that she didn't trust herself if she stayed. "I'm going," she said. "Tonight was not completely terrible."

Then she made herself leave before Brad's open, earnest face made her change her mind.

CHAPTER 10

LINDSAY SAT AT A TABLE near the front window of Pop and ordered a martini as the waitress walked by. Pop was best known for its extensive martini menu, and most of the drinks were really just sugary ingredients with a splash of alcohol, but they were all tasty. Her personal favorite was called the Dirrrty Martini, which was, well, a dirty martini, but with a little citrus added to brighten up the brininess of the olive juice.

Lauren and Paige were both working the late shift at the café, so they wouldn't be along for a bit. Evan had texted that he was running late because something had gone terribly awry on the subway. So Lindsay sat alone and nursed her martini and played a puzzle game on her phone while she waited.

And who should walk in but Brad.

He looked around, spotted her, walked to her table, and helped himself to a seat.

"What are you doing here?"

He grinned, which was unnerving. "I brought Hamilton home yesterday and realized I forgot to get his immunization records from Lauren, but I need them before his vet appointment Saturday. Lauren and I are working opposite shifts the rest of the week, so she offered to meet me here tonight to give me the paperwork. She said you'd be here."

"You're early. She won't get here for another hour, probably. I'm waiting for Evan."

"Uh-huh."

"You already knew that, didn't you?"

He shrugged.

"Did you come here to see me?"

"Do you see anyone else here?"

Lindsay was not happy to see him. She wasn't ready to talk to him yet. If she ever would be. This was ridiculous. Why did he keep popping up in her life? She sipped her martini and looked around, trying to find something to focus her attention on.

"So you don't want to talk about what happened?" he asked.

"What, the sexy bits?"

"And you freaking out afterward."

Lindsay sighed. No, she didn't want to talk about any of this, not at all. She ground out, "We're not getting back together."

"No?"

"No. The sex was good and all, but as far as I can tell, you're still the same charming, flirty mess I broke up with five years ago."

He had the good grace to look mildly offended, but his eyes sparkled as if he were laughing at her. "Good? The sex was *great*."

She rolled her eyes. "Sex was never our problem."

He nodded. "So you said the other night." When the waitress slid a basket of chips onto the table, he took one and popped it in his mouth, a gesture that looked casual and relaxed. "So what was our problem? That you are so jaded from your parents' divorce that you don't trust yourself to be vulnerable with anyone, and that you used Phoebe making out with me as an excuse to end the good thing you and I had going?" He popped another chip in his mouth.

Lauren stared at him for a long moment and then realized her jaw was hanging open. She closed her mouth hard, her teeth clacking together. She must have looked like a cartoon character.

How dare he? How could he just sit there and casually psychoanalyze her, think he knew her so well and spit out a proclamation like that?

But also, she was shocked at how well he'd nailed her.

She realized, then, that despite his casual demeanor, he was mad. She'd been within her rights to walk out on him the other night; she wasn't ready for anything more with him than that one dumb night. But he was mad that she'd bailed with him.

He should have understood. She knew that being the child of an acrimonious divorce did not make her unique, but she'd confessed that much to Brad one night when they'd been dating. Her mother had been a mess emotionally for a lot of Lindsay's childhood, and Lindsay had always been reluctant to put herself in the position to be that vulnerable. Enough of her friends were in good relationships now that obviously love and happiness were achievable, but Lindsay often wondered if they were really in the cards for her.

Lindsay's father and Brad had a lot in common. Brad was far kinder, but like Lindsay's dad, he was an incorrigible flirt and women seemed to gravitate to him. Brad knew all this because Lindsay had told him, partly to confess something about herself and partly to explain why she had trust issues. She'd seen first-hand how much her mother had been destroyed by her father's philandering, and Lindsay didn't want to repeat that old pattern. Brad had acted sympathetic at the time. He'd even told her he was glad she'd told him because he understood her better.

Lindsay's father often partook of what was offered. She hadn't thought Brad had ever done that…until the night she caught him with Phoebe.

"What I was going to say," Lindsay said, recovering, "was that you flirt with anything in a skirt and don't know when to rein it in."

"We've had this conversation before. We had a variation on it the other night. We figured out that we don't trust each other. You don't trust me because I'm an unrepentant flirt, and I don't trust you because you don't trust anyone."

"That's not true. I trust my friends."

"Have you ever been in a romantic relationship in which you trusted the guy you were dating?"

Lindsay crossed her arms because he probably already knew the answer to that question. Clearly it was no. It was why she wasn't involved with anyone right now. The fact that he kept bringing it up pissed her off.

"In my defense," said Brad, "I am a functional adult now in a way I was not five years ago. You may have noticed that I have my own place now."

"The only art on your walls is a Star Wars poster."

"That I put in a frame. See? Adult."

Lindsay tried to decide what she really wanted here. She sensed that Brad was trying to woo her in his own very Brad way. She couldn't quite understand why.

"Anyway," he said after he ate another chip, "you agreed you could spend time in the same room as me without us stabbing each other, so I partly just came by to say hi while I wait for Lauren. So, hi."

"Hi."

Brad ate another chip. "These are good. What do you usually drink here?"

"We come here for the martinis."

Brad picked up the drink menu and grimaced. Lindsay suddenly remembered that, though he had a sweet tooth, Brad hated sugary drinks. When the waitress came by again, he ordered a scotch on the rocks.

They'd known each other inside and out once. How much of that knowledge had changed over time?

Some things probably hadn't changed. Brad had a tattoo of two rolling pins that formed an X on the inside of his forearm now—that had definitely been added in the last five years— but she suspected a lot of other things were the same. He hated green olives but liked black ones. He added milk but not sugar to coffee. He had an allergy to horseradish he didn't know about until he ate some one day in culinary school and then broke out in hives. He loved sci-fi movies and watching baseball games while snoozing on his sofa and reading thrillers. She assumed little of that had changed.

She sipped her martini and eyed him.

"What are you thinking now?" he asked.

"That I know you but I don't. I was just mentally cataloging the things I remember about you."

"Was one of those things my huge penis?"

Lindsay laughed despite herself. "No. I guess I'll put that on the list. I was thinking more how you like your coffee, what foods you're allergic to, which kind of movies you like."

"Ah, okay. You like your coffee light and sweet, like, why even bother with the coffee? You're allergic to pineapple, as we learned during the upside-down cake incident. And you like froufrou rom-coms but will never admit it. There. Did I pass?"

"Yeah, I guess so. What makes you think I like rom-coms?"

"Because despite your aversion to love and commitment, you teared up at the end of every one we watched together. You, my dear ex, are a sap."

"That is not true."

He shrugged.

"These are all superficial things anyway," she said. "Me being allergic to pineapple doesn't tell you anything about my personality."

"No, it doesn't. What does, however, is something I've always admired about you, which is that you are fiercely loyal to your friends, but as soon as someone does anything to cross you or them, that person is dead to you. I know this because I was on the wrong side of that once. And I'd like to be alive to you again."

Brad knew he was running out of time. Evan would get here any minute, and although Brad and Lindsay were not exactly in private as they spoke in the middle of a crowded bar, none of her friends were here to overhear this conversation.

"What does that even mean?" Lindsay asked after a long pause.

"I think you should go out with me again."

"Brad."

"Hear me out. I think you should go out with me again. Not commit to anything, just go on a date or something, so that I can demonstrate to you that I am a good person and that we could be good together once we figure out that whole trust thing."

"This thing with us didn't work out the first time. What makes you think it will now?"

That was the million-dollar question, wasn't it? "We've learned and grown as people?"

She grunted and crossed her arms.

"We'll never know if we don't try."

"I guess." She shot him a sidelong glance. "You got another cliché for me?"

Brad laughed. "Fake it 'til you make it? Eyes on the prize? Go for the gold?"

Lindsay rolled her eyes.

"Just think about it, all right? And, look, if you just want to use me for my hot body, I'm okay with that, too." Brad wasn't entirely sure why he was throwing himself at Lindsay so hard. Well, he did want her back. No one had ever fit with him or made him laugh or eased the old wounds in him the way Lindsay had, and he'd regretted every moment of his life since she'd walked away from him the first time. Oh, he'd dated other women—he was a man with a pulse, after all—but none of them measured up.

Her mouth twisted in a way that showed she was amused but didn't want to be, a suppressed smile for the ages. He thought he almost had her when Evan walked in.

Lindsay, Evan, and Lauren had been friends since their undergrad days. Brad's understanding of the situation was that Evan and Lauren were very close, but since Lindsay had moved to Brooklyn after culinary school, the three of them and Paige had started spending a lot of time together. It had been clear from their rapport at the adoption party that they were all close now in a way they hadn't quite been five years ago.

Another clue was that Evan sat down and gave Brad the stink eye.

"I'm just waiting for Lauren," said Brad. "She has some paperwork for me. She made me get a cat."

"She does that," said Evan.

"He dropped by to say hi to me, too," said Lindsay.

"Did you guys kiss and make up or what?" asked Evan.

Lindsay looked horrified, so Brad decided not to betray anything. "No, no. She still hates me. Not for lack of effort on my part."

Evan narrowed his eyes at Brad. It was like he was trying to see right through him. The intensity of Evan's gaze was unnerving. "Uh, what are you doing?" asked Brad.

"Everyone at the cat café is in love with you, so I'm trying to figure out why."

"I make good scones?"

"You're not hard on the eyes, I guess," said Evan.

Brad smiled.

"There it is," said Lindsay.

"Oh," said Evan. "That's a persuasive argument."

"What did I do?" Brad asked.

Evan laughed. "Not to be, like, a creepy guy on the street, but you should smile more."

Brad filed that away for later.

"Anyway, sorry I'm late," Evan said, his tone lighter. "The subway is pandemonium. Also, it's a day ending in *y*."

"Is Will coming?" Lindsay asked.

"No. I told him I had meetings all day, which is not really a lie."

"Do you not want to see him?"

"I don't know. I'm reevaluating."

Brad sensed there was something going on here that Lindsay already knew about, but it felt invasive to ask, so he sat back and listened. He munched on a few more chips.

"Does Will know you're reevaluating?" asked Lindsay.

"Not exactly."

"Was Will at the cat adoption party?" asked Brad.

"No, he had other plans," said Evan.

"Just curious if I've met him."

Lindsay shrugged. "He is a nice guy. He's sweet and affectionate."

"He gets me into good restaurants," said Evan.

"If that's your standard," said Brad, "you don't need your boyfriend for that."

Evan raised an eyebrow. "Are you saying *you* could get me into good restaurants?"

"I meant Lindsay, but… Yeah, I can do that. I have a lot of contacts in the industry. Not everywhere, of course, but I've got friends."

Evan laughed. "All right. I mean, Will is pretty good company at those restaurants. He knows a lot about food."

"What does he do?"

"He's a cookbook editor." Evan mentioned the name of the publisher.

"Wait, your boyfriend is Will Feeney?"

"So you know him."

"Not well," said Brad. "We've met a few times. He's pretty well-known among New York foodie types, though. Seems like a nice guy."

Evan nodded. "He is. I'm just being stupid. And if he were here, he'd try to talk you into writing a cookbook with cat-friendly recipes."

Brad felt maxed out as it was and couldn't imagine finding time to write a cookbook, but he said, "That's not a bad idea."

"If Paige were here, she'd tell you to go for it," said Lindsay. "Great publicity for the café."

"Let's not mention this in front of Paige, then," said Brad. "I've only been at this job a month."

Lauren and Paige arrived a few minutes later. Lauren stood at the table for a moment, surveying the scene, before sitting and said, "Well, Brad, I'm glad to see you here, and not your bloodied, mutilated corpse."

"I think Lindsay and I have made a truce." Brad looked at Lindsay to verify if this was true.

She shrugged, but he'd take that.

CHAPTER 11

AFTER HER MORNING ROUTINE, LINDSAY sat down at her desk with a cup of coffee and yawned as she turned on her laptop.

Fred wandered over and hopped up on the desk. He sat right behind the laptop screen as if to say, *If you're looking in this direction, you should look at me.* Lindsay reached over and petted his head. "Hey, buddy. Did you have a good breakfast?"

He rubbed his chin against her hand affectionately.

"I bet your dreams were about nice things like catching bugs and eating fish and not about things like certain ex-boyfriends."

He started to purr.

She turned her attention back to her computer. Her email was mostly inane, so she clicked over to a newspaper website. And there was the breaking news: New York Forum *reports second-quarter losses; layoffs expected.*

The *Forum* was one of the last independent media companies in the city. It had spent the last decade building up alternative revenue streams, particularly online. The editor in chief had been fighting to keep the print edition circulating even while some shareholders had been putting pressure on the organization to go fully online.

And, yeah, the *Forum* could be a little trashy. Most people bought it for its popular celebrity gossip column. But it published some good journalism, too, and it was one of about five newspapers and magazines that were popular among the morning straphangers. Declining print circulation and ad revenue put the print edition in danger, so if the *Forum* was having trouble, Lindsay had always guessed that would be the first thing to go.

But what did this mean for her own job? She didn't have much seniority or really any history with the company. Her byline had only appeared four times, although she'd assigned out a dozen stories to other writers. But the *Forum* was more likely to keep editors like Erica Sanchez and dump the younger, newer people. Right? It wasn't like there were a plethora of opportunities for food writers, even in New York.

She had other skills to fall back on, of course. She hadn't enjoyed flipping burgers in someone else's kitchen, but it was an option if this fell through. The idea of cooking again pulled at her for a moment, but she shook it off.

But maybe it was premature to think that way. She grabbed her phone and called Evan, the only person she could think of who understood how New York media worked. He worked in advertising and graphic design, after all.

After Lindsay explained the situation, she asked, "How worried do you think I should be?"

Evan was silent for a moment, then said, "Hmm. How did that story on Brad do?"

"Pretty well. Lots of clicks on the website. You put cute cats in the featured image, and people will click on it."

Evan laughed. "You may have just unlocked the key to advertising success. I'm going to start putting cats on everything. And I'm assuming the hot guy in the photo didn't hurt."

Lindsay didn't want to dwell on that. "What do I do, Evan?"

"Okay, here's my thought. You need to make yourself indispensable. You need a big story to show them how good and valuable you are. Something that'll attract a lot of attention. Or you need a big scoop, some bit of breaking news that no one else has cottoned on to yet."

"Like what? The culinary world is not exactly teeming with scandal. I don't think 'Jean-Georges put a new pear dessert on his tasting menu' is a thing many people care about."

"Not sure. Can your handsome ex-boyfriend get you into some new restaurant that no one else can get into? Can he connect you with some friend of his, since he seems to know everyone?"

Lindsay sighed. "I don't want to ask Brad."

"What's going on with you guys, anyway?"

"I don't know." And Lindsay really didn't. Her feelings where Brad was concerned were all over the map. She hadn't ever responded to his plea to go on a date. He'd texted her a few times, and she'd ignored him.

She just couldn't see how they could get back together and not repeat their old patterns and end up just where they'd been five years ago.

And did he really want her back? Or was he just being his old flirty self with her? She couldn't figure that out, either.

"Given what I saw of him the other night," said Evan, "I'm guessing he'd help you."

"Probably. I just don't want to owe him anything."

"Who says that's how it would be?"

"'Save my job' is a pretty big favor to ask someone."

"Well, you can suck it up and ask the one person in your life best equipped to help you, or you can continue avoid him and try to find a scoop on your own. I can ask Will. I'm sure he's got a stack of new cookbooks he'd love for you to review."

"I don't think a cookbook review is going to do it, either, but thanks."

"Will knows lots of chefs, was my larger point."

Lindsay considered. Will did know a lot of people in the restaurant biz, but if Evan was thinking they might break up, asking Will seemed highly inappropriate. She wouldn't have felt right asking him for help right before Evan dumped him and then disappeared from her life. If Evan dumped him.

"You're not..." Lindsay started to ask, and then thought better of it.

"I'm not what?"

She decided to just go for it. "You're not settling, are you? You're not just staying with Will because you don't want to be single or because at least he's someone and he's a decent fellow, are you?"

"I honestly don't know. If I'm not feeling it, I should stop stringing him along, but I don't know what I feel. This is all very confusing. I mean, there's nothing wrong with him."

"But he doesn't light you on fire."

"Does Brad light you on fire?"

God, yes. "You've seen him."

"That's not an answer. Will is objectively attractive. So is Brad."

Lindsay closed her eyes and remembered the night she and Brad had spent together recently. Those sheets could have gone up in flames. "Yeah. He lights me on fire. But that's no reason to get back together, if that's what you think."

"It was really more of a survey question. For research purposes."

Lindsay laughed softly. "We're both a mess."

"I know, honey, I know. But if Brad's going to try to worm his way back into your life, I don't think it's unfair of you to ask for his help. Then maybe take the time to think about what you really want with him."

"Yeah, yeah. And I'd give you the same advice, without the asking-for-help part."

"So you're gonna ask Brad for help?"

She sighed. "Yeah, I guess so. But I'll also stress that it doesn't mean we're getting back together. But he wants me to go on a date with him. What if that's what he wants in exchange?"

"Hold your ground, Linds. Be strong. Unless you want to go on a date with him."

"I don't."

"Are you sure?"

No. "Yes."

"All right. You can totally take him. Although that grin of his is *disarming*."

"That's how he got me the first time."

"He's got a powerful weapon in his arsenal. But you, Lindsay, are a strong, confident woman and a professional. You know how to put him in his place."

She was not at all confident she would be able to resist Brad's stupid-handsome face, but she said, "Thanks."

"You're strong. You're a warrior! You're a fierce woman! You're a Taylor Swift song!"

Lindsay laughed and shook her head.

When Lindsay got off the phone, she stared at her computer for a while. Fred moved like a snake around her laptop and settled onto her lap. She petted him, thinking. Making herself indispensable would probably mean pulling out all the stops, and Evan was right—Brad knew everyone. If something was happening in the New York restaurant community, Brad or one of his friends would know about it. So if she wanted a scoop, he'd be the guy to ask. Even if it meant swallowing some pride.

And maybe the prospect of going on a date with him was not *completely* repellent. Because, well, that passion Evan felt was lacking for Will? Lindsay still had it for Brad, somewhere deep down. But that passion wasn't enough sometimes.

———————

Brad brought the last batch of sandwiches from the kitchen to the front of the café. For the last few days, he'd been using leftover croissants—usually the last bakery item left after the breakfast rush—to make little sandwiches with thin-sliced ham or tuna salad or whatever was on sale at the organic market up the street. They'd proven to be a pretty big hit around the lunch rush.

Doug Francis, one of the veterinarians from the clinic next door, walked in just as Brad was putting the last of the sandwiches out.

"What have you got today?" asked Doug.

"Ham and gruyère," Brad said, pointing to one half of the tray, "and organic chicken salad. I have a couple of croissants left, so I could whip up something vegetarian if needed. I've got some vegan cheese and miscellaneous greens in back."

"Not necessary. The chicken salad sounds good."

"Isn't one of the vets vegetarian?"

"Olivia," said Doug, eyeing his sandwich. "She's off today, though. The rest of us carnivores will drift over for one of these sandwiches this afternoon as we get breaks."

Brad bagged a sandwich as Monique rang up Doug's order.

"I'm thinking about doing a roasted vegetable thing," said Brad. "Not on a croissant, though. Roasted vegetables have a lot of moisture. These poor croissants would be mush."

"Sounds healthy," said Doug, sounding suspicious.

"Roasted eggplant, roasted red peppers, balsamic vinegar, fresh mozzarella optional. On sourdough, maybe. I've got my own starter."

"You could go full vegan and make vegan bread."

"Great idea!" said Brad, liking it even though he suspected Doug was joking. "I've been doing some experimenting at home. As long as the yeast does its job, you can make a good, chewy bread without milk or eggs."

"I believe you," said Doug, handing Monique a few bills. "But does it have any flavor?"

"I know vegan food is lost on *you*," said Monique, "but we do have vegan customers. It's good to have options."

"My wife eats mostly vegan. I get it. My son thinks he wants to be a vegetarian now. I think he'll miss bacon within a few days, but as long as he's eating nutritious meals, I don't care."

That sounded like a classic dad.

Or not. Brad's own father would likely never get anywhere near something vegan. Dad was a meat-and-potatoes kind of guy who seemed to think steak was gendered somehow. As Brad had told Lindsay, he still thought pastry making was a girlie profession. He likely expected Brad to bring a man home one of these days—even though Brad was pretty firmly heterosexual—because that was just how Dad thought. Brad had long kept that from Lindsay; he figured if he mentioned it, she'd probably give him some lecture out of one of her undergrad women's studies classes about gender being a construct. It wasn't that Brad disagreed—he loved his job—but his father still took up a lot of mental real estate that Brad tried and failed to deny him. Things had come to a head one weekend in culinary school when Brad's parents visited and Brad had to warn Lindsay.

Brad handed Doug his sandwich.

"I don't want to tell you what to do," said Doug, "but the grocery store on Whitman and Court Streets has the best cheese counter in Brooklyn."

"Good to know," said Brad.

"I like cheese."

"So if I made, say, a cheddar and onion scone or some kind of cheese-encrusted bread, you'd be over here buying it?"

"Count on it," Doug said, giving Brad a thumbs-up. "All right, I've got a dog to neuter in about ten minutes. Wish me luck."

"Good luck?" said Brad.

Doug laughed and left.

"He has a weird sense of humor," Brad said to Monique.

"All of the vets are weirdly casual with how they talk about surgery on cats and dogs. I guess if you see sick pets all day, you develop some defense mechanisms."

Brad nodded.

Lindsay walked in then, which surprised the hell out of Brad. What surprised him even more was when she said, "Oh, good, you're still here."

"You're here to see me?" Brad asked.

"Yeah, I need to ask you something."

"I've got this," said Monique, gesturing toward the register.

"All right. Let's go sit in the cat room," Brad said.

Lindsay had never given him an answer to his question about going out on a date. He hoped she was here to ask him out but doubted that was the case. Her expression was serious. Possibly hesitant. He watched her as they sat and got the sense that she was very reluctant to ask him whatever she was about to ask him.

Several cats were milling about. None of them followed Brad around the way Hamilton had, so they mostly looked on with disinterest as Brad gestured for Lindsay to sit with him at a table.

"What's up?" he asked.

She tucked a loose strand of her dark hair behind her ear.

She had her hair up in a ponytail, but the hair around her face had fallen in soft tendrils that made her look very pretty. She was wearing a cute purple shirtdress that was a bit on the short side, giving Brad a good eyeful of her shapely legs.

She was gorgeous. But she probably would get mad if she saw the direction his thoughts were going, so he focused back on her face.

"I need some help."

Really? "Interesting," he said.

"It's not interesting. It's very mundane. This is not a prelude to anything."

Ah, already on the defensive. He nodded. "What do you need help with?"

"Well, the short version is that the *Forum* is having financial trouble, and there are rumors they will lay people off soon, so I am trying to make myself indispensable. I need a big scoop or some kind of story that will get me the kind of attention to make the *Forum* keep me on. Because I just got this job, I'll probably be the first to go if there are layoffs, but not if they think I'm good for their bottom line. And I love this job, Brad. It's fun and exciting, and it actually pays well, and I love the work I'm doing."

"All right," said Brad. He sensed where she was going, but he wanted to make her say it, to ask him formally. He would, of course, help her however she needed, but he needed her to do a little work here. If they were ever going to get back together, there would have to be some give and take.

"I was hoping, because you know everyone, that you might be able to point me toward a story."

"You were hoping."

She nodded. "Please can you help me, Brad? I'm only asking because you're the best-connected person I could think of. You have a zillion contacts, you know the restaurant industry really well, and I thought you might know of some budding story I could go cover before the *Times* or even *Eat Out New York* gets to it."

He wondered if he should ask her for something in return. Maybe use this as leverage to get her to go out with him. But, no, he didn't want her to go out with him because he'd pressured her into it. He wanted her to go out with him because she wanted to go out with him.

"Okay. Let me think."

"That's it? Okay? You'll help me without any conditions?"

"I mean, you'll owe me. I'll think of some way to have you return the favor. But yes, I will help you."

"I'm grateful, Brad, really."

"Okay. Um..."

He sat back on the sofa and looked at the mural on the opposite wall for a moment. It was a bright, colorful painting depicting cats sitting around a café table drinking coffee, and it had a cool, midcentury-modern retro aesthetic. Brad stared at the colors and tried to think of who he knew and how he could help Lindsay. Then an idea popped into his head.

"What about this? You remember Aaron Ramirez from culinary school? Of course you do; you asked about him last week."

"Yeah, I remember him."

Brad couldn't read her tone. "What does that mean?"

"Nothing. I'm just saying I remember him. And what I remember is Aaron being your bro."

Brad sighed. "Right. Well, as I mentioned, he works at the Food Channel now and is about to start filming a new show. I might be able to get you into a taping, or hell, maybe he wants the *New York Forum*'s food editor as a judge."

Lindsay's whole face lit up. "Are you kidding?"

"I'm serious. I can call him right now and see if he'll do it. He owes me a favor."

She raised an eyebrow. "In return for what?"

"I introduced him to his current girlfriend. Hang on a sec." Brad picked up his phone and dialed Aaron.

"Hey," Aaron answered.

"I'm calling in my favor," said Brad. "For Bianca."

"Oh, no. Am I going to like this?"

"You need judges for your new show, right?"

"You want to judge a savory cooking challenge?"

"No, not me. Although if you did a pastry edition of the show, I hope I'm your first phone call."

Aaron laughed. "All right. Or better yet, you should *compete*."

"I still don't think I'd be good on TV, but we're not talking about me."

"Sure, sure. Who should I hire?"

"Lindsay."

"Your ex-girlfriend Lindsay? The woman you're trying to woo back Lindsay?"

"Yes. That Lindsay."

"Really."

"Can you do it? Not just for me, but because she's the *Forum*'s food editor and a long-time restaurant critic with a culinary degree and is therefore very qualified." He glanced at Lindsay, who stared back at him with her eyebrows raised.

"I mean, yeah, I can do that. We're actively recruiting judges right now, actually."

Brad gave Lindsay a thumbs-up. The expression on her face was pure joy. He wanted to take a picture and frame it. She hadn't looked at him like that in five years.

"Let me just look at my schedule," said Aaron.

Ten minutes later, Lindsay was all set up with a date to report for filming.

"This is perfect," she said. "Getting my face on TV will be great publicity for the *Forum*, plus I can write a little preview of the show for the website and hopefully get some clicks. People love food competition shows."

Brad slipped his phone back into his pocket and spread his arms. "Who came through for you, babe?"

"All right, all right. You did me a solid. But this doesn't mean anything."

Brad begged to differ. She had come to him when she could have gone to one of their other classmates or to Will, for that matter. Evan's boyfriend must know a lot of food people. But she'd come to Brad. And, well, he didn't regret calling in this favor, because he wanted to do something nice for her, and the expression on her face for those few seconds had been reward enough.

Of course, he had an ulterior motive. He liked having made her happy, but he also liked being able to do a favor for her, something for which she'd be grateful. That was, he wanted to help her, but he also wanted her to trust him again. Or for the first time, maybe. She'd asked him for something, and he'd come through for her.

"It doesn't mean anything," he confirmed. "It's one friend doing a nice thing for another friend."

"Friend?"

"I mean, are we friends? At least?"

She frowned. "Yeah, okay. But don't get a big head about it."

He just smiled at her.

She looked at him and smiled, almost like she didn't want to. "I'm going to be a judge on a Food Channel show! I'm going to be on TV! That's so exciting!"

Brad laughed, appreciating her excitement. "You'll be great. You know a ton about food. You certainly knew how to tell the chef at Pepper that his food was flavorless and terrible using a lot of clever wordplay."

Lindsay nodded, still smiling. "This is so awesome. You came through better than I hoped. I can't wait to tell my boss."

"What are friends for?"

She surprised the hell out of him by leaning over to kiss his cheek. He didn't want to let the opportunity pass him by, so he turned his head at the last second and captured her lips.

He half expected her to slap him, but instead, she sank into the kiss. Brad opened one eye to make sure no one else was in the cat room—it was the beginning of the midafternoon slump, so it was indeed empty except for the cats—then he put his hand on Lindsay's cheek and held her there.

She had protested a lot for a woman who kissed him like this, hot and passionate and, well, with a lot of tongue.

Then she pulled away. He tried to follow her, but she put a finger on his lips. "That's enough," she said softly.

"Is this how you kiss your other friends?"

She smirked. "Just you, apparently."

"I'm not a bad guy."

"I know." She leaned away and shook her head. "It's not about good and bad, Brad. It's not that simple. We broke up for good reasons. I don't see any reason we could make it work a second time when we couldn't then."

Brad nodded, even though he had a counterargument ready to go. They could live happily ever after if they just figured out how to trust each other. Not an easy thing to do. Brad wanted to tell her this, but they'd had a nice moment, and he didn't want to push it.

"Anyway, I have to go," she said, standing and shouldering her bag. "I am grateful for your help. I'll find a way to make it up to you. But I need to go tell my boss what's happening and get some other work done." She leaned down and kissed only his cheek that time.

Then she was gone.

She didn't see any reason they could make a relationship work now? Well, he'd have to show her some reasons.

CHAPTER 12

THE WHITMAN STREET CAT CAFÉ was the property of Diane, a retired lawyer who also owned the whole building. She kept things pretty loose and let Lauren run the café however she saw fit, but all significant financial matters went to Diane. Brad had only met Diane a handful of times, but they'd developed a bit of a rapport. She breezed into the café now like she floated in on a cloud.

Diane was in her late sixties, with short bottle-blond hair and an apple-shaped figure. She often wore flowy dresses and caftans, and today was no exception. She wore a loose purple tunic over a pair of white jeans, and Brad could see from her sandaled feet that her toes were painted an iridescent opal color.

He was helping out at the counter because they'd been having a busier-than-usual afternoon. Diane walked up and ordered a tea from Monique, who didn't even bother to ring her up. Diane handed Monique a purple travel mug with pink flowers painted on it, and Monique dropped a tea bag into it with a practiced hand. That Monique didn't need to ask which of the dozen available teas Diane wanted said something about Diane's regularity as a customer.

A brunette woman trailed Diane up to the counter.

"Oh, Bradley, you're here," Diane said as if she'd just noticed him there. "That's fortunate. This is my friend Heather. She's a reporter for the *New York Times*."

"Wonderful to meet you," Brad said, sensing that Diane had a motive in introducing them.

"Heather is a features writer, and she's been hearing things about you and this café."

"Good things, I hope." Brad winked at Heather, who seemed a little dour.

"Oh, of course," said Diane. "The whole city is buzzing about the cute baker who makes treats for humans and cats at the Whitman Street Cat Café!" She sounded like she was inside a commercial.

"I'd love to chat with you," said Heather, her affect disturbingly flat.

"Yeah, sure. Uh…" He glanced at Monique.

"I've got this under control now that the crowd has thinned," she said. "You can talk now if you like."

"Wonderful!" said Diane.

Diane led Heather and Brad into the cat room. They sat at the only available table, and Heather whipped out a notepad.

She asked him a bunch of softball questions, mostly the same ones Lindsay had about why he'd wanted to work here and what made him try making cat treats.

Diane excused herself to go back to whatever she'd been up to before walking into the cat café—Brad was vaguely curious about what a semiretired person got up to with her idle time but hadn't wanted to ask—and after Brad bid her a friendly farewell, he turned back to Heather, who lobbed a few more softballs at him.

During a lull in their conversation, Brad's phone buzzed, so he checked it because Heather was busy writing notes. It was a text from Lindsay: On my way to Food Channel. Anything I need to know?

He gave a quick response about being in a meeting but also that he couldn't think of anything. He then hastily added, Good luck!

"Anything interesting?" Heather asked, gesturing at Brad's phone.

"Oh. Yeah, I, uh… See, a friend of mine is a producer at the Food Channel."

"I've been trying to get tickets to *Champion Chef* for eons! You know a producer there?"

Brad knew there were only so many favors Aaron could do for him before the higher-ups started to get suspicious. He'd already gotten Lindsay in the door; he couldn't do the same for Heather. Nor did he really want to, since they'd just met.

"Yeah, uh, he's buddy of mine. I just connected a writer friend of mine with him."

"Oh, could you do that for me?"

Brad pressed his lips together. "I mean, he doesn't work on *Champion Chef*, so I don't know what good that would do."

"Who's your friend?"

"Aaron Ramirez."

"I know him by reputation. His shows are usually really innovative. You know him?"

"I mean, we went to culinary school together."

"Sure. It seems like all the chefs I've met between the ages of, like, twenty-eight and thirty-four know each other. Usually from culinary school, but also six degrees and all that."

Brad nodded. That was pretty true. "The culinary world is smaller than you'd think."

"You think you could introduce me?"

Brad frowned. He didn't know how to put her off. How did he usually turn down a woman? Well, he'd fake number her, or he'd gently turn her down. *This is just tonight.* Or, *Oh, actually, I'm not looking for a relationship.*

"I don't know if I have enough clout with him to get you in, and also, you and I *just* met."

Heather leveled her gaze at him. "Really? You're going to turn me down."

"Look, I agreed to an interview about my work here at the café. I happen to have an old culinary-school classmate who works at the Food Channel, and I wouldn't even have mentioned it had I not just gotten a text, but my friend and I are not that close and you and I are strangers." Brad hated lying, especially since Aaron was probably his closest friend, but he was starting to really dislike Heather.

"I'm a reporter for the *Times*!"

"Again, I'm sorry, but we just met, and I don't have that kind of leeway."

She glowered at him. And, all right, now she was pissing him off. She was either here to interview him or she wasn't, but if she was going to be this belligerent, he wouldn't help her.

"Fine," she said, standing. She had a snotty note in her tone. This wasn't like fighting with Lindsay. Lindsay had passion and stubbornness, but this woman only had spite. "This article may not even run. I don't know if my editors at the *Times* are even going to care about some baker at a cat café."

"All right," said Brad. He understood now. She wanted something in return for publishing this interview. He wasn't going to bite. He wondered if Diane had been aware that Heather would try to barter something from Brad, who'd apparently gained a reputation for being connected in the industry, or if she had just latched on to his comment and not let go. Either way, he wouldn't lose any sleep over letting her slip out the door.

She gathered up her stuff. "Good day, Mr. Marks." Then she stormed out.

Paige walked into the room after she left. "Did you insult her mother or what?"

Brad sat back in his chair and rubbed his eyes. "She wanted me to do her a favor in exchange for publishing an interview with me in the *Times* about my work here."

He dropped his hands to see Paige's facial expression. She looked back at the door, as if she was sorry the reporter had left. Then she looked at Brad. "A sexual favor?"

"What? No, no, nothing like that. Why would you think that?"

Paige shrugged. "I don't know. You're a very attractive man, which you probably already know."

Brad didn't know what to do with that, so he shook his head and tried to pretend she hadn't said anything. "She wanted me to introduce her to my friend at the Food Channel, except she was an asshole about it. And also, I *just* got Lindsay an opportunity there. I don't have the kind of magic to get my friend to do me another favor, particularly not for a stranger. I'm a nice guy, but I'm not that nice."

"Oh. That does seem unreasonable. So no interview in the *Times*? Diane said she knew someone there."

"That was Diane's friend."

"Oh. Whoops."

"Are you mad? I know you like getting publicity for the café."

"Not at the expense of your ethics or professional connections. It sucks that we lost the interview, but on the other hand, this is not exactly a huge space. Traffic is already up since that story in the *Forum*. It's dead now, but the weekend crowds have been insane. Lauren is thinking about setting up a reservation system."

"Wow, really?"

"Yeah. I think it'd be easy enough to do. Evan did our website, so I think he can help."

"So you're not mad I ran off the *Times* reporter?"

"I mean, that's a terrible opportunity to lose, but we'll survive."

Brad had the sense that Paige regretted what had happened, because she was always trying to get good publicity for the café, but he didn't. That woman had been awful. And if Brad only had one favor with Aaron, he was glad he'd used it on Lindsay.

"You got Lindsay an opportunity at the Food Channel?" Paige asked.

"As a judge on my friend's new TV show. She didn't tell you?"

"I've been busy the last few days and haven't talked to her. I pretty much spend all my days off wedding planning. It's enough to make me want to elope."

Brad didn't really want to hear about wedding planning, but he braced himself for the incoming rant, which Paige had been prone to share with Lauren recently.

But Paige laughed instead. "I'm sure you don't care. But the drawback to being an event planner is that I know what things should cost, so I've been fighting with the venue and all the vendors I want to hire. Josh says I've gone all type A on the wedding. I think I've scared him a little."

Brad laughed. "I can only imagine," he said, trying to be polite.

"But that's really cool! Lindsay's going to be on TV?"

"Yes. On a cooking competition show."

"Oh, I should organize a watch party! We can have people over at Josh's and my place. It has a great kitchen we never use."

"You don't use it?"

"I'm a decent cook, but I've been working evenings a lot lately, so I haven't been cooking much. Josh can...heat things up in a microwave. Most of the time."

"Ouch."

"Yeah. He was mostly surviving on takeout when we met. But this is finally my opportunity to talk Lindsay into cooking for us."

Brad laughed. "Is this a long-term goal of yours?"

"Lindsay is a *great* cook, but her apartment is too small to have many people over at a time. I do not have that problem."

"So you're going to throw a party for Lindsay but make her cook for it."

Paige pursed her lips. "I mean, not if she doesn't want to. There's this really great little cheese shop near me that sells charcuterie platters that would get the job done. But, like, if she *volunteered*, what kind of person would I be if I turned that down?"

"Right." Brad looked back at the door. "Is Diane going to be mad I ran off her friend?"

"She'll get over it. Be nice to her the next time she comes in, though. Diane is a mama bear when it comes to her employees, and she'll defend you to the death, but she might be irked that her reporter friend ran out. But I agree, the reporter was unreasonable. If you explain as much to Diane, I'm sure all will be forgiven."

"All right. Good."

Paige patted his arm. "I gotta go get my laptop and work on next week's schedule. But I wanted to say, those apple cinnamon muffins today? *So* good. I'd say the only appropriate time to use the word 'moist' is to describe those muffins."

"Thanks."

Paige got up and left, leaving Brad alone with his thoughts. He still felt a little bad about running off the reporter, but not bad enough to dwell on it. Instead, his mind shifted toward Lindsay, as it always did lately when he had any idle time. He hoped she got on well as a judge.

His phone vibrated in his pocket. It was Aaron calling.

"Crazy idea," Aaron said when Brad answered. "One of my chefs canceled at the last minute. You want to come substitute?"

"Didn't we talk about this?"

"Are you working tomorrow?"

"No, it's my day off, but—"

"Look, not gonna lie, you were my fifth call. So far everyone has turned me down."

"I'm not really a savory chef, though."

"We have a dessert round. And anyway, you don't need to win, you just need to be on the show."

"So I'm a warm body." Brad sighed. After blowing it with the *Times* reporter, he was worried about turning down another opportunity. "I'll do it, but my boss is going to want me to drop the name of the cat café about a hundred times."

"If you can come film tomorrow, I'll make the entire episode about the cat café."

"Okay, fine. Wait, isn't tomorrow the day Lindsay judges?"

"I was kind of hoping you wouldn't remember that."

"*She* won't judge me, will she? Don't you film more than one episode a day?"

"Priya Kapoor's sous-chef showed up one day when she was judging."

"Not *exactly* the same."

"I can rig it so she doesn't judge you. We're filming three episodes tomorrow."

"Okay. Okay, fine. But you owe me again."

"Yeah, yeah. I'll see you tomorrow."

———

"You'll sit here after hair and makeup," Aaron explained to Lindsay as he gave her and the other judges a tour of the set. "We should be ready to start taping in about forty minutes."

Lindsay's whole body had been thrumming with excitement

since the previous night, when it became clear she was too wound up to sleep.

There were actually three episodes being taped today and six judges on hand that would be rotated for the episodes. That was a lot of eating, but Lindsay was game.

Now that they had a handle on the layout of the studio, Aaron led the judges to the makeup room, which was adjacent to the green room where they'd hang out between tapings. Once Lindsay had her makeup done—caked on would be more accurate—she walked into the green room, which was nicely appointed. There were a few big sofas and overstuffed chairs, a TV in the corner showing what was currently airing on the Food Channel, another TV right above it showing the live feed from the *Mystery Meal* set, and the one entire wall dominated with a huge spread of food, with a coffee urn and a water fountain on one end. Lindsay got a cup of coffee and settled into one of the chairs to wait.

The other judges drifted in gradually. Two of them were Food Channel regulars. Amanda Dreyfuss was a sunny blond restaurateur who owned a few restaurants in Manhattan that specialized mostly in southern-tinged New American cuisine. Pedro Santos hailed from Mexico and was the executive chef of a popular Latin fusion restaurant in Harlem. Both had been judges on a half-dozen Food Channel shows and contributed recipes to the Food Channel website, and Lindsay was a little starstruck. Priya Kapoor was an Indian chef who was also a sometimes judge or talking head on various Food Channel properties. She was also breathtakingly beautiful, with shiny black hair and brown skin and big eyes. Lindsay found it hard not to look at her.

Then there was Zachary Talmadge, whom Lindsay instantly disliked. He'd written a series of pretentious vegetarian cookbooks, although he was not a vegetarian himself as far as Lindsay knew. It would be hard to judge this show if he was. He also had a condescending note to his voice that got Lindsay's hackles up. Rounding out the judging pool was Claudia Rowe, a fortysomething actress best known for her role as the First Lady on a popular primetime political drama that had aired about ten years ago. Lindsay had watched that show religiously and was working up to asking her for a selfie as they all sat together.

As they were chatting and getting to know each other, Pedro pointed at Lindsay and said, "You're the one that wrote that review of Pepper!" He had a heavy accent but was easy to understand.

"Yes," said Lindsay.

Pedro laughed and slapped his knee. "I read that review. My cousin is a line cook there."

"Oh, I'm sorry."

She meant she was sorry if she'd offended Pedro or his cousin, but Pedro seemed to take it as she was sorry his cousin had to work there. He laughed harder. "The head chef there is a hack. Hardly knows the difference between a jalapeño and a bell pepper. Julio is only working there until he can find a better job. I'm not surprised the food is bland."

Well, that explained some things. "The restaurant seems to be doing okay. My friend manages the café across the street, and every time I go by, there are plenty of diners."

Pedro shrugged. "I give it six months."

"Yeah?"

"Yeah. It's owned by some boy-band singer, right? So it'll get some traffic just from his fans or people who want to see what a celebrity restaurant is like. And you'll get the crowd who read your review and want to see if you were exaggerating. But it's in Brooklyn, so you won't get much of a tourist crowd because the folk who come to New York to see a Broadway show or the Statue of Liberty don't generally go to Brooklyn, and soon enough, there will be some new novelty restaurant everyone is going to. So, yeah, six months. Tops."

"Where is the restaurant?" asked Amanda.

"Whitman Street," said Lindsay. "About halfway between the Barclays Center and the river."

"Ooh, yeah. That's a tough area for a tourist trap. Chef Sakai used to have a sushi place there and struggled to keep it open."

Lindsay didn't know who Chef Sakai was, but she assumed he was another Food Channel personality. There seemed to be about thirty of them, and they were all contractually obligated to act like they were great friends with each other. The affection between Amanda and Priya seemed genuine, and everyone seemed to like Pedro, so maybe the camaraderie was authentic.

Lindsay would judge the first and third episode filmed that day. The first panel called was Lindsay, Amanda, and Priya. An all-female panel sounded fun. They were escorted to the judge's table. Lindsay settled into her seat as the host walked over.

The host, Ben Hawthorne, had gotten his start as the food guy on a makeover show where he'd helped the makeover candidate, usually a hopeless straight dude, cook a nice meal for their romantic interest. So he had some food credentials—and a culinary degree from the same school Lindsay had attended, she learned via small talk while they waited to start—but had opted to be a TV personality instead of a restaurant chef. He was cute but definitely batted for Evan's team.

And then the show got started. The first episode featured four chefs who marched out in their show-branded black chef's jackets and took their places at each of the four stations. Ben had explained he'd record a voice-over with the bio for each chef after the fact, but for now, he read each chef's name and the city they came from.

Then Ben walked to the center of the room, where a huge table had been set up while the judges had been hanging out in the green room. It was covered with a giant metal cloche that was attached to a cord that went to the ceiling.

"Here's how this will work," said Ben to the camera. "We've got four chefs. In the first round, we'll give them a mystery ingredient that must be featured in an entrée. They'll have an hour to prepare that entrée. Our illustrious judges will taste each dish and choose two or three chefs to advance to the final round. For the final, the chefs will have thirty minutes and a new mystery ingredient from which they must make either a dessert or a small plate. The best chef will win ten thousand dollars! Are the chefs ready?"

The chefs each murmured their assent.

Ben said, "Today's *Mystery Meal* must include…"

The metal covering began to rise to the ceiling. The judges had no idea what the ingredients would be. Lindsay hoped this one was something she liked. She'd had to provide her allergies to the show in advance—she was sitting out the second episode because, she suspected, the mystery ingredient was something from her allergy list, probably lobster—so the meal would be something she could at least eat.

The table was covered in lovingly displayed large cuts of what looked like beef.

"Skirt steak!" Ben said triumphantly.

Well, that was disappointingly mundane.

"And your time starts...now!"

Ben then did a bit where he introduced each judge. "*New York Forum* food editor, Lindsay Somers!" sounded pretty amazing coming from Ben's lips.

Erica Sanchez had been over the moon. When Lindsay had told her boss she was going on a Food Channel show, Erica had actually said, "Wow, this could save your whole department." Lindsay doubted that, but it was very good publicity for the *Forum*.

Brad may very well have saved Lindsay's job. And for no reason other than that she'd asked him.

Well, okay, she suspected that he helped her because he wanted her to like him and take him back. He'd come through for her in a spectacular way. She'd spent the better part of the last week trying to work out what that *meant*. Was he trying to show she could trust him? That she could ask him for something and he'd deliver? Was he trying to impress her? Did he genuinely care about her success?

It almost didn't matter, because the larger question was what *she* wanted. Did she want him back? And if so, could she trust him to be faithful to her? He talked a good game, but did she believe it? And if she was even asking herself these questions, did that mean she *did* want him back in her life?

She had more pressing matters now, so she focused back on the proceedings. Her role was mostly to watch the chefs cook and chat with the judges about what was happening, not to obsess over her ex-boyfriend.

"Skirt steak is an interesting choice, eh?" said Ben.

"I think it's a good challenge," said Amanda. "It's difficult to make skirt steak tender and very easy to make it chewy. So this will be a test of technique more than about cooking a weird ingredient."

"And it's a challenge of creativity," said Priya. "Easy enough to grill a steak and slap some rice and beans next to it. You can eat that meal in any Mexican restaurant. I'd like to see these chefs do something we haven't seen before."

Lindsay watched one of the chefs grab garam masala from the pantry. "I think Chef Langley is pandering, Priya."

Priya laughed. "If he *really* wanted to impress me, he'd make his own garam masala. Any Indian chef worth his salt, or his curry powder, can make good garam masala."

And so it went. A massive digital clock behind the judge's table kept time. The judges watched the chefs work. Priya and Amanda had some practice in providing commentary for contests like this, and Lindsay didn't know how snarky she was allowed to be, so she held back. But then Priya made a dry comment about one of the chefs slicing an avocado, and Lindsay felt more in her element.

For the next twenty minutes, the three judges made food-related jokes and cracked each other up. When the chefs were down to five minutes, though, the whole room filled with tension. Lindsay worried the chefs wouldn't get their dishes done on time. It was a close call for the guy who had made some kind of Indian marinade for his steak; he literally threw pieces of sliced steak at the plates to get everything done on time, and sauce flew all over his station.

Next: tasting.

Each chef presented the judges with a plate of food and explained their thinking. One chef had, quite predictably, basically made fajitas and overcooked the steak while he was at it.

"I could get this meal at any chain suburban restaurant," said Lindsay.

"I agree," said Priya. "It's...fine, but not very imaginative."

The garam masala guy admitted that he'd seen Priya on the panel and decided to go in an Indian direction. He'd made a marinade for his steak with Indian spices and served it with a side of wilted spinach and basmati rice. Everything was cooked competently, but Lindsay said, "I'm not 100 percent sure this works. I like the flavors, but I'm not sure skirt steak is the right vehicle for them."

The third chef nailed it. He'd served his steak with fingerling potatoes and a leafy greens salad, and he'd made a savory marinade that had a lot of vinegar in it, but the steak was tender and perfect, and Lindsay loved a well-seasoned potato. "You're also not thinking very far outside of the box," Lindsay said. "But I want to eat all of this. The steak is cooked perfectly."

The fourth chef had made a steak salad, presenting the steak in a bed of romaine with a ton of chopped veggies and shaved Parmesan on top, and though the dish also wasn't very imaginative, he had cooked the steak perfectly.

The chefs were ushered out, giving the judges time to discuss. They agreed pretty quickly that the third and fourth chefs should advance, and they'd give them a pass on the lack of creativity because there were only so many things you could do with skirt steak, and that one chef's attempt had gone pretty badly awry.

Lindsay felt terrible eliminating two chefs. Priya said she'd get used to it.

The four chefs were brought back in. Ben announced the results with a practiced look of regret on his face. Two chefs left, and the other two went to their stations.

Round two was then a face-off, and the mystery ingredient was...heavy cream.

One chef quickly got shortbread in the oven, and while it was baking, he whipped up the cream and made little strawberry short-cakes. The other chef found some clams in the pantry and whipped up a small plate of steamed clams with a cream-based sauce.

When the judges were presented with the dishes, Lindsay was most nervous about the clam dish. She knew that, although they were an unusual pairing, dairy and seafood could go well together if done thoughtfully, and she had in fact tasted very good dishes with both, but the concept had always turned her stomach. On this chef's dish, though, the sauce ended up being delicious, and the clams were steamed just right. Compared to the creator of the strawberry shortcake, which was good but not mind-blowing, the other chef was a clear winner, Lindsay thought. "You should bottle this sauce," she said. "I would just drink it right out of the bottle."

The chefs were sent out again, and Priya and Amanda agreed with Lindsay, so in another unanimous decision, they declared a winner.

Once filming concluded, the judges left to change clothes so it wouldn't look like all the episodes were filmed on the same day. Amanda and Priya had to get back out for the second episode, but Lindsay took her time. When she returned to the green room, Pedro and Claudia were flirting heavily with each other. Lindsay greeted them both amiably, but mostly she was glad she wouldn't be stuck judging or sitting with Zachary, who made her uncomfortable. He seemed like the sort of guy who hit on his kitchen staff constantly.

She turned her attention instead to the monitor, where filming of the episode was already in progress.

And suddenly there was Brad.

This was clearly why Lindsay had been told she couldn't judge the second episode. She was annoyed Brad hadn't said anything, but glad she didn't have to judge him. That would have been impossible. Well, also unethical for, like, five different reasons.

She decided to ignore Pedro and Claudia and instead focused on the screen.

Brad and the other chefs were running around the kitchen, grabbing ingredients, chopping vegetables, tossing stuff in pans. The secret ingredient had indeed been lobster, and Lindsay wondered how much Brad had to stretch himself to cook seafood.

Apparently not that far. He appeared to be grilling the tails to make lobster rolls. She watched, somewhat in awe, as he whipped up an aioli like it was the easiest thing. He didn't have time to bake his own rolls, but she bet he would have otherwise.

She realized she hadn't seen Brad in action since culinary school. He was efficient, he kept his station clean, he thought fast on his feet. His face showed only complete focus on what he was doing, but every now and then he'd glance up in a way that made her feel like he was looking right at her, although probably he was just self-conscious about the cameras.

His plates looked immaculate as the round ended. He'd made coleslaw, too, and it sat in a neat little pile beside the lobster roll, which was stuffed with big chunks of lobster, celery, green onions, and some kind of seasoning. Lindsay had eaten a lot during that previous episode, and she was violently allergic to lobster, but looking at the camera close-up of that lobster roll made her mouth water.

She worried for Brad, though. Maybe the dish was too simple.

Priya praised him for cooking the lobster perfectly. Zachary really liked the balance of flavors in the slaw. Amanda said she wanted to lick the aioli off the bun. They all agreed, though, that a lobster roll wasn't much of a risk.

On the other hand, one of the other chefs brutally overcooked their lobster, and the judges agreed it was chewy. Another of the chefs had gone a little experimental with the seasoning, and the judges disagreed about whether it tasted good. But one chef had managed a lobster bisque in a short amount of time that the judges were positively orgasmic over.

When it was time to announce who would be moving on to the next round, Lindsay leaned forward to watch the proceedings on TV, hardly able to breathe in anticipation. She wanted Brad to have a chance to knock the judges' socks off with a dessert.

When he made it through to the second round, the look of surprise that came over her face hit Lindsay right in the solar plexus.

Could it be that she wanted good things for him?

Of course she did. Of course. But her feelings were complicated. It reminded her of when she heard he'd gotten the job at Milk Bar. Part of her was excited someone she knew had gotten a job somewhere famous. She was glad he was successful, she was happy for him. But she was jealous, too. She'd imagined she'd have a career cooking in great restaurants, but that just wasn't how her life had played out. She had a lot of regrets about her life, and that was one of them. So learning about Brad's successes had hurt in a way; here he was having this amazing life in the industry she loved, too, and she was... what? Writing restaurant reviews for a few cents a word? She'd made the right choice for herself at the time. She knew that in her gut. But maybe, deep down, the reason why she found Brad's arrival back in her life so disturbing was that he made her feel like failure all over again.

He hadn't even done anything. He just...existed. And these were Lindsay's own issues apart from him. But seeing him again brought all her old insecurities roaring back.

The secret ingredient for Brad's dessert round was arbol chiles. The camera zoomed in on Brad's face the moment he started turning over ideas for how to put a fairly hot pepper into a dessert.

What he came up with was a Mexican chocolate cupcake.

Lindsay worried he couldn't get the cupcakes baked in the allotted time, but he got them in the oven immediately before turning his attention to making frosting. He got those cupcakes out of the oven in time to shove them in the freezer to cool before he frosted them. Lindsay wondered if his time working in a cupcake shop had taught him how to do all this quickly.

The other chef went in a savory direction and made a chicken dish. It did look great when he finished it.

But while the judges found the dish tasty, arbol chile plus Mexican-inspired chicken thighs and rice wasn't really reinventing the wheel. Everyone seemed tremendously impressed by the cupcakes, though. Amanda said, "I can't believe you made cupcakes that fast," about eight times.

The cameras kept running while the judges deliberated. Lindsay's heart started to race as she realized that, though the judges liked both dishes, they were more impressed by the cupcakes.

Aaron snuck into the green room. "I thought he was a seat filler," he said. "I asked him yesterday to sub in because one of my chefs canceled. He didn't want to do it, but I talked him into it. He assumed he'd flame out in the savory round."

Lindsay let out a heavy sigh. "Isn't it just like Brad to win the whole thing."

"You know him?" asked Claudia.

"We used to date." Lindsay turned to Aaron. "I kinda feel like you kept me out of that round more because of Brad than because eating lobster makes my whole face swell up."

Aaron smiled sheepishly. "I did engineer the lobster round to coincide with Brad's presence on set."

They watched as the judges came to an agreement. Aaron stood next to Lindsay as they watched the chefs go back in for judgment.

The undeniable thing about watching Brad cook is that he was good and he deserved his success. When the judges declared him the winner, he accepted it humbly and thanked them.

He was right, about everything. Lindsay didn't have much

faith in love or romantic relationships. She'd spent that entire year they'd dated waiting for the other shoe to drop. It never did, but when their graduation was pending, when she knew the culinary-school bubble would pop, making plans suddenly felt essential. So when Brad kept putting her off, she figured he wasn't in it for the long haul. And he was right, Phoebe was an excuse. Lindsay could have let him explain himself. She could have forgiven him, even. She chose not to.

She'd wondered for five years if she made the wrong choice.

A production assistant stuck her head in the green room and said, "Hey, guys, we're ready for you on set."

The third episode featured judges Lindsay, Pedro, and Claudia. Lindsay worried she wouldn't be able to come up with anything intelligent to say, given how distracted she felt. Was Brad still here? Did he know she was here? He must have. Should she talk to him?

Cameras were rolling, though. Nopales was the mystery ingredient, which felt like the show was pandering to Pedro. One of the chefs that round worked in a vegetarian restaurant and made a Mexican-inspired entrée in which the nopales was grilled and treated like a steak. He was an easy pass into the second round.

The two final chefs cooked plantains. One went in a caramelized dessert direction, and the other went in a savory, deep-fried direction. Both were delicious, but the dessert eked out the win.

The whole day had taken almost eight hours. As they wrapped up and got ready to head home, Aaron walked over to her and said, "*Great* job. Just the right amount of snark and compliments for the chefs. I'm way impressed."

"Thanks!" Lindsay hadn't expected a compliment like that, but she appreciated hearing it.

"I've got judges booked for the rest of the season, but can I call you if I have a cancellation? I like to have a couple of locals on standby."

"Yes, absolutely. This was really fun."

"I'll email you when I confirm the air date, but I think it will be in a few weeks."

"That soon?"

"Yeah, we got bumped up on the schedule because the shooting schedule for Billy Watts's new travel show got gummed up by bad weather." Aaron rolled his eyes. "He won't do outdoor shots if it's raining."

"I guess the rain would mess up his hair."

Aaron laughed. "True story."

"Anyway, I'm really grateful for this opportunity."

"Oh, no problem. Happy to help anyone I survived culinary school with."

"And Brad."

"Sure. He did ask on your behalf. I won't pry into what's going on there."

"Good, because I don't know. But it was great to see you again, and I'd be happy to judge anytime."

Aaron smiled. "Sure. Thanks, Lindsay."

"Is he still here?"

"He hung around to watch the last episode film, yes. I think he's in the contestant green room. You want me to bring you there?"

"Could you?"

Aaron winked. "Sure. Come with me."

Brad was alone in the contestant green room. He'd changed out of the show's standard-issue chef's jacket and into a T-shirt and skinny jeans.

"So, hey, why didn't you tell me you were here?" was the first thing that flew out of her mouth. She hadn't intended to be so adversarial. It was...unhappiness. Loneliness. Shame. Joy. Love. All of her emotions swirled around when she and Brad were in the same room.

"Could you give us a second?" Brad said to Aaron.

Aaron nodded. "I need to clear you all out of here in ten minutes, but I'll be right outside."

Lindsay took a deep breath. "Congratulations."

"Thanks. Sorry I didn't tell you I'd be here. Aaron called yesterday to ask me to do this. When I got home last night, I kinda passed out before I could call you. Working the morning shift, man."

"It's okay," she said, meaning it. She understood. She was going to have to dial back the hostility if she had a chance of forgiving both of them. "It was nice seeing you cook again."

"Good. Okay. Thank you."

She wanted to apologize to him, but she couldn't quite make her mouth make the words. "That was really all I wanted to say. I liked watching you cook, and it felt rude not to say hi if you were still here."

"You've probably eaten your fill, but you want to get a drink or something?"

"I can't tonight. A couple of the other judges invited me to get drinks with them, and I want to pick their brains about stuff for the story I'm writing. Rain check?"

He seemed bewildered. "Yeah. Of course. Give me a call sometime."

"I will."

He narrowed his eyes. "For real? Or are you just being polite?"

"I may have some nonsense to deal with, and I'm still not convinced that you and I can have a functional relationship, but if we *are* going to try being friends, then I need to put in a little bit of effort."

He smiled. "Just a little."

There was a knock at the door, and then Aaron stuck his head in. "Kids? We gotta shut this down."

"Later, Brad," Lindsay said, feeling fairly confident he didn't believe she meant it.

CHAPTER 13

BRAD THOUGHT HE MIGHT FALL over when he hit his intercom button and his visitor said, "It's Lindsay."

He let her up without question, but he was very curious about what she was doing at his apartment.

"We're neighbors now, basically," she said as he let her in.

"Sure," he said. "You need a cup of flour or..."

She walked in and kept going until she was in the middle of his kitchen, and then turned around. "I wanted to thank you."

"Okay. You're welcome?"

She kept walking as if this were her apartment—right into the living room—and flopped down on the sofa.

"I was too dazed after taping to say anything coherent. But filming at the Food Channel yesterday was *amazing*. I had so much fun. I mean, it was pretty scary at first. I wasn't totally sure what to say on camera. But I ran with my instincts, and Aaron told me afterward that I did well. And my boss is over the moon. Me being on the show is good publicity for the *Forum*, especially now that they're doing more digitally and have a wider reach."

"Oh, good." Brad sat next to her on the sofa. He'd been watching a baseball game, so he picked up the remote and switched it off.

"I wanted to thank you in person, because not only did you give me something really fun to do, but I think you saved my job."

"I was happy to help. Really."

"And you got, what, a big cash prize out of it, too?"

"Well, after taxes and everything, it's not *that* big of a prize. But I really thought I'd lose in the first round, so that was a nice surprise. Who knew you could win a lobster-cooking contest by making lobster rolls?"

"Priya Kapoor said last night that it was the best lobster roll she's ever eaten."

"Wow, really? That's wild. Guess that seafood knowledge from culinary school is still rattling around in my head. But enough about me. I was happy to help. I'm glad you had a good time."

Lindsay smiled. Then she kissed him.

Kissing Lindsay was always wonderful, so he wasn't mad that she was kissing him now, but he couldn't help but wonder why.

But then he forgot about his reservations. He cupped the side of her face and deepened the kiss.

She pulled back slightly and smiled at him.

Oh, right. Why was she kissing him? He looked into her eyes but couldn't read her expression. Did she think she owed him in some way? Was she just kissing him to thank her for getting her on TV?

"I hope you know," he said, "I didn't expect anything in return. I wanted to help."

"I know. You make it hard to hate you when you're selfless like that."

"Well, good. I don't want you to hate me."

She looked away for a moment before meeting his gaze again. "I don't...understand."

"What don't you understand?"

"Why you want me back."

Brad debated how much to say. He'd loved her once. She'd been his favorite person in culinary school—in the world—for the year they'd been together. She was still one of his favorite people, even before she walked back into his life. He thought she was great—beautiful and smart, loyal and fierce, stubborn and challenging, angry and edgy sometimes. Once upon a time, he'd been in love with all of it, but she had harder edges now, was a little more cynical. But he wanted to know the woman she'd become, which told him he wanted to be with her again.

"You got under my skin, I guess. I never stopped thinking about you."

Lindsay frowned. She opened and closed her mouth a few times like she didn't know how to respond to that.

"I want another chance," he said, deciding to just go for it. "You and I were great together. We had a lot of fun together, didn't we?"

"Well, sure, but relationships are more than just fun."

"I know. That's why I want a chance to prove that I'm an adult now. I want to think about the future and make plans. And I want you to be a part of that, if you'll have me."

She looked down and, if Brad was not mistaken, blinked away tears. "But didn't I... I mean, my heart, it... When I saw you and Phoebe, I just... It shattered."

Brad felt that deep in his chest. He hated that he'd hurt her. He'd never wanted to. But he'd gotten her point, what she'd told him the other day about how Phoebe had been setting them up, and he'd been too self-absorbed to see it.

"Yes," he said softly. "You broke my heart when you left me. But I understand why you did. And I want to make it up to you. I've missed you, Lindsay."

She frowned. "I missed you, too."

He kissed her. He had no idea how to show her that he was sincere, that she could trust him, that he could be the man she wanted and needed him to be. But he could do this.

She sighed into his mouth and put her arms around his shoulders.

And so here they were, making out on his sofa again. He leaned over and she leaned back, and then he was on top of her on the lumpy, too-small sofa.

This he knew. This was familiar. The feel of her fingers in his hair, the taste of her lips, the curves of her body under his hands. They felt *right* together, like some order had been brought to their chaotic universe, like the planets were aligning. In some ways, this part was easy. It was the emotional stuff they kept messing up.

He'd fucked it up once. He was determined to get it right this time.

But first, he had to respond to this immediate moment. Lindsay pulled his shirt off and ran her hands over his chest, pausing on the sun tattoo.

"Okay, wait," he said. "I can't believe I'm about to say this, but maybe we should talk about this before, you know."

She frowned at him. "Brad."

"I just don't want us to do something we're going to regret later."

Lindsay didn't quite back off, but Brad could feel the hesitation wafting off her. Then she said, "Watching you cook reminded me of the good old days, I guess. I know I've been...unfair to you. I've got some shit I'm dealing with, and none of it is your fault. Okay?"

"Sure. Do you want to talk about it?"

"No."

He wondered if he should let it go. If he should accept her affection now. If this were a short-term thing, he'd let her stay mum. But he wanted her back for the long-term, so he pushed her. "Do you think we should talk about it?"

She rolled her eyes, but then she looked at him. "It's just... Okay. The thing is, when I was watching you cook at the taping, it occurred to me that I made a choice when I walked out on you, and I've felt many times that it was the wrong choice. And I don't know if what I want is to get back together, but that second-chance thing, maybe I could do that."

"Not sure if you noticed, but you were about to jump my bones. Not sure if that counts as a date."

"It counts as something."

He laughed. "Linds, I—"

"Do we *have* to have a big talk about our feelings?"

"Are you gonna freak out if we have sex again?"

"No. Not this time."

He kissed Lindsay again, testing the waters. She groaned and bucked her hips against him.

Well, far be it for him to deprive her of what she wanted.

The couch was a problem, though. He made a mental note to invest in a bigger couch in the near future. Then he slid off, stood, and scooped her up in his arms.

He carried her into the bedroom, and she laughed as she threw her arms around his neck. He laid her gently on the bed and went about stripping off the rest of his clothes. She peeled off her own clothes. She looked like she'd come from working in the office, wearing a pretty pink blouse tucked into a black pencil skirt that showed off the shape of her body, but the relative sexiness and professionalism of her clothes stopped mattering the moment they hit the floor.

He slid on the bed beside her naked body. He ran a hand from her neck, over her collarbone, to her breast. He cupped her flesh and pinched her nipple. She hissed in response.

"So here we are again," he said.

"This is not because you saved my job."

"I know."

"It's because I want to do this."

"Uh-huh." Brad tried to put something wry in his smile, but he believed her.

"We do this part pretty well."

"I recall saying as much a few weeks ago."

She rolled her eyes and reached for his nightstand drawer. She pulled out a condom and handed it to him. "Don't look so smug."

"Smug? I would never."

"Brad?"

"Lindsay?"

"Be with me tonight."

Brad groaned and kissed her neck. "Happily."

Her body was doing a number on him. Her creamy skin contrasted with her dark hair, her pink nipples, the rise and fall of her curves, all of it beautiful and arousing. His own body felt electrically charged, and he longed to sink into her. So he was distracted and hardly heard her. But somewhere in his mind, he registered what she'd just said.

"Okay," he said.

"Okay?"

He tried to focus on her face and not the growing need within him, although he couldn't seem to stop his hands from stroking her body. "We're not getting back together. Yet."

"Yet?"

"Once we finish with this, my intention is to convince you that we should be together. If not for the hot sex, then because we like each other."

"What makes you so sure of that?"

"I like you. You are currently naked in my bed, so either you just think I'm dead sexy or you like me, too."

"More the first one."

"Uh-huh." This time he didn't believe her.

But the longer they lay there, the more his body cried out for him to move against her. He rolled on the condom, tossed the wrapper over his shoulder, and then grabbed Lindsay. He rolled them both so that she was on top, and she fell forward onto his chest with a laugh.

"Oh, is that how it is?" she said, staring down at him with a sly expression on her face.

"I put my fate in your hands."

He wanted to persuade her that they should be together, but he wanted her to agree with that as fervently as he believed it. So he gave her control.

She kissed him. Unable to resist, he put her arms around him. She started to shift against his upper body, then she slowly slid away. She sat up. Then she sank onto his cock.

Brad groaned as he sank into her. She was hot and tight, and this was like relief and agony all rolled into one. Having her arms around him felt like coming back home again, and he wanted to remember this moment in case he never got another. Even though everything in his body screamed to go faster, push harder, get to the finish line faster, he wanted to slow it down, savor it.

He kissed Lindsay, took her lower lip into his mouth, nipped at her with his teeth, wanted her to feel it. He touched her everywhere he could reach, tried to memorize the feel of her skin under his hands. He pumped his hips slowly, slid in and out of her, and wanted to make her feel it all, too.

As far as he could tell, they were back together right now. But he didn't dare point that out to Lindsay.

She rode him. She stretched her arms into the air, making her beautiful body long, making her breasts stand out. God, she was perfect. He put his hands on her hips but didn't try to control her pace. This was all Lindsay. Her body squeezed his, she let out cute little sighs, and his heart pounded so hard he thought it might beat out of his chest. She looked beautiful, powerful, stunning. And she was making him feel, well, everything. He needed her in his life. He wanted her like this every day. He would not stop until he found a way to show her that the two of them were perfect together.

He wasn't there yet. So he'd keep trying.

"God," she panted.

"Yes, dear."

He couldn't not touch her, so as she rode him, he pressed a thumb against her clit. She rode against him and touched her breasts, cupping them, squeezing her own nipples. "Right there," she said.

He was going to make her go off like a rocket.

His secret was that he still remembered. He knew what set her off. He knew what she liked. He'd held on to that knowledge in case it proved useful again, and it definitely had. He moved inside her, drew his thumb in circles, pressed with just enough force to make her really feel it, and then she groaned. The way she shook, above him, around him, told him he'd achieved his goal. It was the most amazing thing he'd ever seen. She was flying apart, and braced a hand on his chest to support herself. As her orgasm waned, she pinched his nipples, and that was all he needed to get the rest of the way there. He threw his head back and lost himself in her, coming hard, seeing stars.

A few minutes later, they were both lying on their backs, still panting.

Lindsay hadn't eaten, and when her stomach growled, Brad suggested they get dinner delivered.

And so, dressed in one of Brad's old T-shirts and her own

underwear, she sat cross-legged on the sofa and shoveled green curry into her mouth, because that bout of sex had left her starving.

Brad twirled his fork through a plastic container of pad thai. "So riddle me this," he said. "Why are we not getting back together?"

Brad wore only a pair of soft-looking sweatpants. He'd answered the door when the delivery guy came wearing only those sweatpants, probably giving that poor guy an eyeful. His chest was distracting. Lindsay struggled not to stare at it.

"We didn't work out the first time," Lindsay said with a shrug. That was an inescapable fact. That Brad didn't agree was a little disconcerting. "I never felt like I knew where I stood with you, because you were so flirty with everyone. You still do it, you know."

"What, flirt?"

"With *everyone*. At that adoption party, you had every woman there in the palm of your hand. Some of the men, too."

"Jealous?"

"Not now. We're not a couple now. Back when we were dating? Yes."

Brad sighed. "Okay."

Hamilton trotted into the living room with his nose in the air. He hopped up on the coffee table to investigate the spread. Brad quickly put the tops on all the open containers and tried to shoo away the cat, but Hamilton just lay down on the empty end of the table.

"Cats don't like Thai food," said Brad.

"I don't think he knows that."

Brad sighed. "I fed him when I got home and have not seen him since. Of course he shows up again at mealtime."

"How is having a cat?"

Brad's lips twisted in a way that showed he was clearly trying to suppress a smile. "It's actually fun. Most evenings, he hops up on the sofa and watches TV with me. He likes to sleep on the corner of the mattress near my head at night. I keep forgetting he's there and wake up next to this orange ball of fur, which is a little weird, but I'm starting to get used to it."

"And he tries to steal your food."

"Always. Cat after my own heart. Loves a good meal."

Lindsay reached over and petted the cat and tried to remember what they'd been talking about before he jumped up on the table. Oh, right. The past. After mulling it over for a moment, Lindsay said, "If I'm going to give you another chance, I need to know that you'll come home to *me*. I'm not saying you can't look or you can't flirt because that would be unreasonable. But I need to have faith that, no matter what you do, it's me you come home to. It's me you love."

"It was always you."

He sounded earnest, and his words squeezed her heart, but she didn't have complete trust in them. But was that her, or was that him? Hadn't he been trying to show her things were different? "It's not that I don't trust you—"

He sighed. "You don't."

"I need some time, okay?" And that was the truth. Everything about Brad's presence in her life confused her. Did she trust him? She couldn't tell. She wanted to. Could she be with someone who made her feel like she'd failed, albeit through no fault of his own? She was less sure of that. Could they make this work, or were they just tangled up in their old feelings for each other? "I'm just... I don't feel like I'm on steady ground with you. I need to think about things, okay? I'm willing to see where this goes, but I need more time to decide what I want."

Brad gave her a long look, like he was mulling that over. "Okay. I can give you time. But I need something from you."

Lindsay steeled herself, although she guessed what he'd say. "What is it?"

"Try to trust me."

"I am trying."

"Look, I want you back in my life in whatever form you will have me. Given that we just had sex, again, I am guessing a friendship is probably not in the cards. So I will do everything I can to prove myself trustworthy. But you have to do the same. You have to show me that I'm putting my faith in someone who wants to be with me, who is willing to be vulnerable with me. And if you can't do that, there really is no hope for us."

She fidgeted, uncomfortable with how intensely he looked at her now. She hated that word. *Vulnerable.* It was unsafe. It terrified her.

He kept talking. "I know how hard it is for you to open up and trust people, but trust is not a one-way street. I think part of you always expected me to leave you, so you left me first, and I'm telling you now that I need you to trust that I won't. Trust that I want you and I will be here for you, but only if you are there for me, too. I will do everything in my power never to betray your trust, and you have to do the same, or this will never work."

She nodded slowly. She recognized the dilemma here. She had to open herself up to trusting him, something her mind and her heart were screaming at her not to do, but in return she could have a life with a great man who made her happy. Or she could stay in her safety zone and keep living her life as if he'd never walked into it but lose out on being with a great guy.

"What do you want?" Brad asked.

Lindsay stared at the little plastic tub that held what remained of her green curry. She genuinely had no idea which option was better, and she realized that she'd lose something no matter which she chose. "I don't know. I want to trust you. But it's hard."

Brad nodded. Then he sat back on the sofa and eyed her. "I'm going to prove it, you know."

"Prove what?"

"That you can trust me and that we belong together."

"How are you going to do that?"

"I don't know yet. But I will figure it out."

CHAPTER 14

TV PRODUCERS DID PRETTY WELL for themselves, and Aaron's Chelsea apartment somehow had a wet bar. It wasn't the biggest space, but Aaron had sunk some money into making the space nice. It made Brad think about the sad Post-its on his wall where art should have gone, and Lindsay's crack about his only art being a Star Wars poster. And she wasn't wrong; he had some work to do to make his apartment look like an adult lived there. But Aaron's place looked mature and expensive, even though it was small.

Aaron mixed Brad a manhattan and slid it in front of him. "So. Tell me about Lindsay. Does she still hate you?"

Brad sighed. "She still hates me. Well, no, that's not true. She doesn't trust me."

"It was wild seeing her again. She looks better now than she did five years ago."

"I *know*."

Aaron laughed. "She doesn't trust you because she still thinks you cheated on her?"

"I think we've gotten past that, actually. She doesn't trust me because she doesn't trust anyone."

"That's a pickle. And you still want her back?"

"More than anything in this life. I can't even put a finger on why, just that whenever I see her, I feel…" Brad couldn't explain it. Something in him melted whenever they were in a room with each other, but that was the kind of schmoopy, romantic nonsense Aaron would definitely make fun of him for.

"Turned on?" Aaron suggested.

"Sure, that. But…happy. I feel happy. I think we can make each other happy. But winning her back is turning out to require a lot of effort."

"In what way?"

Brad huffed out a breath and sipped his drink. "Well, she requires some convincing."

"So you contacting me to get her on *Mystery Meal* didn't do the trick?"

"I didn't do that to win her back."

"The hell you say."

"Well, okay, maybe in the back of my mind, I thought she might be grateful, but I genuinely just wanted to help her. Because I still really care about her. If she decided to view that as a reason to give me a second chance, then bonus. Unfortunately, I don't think that's how she saw it."

"Hmm."

"And on top of that, I managed to piss off a journalist in the process." Brad explained what had happened with Heather, the *Times* reporter.

When Brad finished talking, Aaron said, "So let me get this straight. You pissed off a *New York Times* reporter for Lindsay's sake?"

That wasn't exactly how Brad had seen it in the moment, but... Yes, that is exactly what he'd done. But he said, "I didn't think you'd do me another favor."

"Nor could I have without pissing off my bosses. Especially in that case. Heather Chapman is a hack."

"You know her?"

"She took over for Russo when he got promoted, but her writing lacks any life. She writes about food with about the same excitement I have for watching grass grow."

"I'm pretty sure she's a robot. She has no personality."

Aaron nodded. "My boss doesn't like her because she gave one of the Food Channel's regular chefs a bad review. You know Wood Plank in the Village?"

"Yeah. That's Billy Watts's place, isn't it?" Billy Watts was kind of the ur-celebrity chef. He hosted or worked as a judge on a half-dozen different properties.

"Yup. And Billy Watts is a god at the Food Channel. I'm not saying Wood Plank is this amazing restaurant, because I ate there once and it's good but definitely trying too hard. Although the salmon there is..." Aaron moaned. "Well, anyway, her panning Wood Plank effectively got her blacklisted."

"She said she'd been trying to get *Champion Chef* tickets."

"Don't mess with Billy Watts. That is for sure why she keeps getting turned down. He coproduces *Champion Chef*."

"So just as well I didn't try to get her in with you."

"Yeah, that would have been embarrassing for all of us."

Paige was still a little pissed Brad had biffed the interview, but so far no story had run. Brad thought no review was better than a negative one, which he'd been worried about. Heather might have been a robot, but she could have retaliated if she was genuinely mad at him.

He sighed and sipped his manhattan.

Aaron pulled over a stool and sat across from Brad. "Okay. So, let's think about this for a second. You did Lindsay a solid. She was great on the show, by the way. I have zero regrets about setting that up."

"I knew she would be."

"You have it bad, man."

"I know. She doesn't like that I'm flirty with everyone. That's part of her issue with me."

"So stop flirting with everyone."

"If I could just turn it off, I would. I don't even think about it most of the time."

"Yeah, sure. Must be hard to be a good-looking guy with women throwing themselves at you all the time."

Brad rolled his eyes. "It's not like that."

"Then what's it like?"

Brad stared at his drink.

There'd been a time in his life when he'd overcompensated. His family was very conservative. Brad had been a pretty average kid—he'd played sports and got decent grades and had a lively social life—but he and his father had gotten into a knockdown, drag-out fight over Brad's career when he was about twenty.

College was...fine, but Brad hadn't found anything he was passionate about until he got a job at a restaurant to help pay tuition. He'd just been waiting tables, but he became friendly with the kitchen staff and started learning more about cooking.

Men didn't cook, his father had said, which was patently absurd. *Most* chefs were men; sexism in the industry still made it incredibly hard for women to break through to the highest levels. And then Brad had gotten excited about pastry, which his father thought was even less masculine. Brad ultimately didn't care— he'd pursued what he was passionate about, and he loved his job.

But he knew he'd internalized some of his father's bullshit about being a pastry chef and how that made him less masculine, and he supposed he'd gone a little out of his way to prove his heterosexuality. Here at the ripe old age of thirty, he could see how ridiculous and homophobic that had been, but when he'd started culinary school, he hadn't been so self-assured.

So, yeah, subconsciously, he'd probably gotten into the habit of flirting with many women to prove to someone—his father, himself—that he was an adult heterosexual man even though he made cupcakes for a living.

Hell, just the other day, Brad had called home to ask his mother for something, and Dad had gotten on the phone and said, "Still working in that pussy café, huh?" He'd seemed tickled by his double entendre. Brad didn't have it in him to tell his father to fuck off, so he'd gotten off the phone instead and realized after the fact that he'd forgotten to tell his parents he'd won a cooking competition. At least here in New York he was a safe distance from his father's bullshit, but Dad still got into his head sometimes.

Brad sipped his drink. "Residual childhood trauma."

"How's that?" asked Aaron.

"Our parents have fucked us up so much. Me, Lindsay, probably you."

Aaron grimaced. "We never had alcohol in the house when I was growing up because my uncle is an alcoholic."

"Not so unusual."

"Perhaps not. But I was afraid to drink for a long time because I might be an alcoholic. I'm not and I got over that, obviously." Aaron held up his own tumbler.

"And my dad thinks pastry is girlie. And Lindsay's parents hate each other's guts because her dad couldn't keep it in his pants. And all of that garbage weighs on us as adults."

Aaron nodded. "You think all that is at play here now? With you and Lindsay, I mean. You said she doesn't trust anyone."

"I mean, yeah. I don't mean to psychoanalyze her, but that's my present theory on why we can't make things work. So all I have to do is show her she can trust me."

Aaron smirked. "Oh, is that all?"

"Uphill battle, I know. Well, enough about me. My life is stupid and boring and this is some middle school drama, just me waiting for Lindsay to say whether she likes me enough to go steady. How are things with you and Bianca?"

Aaron held up a finger and pointed at Brad. "Oh, no. Don't change the subject on me. You're trying to win Lindsay back. It sounds like a challenge. Are you really sure she's worth all this effort?"

"Yes."

Brad hadn't even hesitated. Aaron gave him a long look. "Bianca's great. I'm gonna marry that girl one of these days. Maybe you can bring Lindsay to our wedding."

"Yeah? You gonna propose?"

"Thinking about it."

Brad sipped his cocktail. "Sorry I'm eating a lot of your time with my romantic nonsense."

"I asked. My bad."

Brad laughed. "Well, thanks for listening anyway."

"Let me get you a refill."

Lindsay sat at one of the stations in the *Forum* office and put on her headphones, although she didn't play any music because she wanted to eavesdrop on conversations around her. She hoped she could pick up more information about the financial status at the *Forum*, but so far, no one had said anything enlightening within earshot.

Erica walked over midmorning with a big grin on her face. Lindsay slipped off her headphones.

"I just got off the phone with a buddy of mine at the Food Channel," said Erica. "They *loved* you."

"Oh, that's great! I'm glad that all worked out."

"That article you wrote about unusual food trucks was also fantastic. We've gotten a lot of positive feedback."

"Great. I'm glad."

"But the Food Channel thing, just you saying you're the *Forum*'s food editor is bound to get the website some attention when the episode airs."

"Brad Marks helped set it up," said Lindsay.

"The cat café baker? That's wonderful. I was meaning to ask if he's as hot as he looks in his head shot."

"More," Lindsay said, feeling resigned.

Erica laughed. "You say that like it's a bad thing."

"Brad and I have some history, is all. From our culinary school days. It's nothing."

"My friend Heather bombed with him."

Lindsay balked. Brad turned someone down? "Really?"

"She's a feature writer for the *Times*. She's been gunning for Ben Russo's job now that he's given up food writing to pen self-righteous op-eds, but I don't think she'll get it. Don't tell her I said this, but she's not that great a writer. But she's my friend, so I support her. For the record."

"Of course."

"She did an interview with him about the cat café, but it kind of fell apart when she asked for a favor and he turned her down. She killed the story in retaliation."

"You're joking. Why did it fall apart?"

"Not clear, but if I'm reading between the lines, she wanted him to do her a favor the way he did a favor for you, and he refused."

"Is that a euphemism?" Did this woman come on to Brad? Well, Erica couldn't possibly know that Lindsay and Brad had slept together recently. Twice. So why was jealousy burning up Lindsay's chest?

Erica laughed. "No, no. Heather's a big fan of the Food Channel and has been trying to get tickets to something so she can write about it for the paper, but someone there must hate the *Times* because they keep turning her down. And I think she took that out on poor Brad."

Lindsay's head spun. Brad had really done her a solid. She suspected that he only had so many favors he could get from Aaron. Aaron had been accommodating because he remembered her from culinary school, but Brad could talk his way into anything. Could he have gotten this Heather woman a judge position on a Food Channel show or set her up with an inside tour to write about one of the shows? Hell, he could have gotten Heather screeners of *Mystery Meal* and called it a day. But Brad had torpedoed it, probably for Lindsay's sake, and blown up a good publicity interview with the *Times* in the process.

She was touched. She knew he wanted her back. And he'd done this nice thing for her, knowingly sacrificing publicity for himself, and he hadn't mentioned it when she'd gone over to his apartment to thank him. If Brad had wanted her to know about it, he would have said something.

As she turned that over in her head, Erica said, "I'm sure you've heard we're going to have to do some reorganizing."

That brought Lindsay's attention back to the present. *Reorganizing* was just a fancy word for layoffs, but Lindsay nodded.

"I have to cut a few contractors, but you have nothing to worry about. My boss is ecstatic you've gotten us so much good publicity. Our circulation numbers are static, but web traffic has gone up a little, and you're part of the reason. So thanks, Lindsay. And thank Brad Marks for me. I can't wait to see the show when it airs."

Lindsay suppressed a sigh of relief, but she was overjoyed that her job was safe. It was funny how the possibility of losing this job had made her think about cooking again, but hearing Erica tell her that this job was safe was a load off her shoulders. Cooking was the great unknown. Would it make her happy? Could she even still cook restaurant-quality meals? But this job she could do well. "I'll let you know the air date as soon as I do. I could write something up about my experience on set, too."

"Oh, yeah, great idea. People love behind-the-scenes stories. I mean, if you had to sign an NDA, don't violate it or anything, but if there's any insight you can share, I'd be happy to publish it."

"I could focus on what it's like to judge a contest like that. Like, they had me sit out the episode in which I was allergic to one of the mystery ingredients. I always wondered about that. Like, if you're a judge who is allergic to shellfish or doesn't eat pork, how can you be a good judge? And now I know."

"Interesting!" said Erica. "Yeah, write that up. Anything you can include about what it was like to be on set would be good. I have a meeting in five, but great job, Linds."

When Erica was gone, Lindsay turned back to her laptop but stared into space for a minute. Her Food Channel appearance had clearly gone a long way toward securing her job. She had Brad to thank for that. Brad, who had torpedoed an interview with the *Times* for Lindsay's sake. She could almost picture how that must have happened. She bet that woman flirted with him, but Brad was so oblivious that he didn't notice. How mad would she have been when he tried to shut her down gently? Maybe it was time to think about Brad in a new way.

What was her problem, anyway? Here was a great guy who cared about her and was basically throwing himself at her. Why couldn't she just accept that? What was making her resist him?

He wasn't perfect. Nobody was. She had some ideal in her head about who her perfect mate was, but she'd never opened herself up to possibilities; she only let men fall short of her impossibly high expectations. She kept herself safe, single, and free from heartbreak, because the one time she *had* opened up, she'd gotten her heart stomped on.

Had Brad measured up to her ideal? Probably not, but nobody could. Brad was real and he cared about her. She couldn't control him, nor did she want to. She just...wanted to feel safe. For a time she had with him, but she'd been constantly expecting the other shoe to drop. Then it had.

The bottom line was that, despite her deeply held conviction that everything was bound to go wrong, she had to open herself up to the possibility that it wouldn't. She didn't need perfect, but she did need faith, and she had to put her faith in Brad.

Brad was right. It was hard for her to trust anyone. But maybe it was time to give Brad a shot.

CHAPTER 15

BY SOME MIRACLE, LAUREN AND Paige were both free on a Sunday because the cat café had no events, so they joined Lindsay and Evan at brunch at a restaurant Paige liked near her apartment. It was a seasonal farm-to-table restaurant, which Lindsay appreciated. They were seated at a table near the rear of the space, which had huge floor-to-ceiling windows that looked out over the back deck. A few diners sat out there, although it was a shade too hot to be comfortable eating outside. But the deck was lovely, with little twinkle lights and floral garlands strewn across the pagoda that shaded the space.

"Josh and I came here on one of our first dates," said Paige. "He ate half the kitchen."

"That checks out," said Lauren as she perused the menu.

"If you don't like the food here, Linds, don't tell me," said Paige. "We still eat here a lot."

"I'm sure it's fine," said Lindsay. "You all agreed with me that Pepper was bad, and besides, I'm not the health inspector. I can't shut it down, and I'm not here to review. I'm just here for brunch. Are the frittatas here any good?"

"Oh, yeah. I like the spinach mushroom one."

After they ordered, Evan asked, "So how is everyone?"

"Hannah is crawling," said Lauren. "Caleb went all crazy overprotective father and babyproofed the bejesus out of the apartment. The baby gate he put on the doorway to the kitchen has some silly trick to it that I have not yet mastered, so I keep getting locked out. I had to vault over it yesterday morning to make coffee because Caleb had an early shift and wasn't home."

"Yikes," said Lindsay.

"Yeah. Then Hank decided this was a fun game and started hopping over it, too." Hank was Lauren and Caleb's yellow Lab mix.

"How is Caleb doing with fatherhood otherwise?" asked Paige.

Lauren's face softened. "He's great with her. He likes to take naps with her on his chest, and it's the cutest thing you've ever seen in the whole world. He talks to her in baby-speak when he thinks I'm not looking, which is remarkable because he doesn't even use that cutesy-wootsy speech with his patients or our pets."

"It figures that a guy as grouchy as Caleb would turn into mush when presented with a baby," said Lindsay.

"I *know*," said Lauren. "It's so cute. And the animals are doing pretty well with Hannah. Hank has decided it is his job to protect Hannah at all costs, so when we put her on her floor mat and let her crawl around, Hank watches her like a hawk. Molly is still not sure what to make of the people kitten and seems extremely skeptical of everything going on, but basically just leaves Hannah alone." Molly was Lauren's cat.

"Your house must just be cute central all the time," said Evan.

"Not so much at three in the morning when Hannah is screaming her head off and nothing I've tried gets her to calm down. But otherwise, yes." Lauren smiled, and it looked genuine.

"And what about you, Paige?" Evan asked.

"My whole life is wedding planning. I should have hired someone to do all this for me."

"You never would have allowed that," said Lauren. "You're too much of a perfectionist."

"True. But that reminds me, bridesmaid dress shopping two weeks from today. You too, Evan."

"I'm wearing a bridesmaid dress to your wedding?" Evan asked. "Because that's not really my thing. Although I look fabulous in fuchsia."

"No, but I thought we could stop at a tux rental place and pick something for you to wear. Maybe we can find a tie and cummerbund to match whatever color we pick for the dresses."

Evan laughed. "Whatever you want, honey."

"Do *you* have a dress?" Lindsay asked Paige.

"Yes! They're doing alterations now. Oh, I have a photo from the fitting I did last week." Paige got out her phone and found the photo. Then she passed her phone around the table.

Lindsay took a good look when she got the phone. The dress was fitted on top and covered with little glass beads. Then it flared out into a frothy tulle skirt. Paige's hair was pinned up out of her face in the photo and she wasn't wearing any makeup, but she still looked stunning.

"Beautiful," said Lindsay. It was a good reminder that not

every romantic relationship ended in disaster. Paige complained about how much work planning her wedding was turning out to be, but she still seemed happy for it to be happening.

"Is Josh helping with the planning much?" Lindsay asked Paige.

Paige laughed. "Oh, no."

"He working a lot these days?" asked Evan.

"Yes, but that's not the reason. He just… Well, he's useless at planning. I ask him questions, and his answer is always, 'Whatever you like best is fine.' So his job is to make sure he and his groomsmen get their tuxes and then they show up at the venue on time. He did help me pick the venue, though. It's going to be at this restaurant near Brooklyn Bridge Park with an amazing view of the bridge."

"The seafood place?" asked Lindsay. "I reviewed it when it opened. It was really good. The fish I ate melted right on my tongue."

"Yeah, Josh and I did a tasting. After the first bite, he said, 'This is it. We're getting married here.' His reaction made it a little challenging to play hardball when we haggled over pricing with the restaurant, but the view is lovely and you'll all eat very well."

"I'm so excited for you," said Lauren. "I have no regrets about my own city hall wedding, but I do like other people's weddings."

Their food was delivered then, and a waitress came over with a glass pitcher full of mimosa and refilled everyone's glasses.

"Shall we go to Lindsay next?" said Evan as everyone tucked into their meals.

Lindsay sighed. "Well, Brad saved my job by getting me

on that Food Channel show, and he apparently killed an interview with the *Times* for my sake. Oh, also, he wants to get back together, and we slept together twice."

Everyone made appropriate surprised sounds. "Are you kidding?" said Evan.

"This is a lot to unpack," said Lauren. "He killed an interview?"

"I witnessed that myself," said Paige. "The reporter was *mad*. I thought she was going to write some scathing review in the *Times*, but so far, nothing."

"Wait," said Evan. "Why did he kill the interview?"

"The reporter wanted favors," said Paige.

"Sexual favors?"

Lindsay groaned. "Why does everyone assume that?"

"Because your future husband is really hot," said Evan.

"No, not sexual favors," said Paige. "Something to do with using Brad's contact at the Food Channel to get another story. She was basically extorting him. Like, 'I'll write a great article about you if you do something for me.' But professionally, not sexually. And he turned her down."

"Was she pretty?" Lindsay asked.

"Oh, don't go there," said Evan.

"She looked fine," said Paige. "Brad told me afterward that he'd hooked you up with an opportunity at the Food Channel and didn't have any strings left he could pull, but Brad knows everyone. He could have gotten her something if he'd really wanted to. Or he could have thrown Lindsay overboard and asked his friend at the Food Channel to get Heather on the judge panel instead of Lindsay. I mean, what's better for his career? Helping the woman who already interviewed him or helping a reporter from the *Times*?"

"So Brad told this woman off for Lindsay's sake," said Evan.

Paige looked at Lindsay. "Yeah. I'm pretty sure that's exactly what he did."

Evan turned to Lindsay, too. "Twice. You slept with him twice."

"Yes. He's...kind of irresistible."

"Sure," said Paige. "And you're not back together because..."

"Why would it work out this time when it didn't the first time?" But even this standard line was starting to ring a little hollow to Lindsay.

"Why wouldn't it?" asked Evan.

Lindsay didn't have an answer for that. The idea was starting to seep in that maybe this time it would work out.

"Do you like him?" asked Lauren.

"Of course she does," said Evan. "She's been hung up on this guy for years."

"I have not!"

"You have," said Evan. "There are restaurants we can't eat at because Brad knows one of the chefs and we might run into him there. Hell, there are whole neighborhoods in Manhattan we couldn't go to for a while. You wouldn't ride the F train for a whole year because Brad lived on the F. You don't do that for a guy you're totally over."

Lindsay sighed. She knew Evan was right. "But I just... What if I screw it up again?" She knew deep down that she was a big factor in their breakup. She hadn't trusted him or listened to him when he tried to explain what happened with Phoebe, and he'd been kind of right that she'd been expecting exactly that to happen. It was hard to trust. "What if we both screw it up? It would hurt even more this time if we…"

"I know, sweetie," said Lauren, patting her hand. "On the other hand, what if it's really amazing? I've been spending a lot of time with him lately, and he's a great guy. I know that's not what you want to hear, but…"

"No, he is. I just don't…trust easily."

"Has this new Brad given you a reason not to trust him?" asked Paige.

Had he? Lindsay replayed every interaction they'd had in the last few weeks, and he'd only been unfailingly honest. "No."

"Then a date can't hurt, can it?" asked Paige. "Just a date, not a marriage proposal."

"I guess not, but I don't know. I need more time to think about it."

As if sensing she didn't want to talk about Brad anymore, everyone nodded. Evan said, "Okay. My turn now."

"What's going on with you, Evan?" said Lauren, playing along.

"Well, I'm pretty sure I'm going to break up with Will."

"What did he do?" asked Paige.

"Nothing, which is kind of the problem. There are just no sparks. Any sparks there were when we first got together have fizzled. Plus, I'm pretty sure he's still in love with his married coworker, and it's surprisingly hard to compete with that."

"Also, Pablo's single again," said Paige.

Ah, Pablo. Evan's longtime crush was extremely good-looking and was a sweet guy from what Lindsay could tell from her limited interactions with him. He and Paige ran an event for kids at the cat café where kids practiced their reading skills on the cats, so she had been spending a lot of time with him recently.

"That's not the reason I want to break up with Will," said Evan. "And I think all these years of me pining have shown nothing will ever happen with Pablo."

"No sparks?" said Lindsay.

"Nada. I mean, mostly we just go out to eat and have sex, which is basically a perfect Saturday night if you ask me, but the sex is…just okay. I don't know. And I thought by now we'd be in love, but… We're not. He's…fine. Which is the issue. Fine is not great or amazing."

"Probably best not to string him along, then," said Lauren.

"Yeah. Pablo's single again? See, I didn't even know that."

Paige grinned. "Yeah, he and that beardy guy broke up. He mentioned it when he came to the café the other day. He was pretty bummed about it, so now is probably not the time to swoop in there. Rebound flings never work out."

"Huh," said Evan.

"Don't get ideas," said Lauren.

"I'm not, I'm not. You're right about rebounds. But, like, this kind of proves my point. If I'm just with Will because he's not Pablo and I don't want to be single, but not because I genuinely like him, then it's not fair for either of us to stay together."

"So you're going to break up with him?" asked Lindsay.

"Yes, I think so." Evan tapped his chin. "Maybe the lesson here is that if there is someone you *do* have sparks with, then you should go for it."

"Subtle," said Lindsay.

Evan leveled his gaze at her. "Are you going to go out with Brad?"

"I will consider it."

"Wow, guys," said Paige. "So much enthusiasm."

"I hate Restaurant Week," Brad said.

Brad and Aaron had just been seated at Olive Tree, an upscale Mediterranean restaurant near Union Square. Brad eyed the prix fixe menu with resignation. There wasn't anything on it that excited him.

"Latent PTSD?" Aaron asked. He looked around the very crowded restaurant.

"Well, sure, that." For a couple of years, Brad had spent every night of New York City's Restaurant Week—which was usually actually two weeks—churning out desserts, which had been its own kind of nightmare. "But actually, it's that the menus are so uninspired. They limit the menu to what they know they can fire quickly and easily. So, look, our options are basically steak or a flatbread pizza, here at a restaurant that is known for good seafood and creative dishes."

"We'll have a good meal for a quarter of what it usually costs here," said Aaron. "That's the beauty of Restaurant Week."

Brad sighed. "I guess that explains why you invited me here. I completely forgot it was Restaurant Week."

"Restaurant Week is not all bad. I had the tasting menu at La Montagne last night. It was amazing. Buttery as hell, and they had to roll me out of there because I ate so much, but so, *so* good."

"See, that I would have appreciated."

Sam, another culinary school buddy, buzzed over to the table and dropped into the third chair. "I'm so sorry I'm late. I had to fire an employee today, which was not the best."

Brad, Aaron, and Sam had lived together for most of culinary school. Sam had followed Brad into studying pastry and currently owned an Upper West Side bakery where mostly he sold cupcakes. They got together for dinner about once a month to catch up. Brad really enjoyed these dinners, but he regretted letting Aaron choose the restaurant this time. He decided to set that aside and hoped the steak would be good.

"This guy just never made it to work on time." Sam glanced at Brad. "You're running a kitchen now, aren't you? What time do you usually get there?"

"Five. It's actually past my bedtime now. I'm only doing this because I haven't seen you in forever."

Sam picked up his menu. "I know what you mean." His gaze ran over the text. "I don't know why I bother to look at menus during Restaurant Week. I'm just gonna order whatever they want me to order."

"You seem cheery tonight," said Aaron.

Sam put the menu down and took a deep breath. "Again, sorry. Firing someone takes a lot out of you."

"My boss is letting me hire another assistant," said Brad, "so you should give me the name of your guy so I don't hire him."

"Oh, I will." Sam rubbed the back of his neck. "It doesn't help that Justin has been out of town on business the last few days." Justin was Sam's husband. "But let's put all that junk aside. How are you guys?"

"Brad is trying to win Lindsay back," said Aaron.

Sam laughed. "I saw her byline on that profile of you in the *Forum*. That surprised the hell out of me."

Brad gave Sam the short version of the story of how Lindsay had come back into his life. He'd been hoping for a distraction tonight, though. He spent enough time thinking about Lindsay; dinner with friends should have been a distraction.

"This feels like a lot of work," said Sam. "Winning her over again, I mean."

"Yeah," Aaron agreed. "Bianca and I went on a date and figured out that we liked each other and have been together ever since. Not that it's all been smooth sailing, but I never had to convince her to be with me."

"You had to convince her a little," said Sam. "I'm sure the TV executive job title helped smooth the way, but you had to talk her into taking your skinny ass home the first time."

"Wasn't that hard. I'm very charming."

"You ask that girl to marry you yet?" asked Brad, hoping to deflect attention from himself.

"No, but I, uh, bought a ring."

"Are you kidding?" said Sam.

"No, I'm dead serious. We're going to wrap filming for the first season of *Mystery Meal* at the end of next week. Then I get a week off and I'm taking Bianca to Florence because she's always wanted to go there. I figured we could eat our way through the city and look at art and I'd find some romantic spot to pop the question."

Sam raised an eyebrow. "You think she'll say yes?"

Aaron frowned. "I did right until you asked me."

"She probably suspects anyway," said Sam. "Justin has a friend who took his girlfriend to Paris, and Justin explained to me that you only take your significant other to Europe if you're going to propose. This friend reasoned they would either come back engaged or broken up. He proposed in front of the Eiffel Tower, though, which is so clichéd."

"Didn't Justin propose to you on the observation deck of the Empire State Building?" asked Brad.

Sam rolled his eyes. "Yes, but during Pride when it was lit up like a rainbow, with a great view of this wonderful city spread out before us."

"There's a nuance here I'm not seeing," Brad stage-whispered to Aaron.

"Maybe what Lindsay needs is a grand romantic gesture," said Sam.

"Like what?"

Sam shrugged. "You're a smart guy. You'll think of something."

When their entrées arrived, Brad mulled over what he could do to impress Lindsay. Not take her to a dinner like this. The steak was cooked well but underseasoned, and the flatbread that Sam had ordered looked a little sad.

"Ah, Restaurant Week," Sam said, picking a piece of red onion off his pizza and tossing it in his mouth. "Food for the masses."

"All right, all right," said Aaron. "Point taken. We'll go somewhere better next time."

"Justin and I ate at this Vietnamese place on Seventy-Seventh last week that was delicious. They have the standard dishes plus a couple of creative things. The chef is first-generation American but went to culinary school in Paris, so it's Vietnamese flavors with Western techniques. And she makes her own fish sauce, which is the salty kick you want with Vietnamese food."

"You're saying we should go there next month?" said Aaron.

"Yes. Especially since I can see the wheels turning in your head. You want to get this chef for your show, don't you?"

Aaron shrugged. "I love Vietnamese. That place on University got a new chef and they're not as good anymore so I've been looking for a new place."

"How do you know all this?" Brad asked. "Did you interview the chef?"

"I asked to talk to her when we ate there. I laid it on thick with the waiter and mentioned I was also a chef. The restaurant's chef came out to the table and we chatted for a bit."

Aaron laughed. "We're all insufferable foodies. There are tourists in this restaurant right now who will go home and tell their friends this was the best meal they ever ate, and here we are whining at the lack of options."

"We come by it honestly," said Sam. "What good is a culinary degree if you can't make fun of how bland or pretentious the food is at restaurants run by celebrity chefs?"

Brad hardly tasted his food anyway. His brain was whirling now. What could he do to impress Lindsay? What was he good at?

Baking, obviously. What did she care about? Food. Her job. His head spun as he speared a potato with his fork.

If Lindsay were here, she'd comment on how dull the menu was, too, because she was just as insufferable as the rest of them.

But maybe he could bake her something that would impress her socks off.

CHAPTER 16

BRAD CARRIED A HUGE BAKERY box into the *Forum*'s office building. He had called Lindsay ahead to make sure she would be there and to explain his actions. Would her office like some cupcakes? She said sure. Brad managed to get as far as the reception desk before Lindsay had to come fetch him. As far as stealthy grand gestures went, it was not a complete success, but hopefully the cupcakes themselves would win her over.

"Why are you really here?" she asked as she led him into the main office area.

"I wanted to do something nice," he said, laying the box on the table Lindsay indicated.

A tall woman with dark hair wandered over. Lindsay said, "Brad, this is my boss, Erica Sanchez. Erica, this is Brad Marks."

"Of the cat café!" Erica extended her hand, so Brad shook it.

"I brought some cupcakes. For the office, not just for Lindsay. As a thank-you for everything." He took the lid off the box.

Erica gazed at them, looking delighted. "What have we got here?"

There were a dozen cupcakes, two of each kind. The cakes themselves were leftovers from that morning's cat café display, but he'd gotten a little creative with frosting because it was easier to make a small batch of frosting than a small batch of cake batter. So there were six kinds of cupcakes. Brad pointed to each and said, "Vanilla, chocolate, cookies and cream, red velvet, cinnamon apple, and maple bacon."

"Oooh." Erica wiggled her fingers as she tried to choose.

Lindsay grabbed one of the maple bacon cupcakes and led him back to her desk, which wasn't so much a desk as a station in the middle of a large table. As she ate it, other workers in the office drifted over and helped themselves.

"I'm wrapping up here in a few," Lindsay said. "I guess we could go get a cup of coffee or something."

The lukewarm reaction was a little less than he'd been hoping for, but Brad would take it.

There was an indie coffee shop near the *Forum*'s offices, which is where Lindsay led Brad. It was full of college students studying, but there were a few empty tables, so Brad snagged one while Lindsay ordered their drinks.

She joined him a few minutes later and handed him a latte, exactly the thing he would have ordered. He hadn't even told her what he wanted.

"So," she said.

"So."

Lindsay frowned. "I heard through the grapevine that you bungled an interview with the *Times* because the reporter wanted you to introduce her to Aaron and you refused."

Brad could only wonder at how small the food world was. "That's true. I didn't think Aaron would do another favor for me."

"So in a roundabout way, you sabotaged a good opportunity for my sake."

"If you want to look at it that way."

"Is that not what happened?"

Brad shrugged. "I mean, yes, I wanted that opportunity for you and not for this reporter, but I wasn't going to make a big deal about it." Which was true. He hadn't planned to say anything, but maybe it was best that it worked out this way. Maybe this would show her he cared, that he was looking out for her.

Lindsay nodded. "The maple bacon cupcake was good."

It still wasn't much, but Brad felt like he was chipping away at her armor. "Thanks. I know you like a good sweet and salty combo."

"I was in San Francisco for a food festival last year, and the hotel had a café that served maple bacon doughnuts that were to die for."

"Everyone says that trend is over, but never underestimate the American love for all things bacon."

Lindsay smiled. "I think cupcakes are also proving to have staying power. A few years ago, all the little cupcake bakeries in the Village started getting replaced with macaron shops, but I think they're going back. Everyone loves cupcakes."

"It seems like a bad strategy to build a business around one trendy item."

"Do you make macarons?"

"I *can*. I haven't for the café yet. Although, I wonder if I could give them little cat ears. I'll have to experiment."

"I have never successfully made a macaron. I caught the flu

this past winter and wound up spending almost a whole week on my couch. I watched like three seasons of that British baking show, and I came away convinced I could make macarons. As soon as I recovered enough to stand upright in my kitchen, I gave it a shot. I failed spectacularly. They came out flat and misshapen."

"It takes some practice. I'll show you the trick sometime."

"We used to talk about cooking together but hardly ever got around to it."

Brad nodded. That was true. In their culinary school days, they did most of their cooking at school or work. Brad still liked the idea of him and Lindsay sharing space in a kitchen, working together to prepare a meal for their friends. He liked that picture immensely.

"We used to talk about opening a restaurant together," said Brad, fully letting himself revel in nostalgia.

"Yeah. I thought about that a lot back in culinary school. We'd be partners, you know? Me as executive chef, you as pastry chef."

"Sure. If we did it now, what kind of food would we make?"

"American, probably. Maybe with a focus on seafood. Mediterranean influences because I really like that flavor profile. Light, delicious, nothing very heavy."

"So, uh, no little crocks of lasagna covered in red sauce."

Lindsay laughed. "God, no. Don't get me wrong. I love Italian food, but for my own restaurant, I'd want to serve food people feel good about eating. Then they can opt to have a decadent dessert if that's how they roll."

Brad liked the sound of that. "You have thought this through. Recently, I mean."

"Yeah, I guess I have. It's been on the brain. I reviewed a

crab shack in Red Hook last summer that reminded me how much I love seafood. It doesn't even have to be fancy. I took the girls and Evan and we ordered this clam-bake-for-four option. It was literally a metal bucket full of seafood, but they used their own seasoning mix and everything was cooked perfectly. Just picnic tables on a deck with a bit of a breeze coming in off the water. Sometimes food like that beats the food at a Michelin-star restaurant. Pretentious doesn't always mean good."

Brad smiled at that. "You know, I spend almost more time talking about food than making food."

Lindsay laughed. "I definitely do. But food is kind of our whole lives, isn't it?"

"Well, not my *whole* life. I like...baseball. And video games. And now cats. I have a pet cat."

"Me too. Those cats do make your life better in ways you don't expect." Lindsay smiled. "And I know you will tell me this is blasphemy, but the food is better at Citi Field than at Yankee Stadium."

"That *is* blasphemy, but I appreciate how you were able to turn one of my nonfood interests back into food."

"Have you eaten at both to compare?"

"As a matter of fact, I have. You remember Sam from culinary school? His brother has season tickets to the Mets, so Sam and I use them sometimes. So, having sampled the cuisines of both teams, I can say that Citi Field has more options near the cheap seats, but you can get a better steak sandwich at Yankee Stadium. I of course did a lot of testing. For science."

"Of course."

"The Yanks are having a great season."

"That's good. I don't care about baseball."

"I know. I don't care that you don't care."

Lindsay shook her head. "I did used to like going to games with you."

"That is a thing we can do this summer. I have season tickets to the Yankees that I end up giving to Aaron a lot because I work all the time. My seats are over first base."

"Is that a thing friends do?"

Brad tried to read between the lines of her question. "Sure. It's a thing people who are dating do, too."

"Brad, I—"

"So, okay, I brought you the cupcakes as a grand gesture. I thought it would go over well in your office. I've been racking my brain about what I can do to impress you, and the truth is, most of what I have is food. I can make really good food. Specifically, good pastry and desserts."

Lindsay let out a sigh. "That's true, you can. And you're surprisingly persistent for a guy I keep turning down."

"You haven't done that."

Lindsay lowered her eyelids. "Haven't I? I'd remember saying yes."

Brad shook his head. "Nope. You keep saying maybe, and you've slept with me twice. This is going to come out sounding creepier than I mean it, but if you really didn't want to ever see me again, you wouldn't be sitting here right now."

Lindsay just pursed her lips and nodded slightly as if to acknowledge that this was a good point.

"You're beautiful and smart and sexy and can talk to me all day about food, which is basically the only thing I know how to talk about. We had fun together once upon a time. I don't know about you, but I'm having fun right now just sipping a latte and talking to you."

"I know, but…"

"So I've put it all out on the table. I have feelings for you. I baked you cupcakes with bacon. I gave you space to think. So what do you think?"

She shook her head, "I don't—"

"What do *you* want, Linds? Do you still want to open that restaurant? I'm game. Let's talk about it. Do you want to keep your current job while I bounce around various pastry jobs until I have enough of a nest egg to open my own bakery? That's cool. Do *you* want to be with *me*? Because I definitely want to be with you. So stop questioning it, believe me when I tell you I'm being sincere, and decide what you want."

Lindsay stared at him. "Oh."

———

Lindsay hated being vulnerable. It was one thing she knew for sure about herself. But accepting Brad back into her life would require making herself vulnerable.

"I'm glad for all that," she said, folding her hands around her coffee cup. "I want to trust you."

He reached over and peeled one of her hands off her cup and wrapped his around it. "The happiest year of my life was that year we were together in culinary school. I've done some great things since then and had some good times and had some jobs I really liked and some I really didn't. But I was never as happy as I was when I was with you. And I kinda suspect the same is true for you. And if that's the case, I think we should try to see if we can be happy together again, is all. Maybe it won't work out. But maybe it will this time because we have a better handle on the people we're supposed to be."

Lindsay let out a breath. She had been happy that year. It had been one of the best years of her life, too.

They'd sometimes worked together inventing new recipes in one of the school's test kitchens late at night. There'd been a night when her friend Ashley and Brad's friend Sam had been working out the best way to make a particular French dessert—some fancy pâtisserie that was beyond Lindsay's comprehension—and it ended with them all throwing flour at each other like a bunch of kids. It had been a bitch to clean up after the fact, but Lindsay couldn't remember ever laughing so hard.

Or there was the time Brad had taken her to meet his parents in Philadelphia, and he'd insisted on taking her to the best cheesesteak place in the city, but they'd gotten lost on the way because Brad had decided to drive there in his parents' car and had taken a "short cut." A fight had ensued in which Lindsay had called Brad a typical male for not wanting to ask for directions. Lindsay had used the GPS on her phone to get them there, and by the time they finally got their cheesesteaks, they were both starving. It was a damned good cheesesteak, though, and the matter-of-fact way Brad had said, "Worth it," once they were eating had made Lindsay smile despite herself.

Or there was the time Aaron had organized a cookout in Prospect Park, and asking a bunch of culinary students to prepare simple burgers and hot dogs on the portable grills someone had brought was somehow too simple. Lindsay and Brad had just sat on a blanket and watched their friends argue over the intricacies of this particular challenge. Lindsay had her head on Brad's lap and was content to let the breeze waft over her, and... Yeah. She'd been happy.

And her life hadn't been the same since leaving him.

If she could find it in herself to trust him, if they both went all in on this, they could have that again.

"I'll go on a real date with you," she said.

He stared at her like he couldn't believe what she'd said. "Yeah?"

"Yeah. You're right, we did have fun. But I don't want to just accept on faith that we will have fun now. I want to get to know the new you. I want to trust you. I'm willing to give us a chance to see if we still have something between us. How's that?"

Brad's face broke into a wide grin. "Sounds great to me! I'm working the rest of the week, but I have Monday off. Maybe I can come up with something to do. You want to eat at that new restaurant Pepper?"

"You *think* you're funny."

But even as they agreed that Brad would call her to make arrangements, she remained deeply skeptical that this could work.

CHAPTER 17

LINDSAY SIPPED COFFEE AT HOME and checked her email. Fred meandered over and settled on her lap. "What kind of food do you like, Mr. Astaire? I saw you eyeing my sushi takeout last night. Should I review more sushi places?" Fred let out a happy little *brrup* in response.

Erica had sent a list of new restaurants the *Forum* hoped to review, so Lindsay did a little research on each one and decided on assignments for the various freelancers who reported to her. For herself, she decided on a new restaurant on Vanderbilt Avenue near her apartment, for convenience.

She picked Thursday night to dine at this place—she preferred weeknights to avoid the weekend/date-night crowds—and hoped to get the review done while the restaurant still had some novelty. Then she texted each of her friends to invite them to join her.

And then the replies came.

Lauren: Caleb is working the night shift Thurs so I'll be home with Hannah.

Paige: Book club at the café Thursday night, so I'm closing at 8.

Evan: I've got a work meeting in Manhattan that will prob go late. Sorry, honey.

Well, that figured. Thursday was two days away, too late for anyone to change their plans. She supposed she could go eat by herself. Bring a book, catch up on her reading.

Then Brad popped into her head.

He'd asked her for a date, hadn't he?

She picked up her phone. He'd be at work now, but he could probably answer a text.

She said, I'm reviewing a new restaurant in Prospect Heights Thurs night. You free?

The reply was a few minutes coming, but Lindsay knew better than to interpret that as hesitancy. This time of the morning, Brad was probably taking bread out of the ovens.

But rather than say yes, Brad replied, What kind of food?

Lindsay laughed. That seemed on-brand. Just like a foodie to think about the cuisine first and the company second. She wasn't even offended, because she probably would have had the same response. Upscale pub food. New restaurant owned by a British chef. Menu is fancy takes on shepherd's pie and fish & chips, etc.

Lindsay was actually looking forward to trying this menu. There'd been a pub near the culinary school where Lindsay and her classmates had hung out after class all the time. The waitstaff all had Irish accents and the menu contained dishes like bangers and mash and a full Irish breakfast. The restaurant was still there, but Lindsay hardly ever went to that neighborhood anymore and she missed it. She wondered if upscale takes on the same kind of food would be delicious or pretentious—it could go either way.

And, okay, if it was pretentious, mocking it with Brad might even be fun.

Brad responded, Sounds good. Gotta keep an eye on the ovens now, but text where/when and I'll be there.

Lindsay considered telling him he'd been her backup choice and this was not a date, but thought better of it. Instead, she texted the restaurant address and told him to meet her there at six. He texted back a thumbs-up emoji.

She hadn't said it wasn't a date. She hadn't said it *was*, either. Would Brad think this was a date or just one friend inviting the other to the restaurant she was reviewing?

She sat back in her desk chair. Was she really doing this? Was she really going to go on a date with Brad?

Her friends were right. She'd never really gotten over him. She'd told herself she had, but she avoided places he'd be, she followed what he was up to, and she still had photos of him on her phone despite their breakup being five years past. She knew deep down that he was a good guy. He was hot, he was talented, and he was caring. And for a year, he'd made her happy.

But Lindsay was very skittish about getting her heart broken again.

Or at all; that was what had made her run the first time.

They'd been out somewhere about three months before their graduation from culinary school. Lindsay couldn't remember where, probably the High Line. One of Brad's favorite leisure activities was getting lobster rolls from a seafood store in Chelsea Market and then walking up to the High Line to eat them outside and people watch.

It had been one of those cool spring days that nobody knew how to dress for, before the warm weather really arrived. As Brad dug into his lobster roll and Lindsay tasted some excellent tuna salad, she commented that although it was still too cool for the guy who rollerbladed by them in shorts, it was definitely too warm for the woman bundled up in a puffy coat with a hat and gloves to be wearing that many layers.

"Judgy of you to point that out, Goldilocks," said Brad.

"I'm just saying."

"What people wear isn't hurting anyone. I'm going to sit here and enjoy my off-season lobster roll."

"Do lobsters go out of season? I thought they caught them in Maine year round."

Brad shrugged. "I always think of lobster as a summer food, but who knows? Did you know that thing everyone attributes to Anthony Bourdain about not eating seafood on Mondays isn't true?"

"What's that?"

"It used to be conventional wisdom that restaurants got their seafood deliveries on Tuesdays, so on Monday, you're eating the oldest fish. Thus you should not eat in seafood restaurants on Mondays. But that's not really true anymore."

"Oh, right. The sushi place near my apartment is closed on Mondays. I wonder if that's why. No one wants to eat sushi on Mondays."

Brad laughed. "Right. True or not, I bet sushi consumption drops off on Mondays."

Brad's gaze snagged on an athletic blond woman who jogged by wearing only a sports bra and bike shorts.

Lindsay snapped her fingers. "I'm over here, buddy."

"Sorry," Brad murmured. Then he turned his attention back to her. "So. Oh, get a load of those two guys by the bar cart over there. Frat bros or gay couple?"

And maybe it was some kind of residual childhood trauma, but something flopped over in Lindsay's stomach. It was a completely innocent thing. Brad wouldn't have gone after the jogging woman. He was just looking. He was a heterosexual male with a pulse; he was allowed to look. It was unreasonable for Lindsay to demand Brad's constant attention when she herself sometimes looked at other men.

And Lindsay's parents' situation was so different. There'd been strain in their marriage for as long as Lindsay had been aware enough to recognize emotions. They fought constantly. Lindsay's mother threatened to leave at least once a week, and then finally, Lindsay's father hadn't bothered to hide the affair with his secretary, and her parents had signed the divorce papers.

She didn't think she and Brad had that dynamic, but they'd only been together for a year. Surely her parents had liked each other enough once to get married. Was Lindsay just doomed to repeat the same patterns?

She could admit that she'd had a foot out the door as a way to safeguard her own heart. She didn't want to repeat her parents' old patterns.

But had that been fair to Brad? Probably not, because even Lindsay could now acknowledge that catching him with Phoebe was more an excuse than a reason to end the relationship. Brad's explanation of what happened with Phoebe, which Lindsay now believed, ran roughshod over the narrative that she'd been telling herself for so long. And he'd shut down that *New York Times* lady. That had to mean something. But could she trust him? Could she trust herself?

She knew love was real. Her friends, particularly Lauren and Paige, had found great, loving relationships, and they seemed so happy. Lindsay was cynical, but deep down, she wanted that, too.

She pushed away from her desk and went to the kitchen to refill her coffee. She hoped she wasn't making a mistake in giving Brad a second chance.

Brad followed Lindsay to their table and looked around. From the outside, the restaurant looked like a pub. It was called the Deer & Goose, like some old British pub, and the signage reflected that. But inside, the restaurant looked like an interior designer had run away with a wilderness theme. There was a huge reclaimed-wood feature wall in the back, from which hung framed watercolor paintings of trees. Each table had a tiny flowerpot with some kind of coniferous tree thing in it, reminiscent of the little trees his mother always bought at Christmastime.

Brad glanced at the menu, then looked at Lindsay. She did look pretty tonight. Her dark hair fell around her shoulders, and she had on a pink cardigan over a floral dress, like she'd actually tried to look nice for this date. Or it wasn't a date. Brad wasn't totally sure.

"So how does this reviewing thing usually work?" Brad asked.

"Well, we don't want them to know I'm a critic, so we definitely don't speak aloud about that."

Brad mimed zipping his lips.

"Order whatever you want, but let's order different entrées so we can try each other's. I've been wanting to try this sausage dish since I saw it on the online menu."

"Ooh, maybe I'll order the toad-in-the-hole."

Lindsay narrowed her eyes at him. "Isn't that just an egg in a piece of toast?"

"Only if you're an American."

"You're an American."

"In England, toad-in-the-hole is a Yorkshire pudding with sausage, onions, and gravy. This menu says they use a chicken apple sausage, which sounds tasty. But partly, I want to judge the Yorkshire pudding."

"I don't think I've ever had one."

"You totally have. I'm sure I made them when we were dating. I was really proud of myself when I mastered making them. It's like an eggy, bread pastry thing."

Lindsay laughed. "You have a way with words. 'Eggy, bread pastry thing'?"

"If they do it right, you'll see."

Brad turned the menu over to see if they had desserts listed. They didn't on the dinner menu, but he spotted that the chef was Michelle McKean.

"Get out of town," he murmured.

"What?"

"I know the chef."

Lindsay sighed. "You know everyone."

That was not at all true, but he did know a lot of chefs in New York between the ages of twenty-five and thirty-five.

A waitress came over to take their orders. Lindsay let Brad order first and then ordered a different appetizer. Before the waitress finished saying, "I'll be right back with your drinks," Brad said, "Is Michelle here tonight?"

"Michelle the chef?"

"Yes. She and I aren't old friends or anything, just casual acquaintances, but I figured I'd say hi if she's here. My name is Brad Marks."

"Ah, sure. She is here tonight. I'll let her know."

Lindsay looked pissed when the waitress walked away.

"What?" Brad asked.

"You might as well have just blown my cover. The whole idea is for me to taste a typical meal at the restaurant. Now that the chef knows you know her, she'll probably put a little extra care into our entrées. So now I can't review a typical meal."

"Oh, whoops. Sorry about that. I wasn't thinking."

"No, you were not."

"Well, now that we're off on the wrong foot, how are you?"

Lindsay looked like she was doing some mental gymnastics behind her strained facade. Likely she was trying to tell herself this was not a mistake. "I'm fine," she said.

So, fine, he'd fucked up. He probably should have waited until after they'd eaten to let the waitress know he was friends with the chef. But Lindsay could turn down her irritation with him a little.

"Hamilton is adjusting well at home," Brad volunteered. "Although during that heat wave we had last week, he slept in my bathroom sink pretty much constantly. Do you think it's because the porcelain or whatever sinks are made of is cool?"

"Probably," said Lindsay. The crease in her forehead started to slip away. "Fred sleeps in the sink sometimes."

"Fred Astaire the cat, right? Does he dance?"

"Not well."

Ah, so that was how this was going to go. He'd stepped in it and pissed her off. She was going to make him pay for it the entire meal. He sighed and sipped his water.

Michelle herself brought their appetizers from the kitchen, plus an extra basket of crumpets. "Hey, Brad," she said.

"Hey, yourself. Long time, no see."

"This is my friend Lindsay. She was actually the one who suggested we try this place. We're excited to try the food." He glanced at Lindsay. He couldn't see a way out of the hole, but he could pull her into the conversation.

Lindsay pasted on a smile and said hello.

"You guys live in the neighborhood?" Michelle had a bit of an English accent that had been flattened by many years living in the States.

"Yeah, we both live a few blocks from here. I had no idea this was your place until I saw your name on the menu."

"Did I hear correctly that you're making pastries for cats now?"

"Well, not just for cats, but I work at a cat café. You should come by sometime! It's over on Whitman Street."

"Maybe I'll do that," Michelle said, touching Brad's shoulder. "Are you the one who ordered the toad-in-the-hole?"

"Guilty."

"I hope my Yorkshire pudding is up to snuff. I know you have strong opinions about them."

"Oh, I'm sure it's fine," said Brad with a wink. "Aren't you actually *from* Yorkshire?"

"I am! It's delightful that you remembered." Michelle smiled wide. "I gotta get back to the kitchen, but it was great seeing you. The crumpets are on the house."

Once she and the waitress were gone, Lindsay was seething. She glared at Brad with her arms crossed.

"Are you going to murder me with your butter knife?" Brad asked.

"I'm thinking about putting the knife through your eye, yeah."

Brad let out a breath. He'd been friendly with Michelle, but Lindsay couldn't really be jealous, could she? He said, "All right. Lay it on me."

She sighed. "No, whatever. Damage done. Nice of you to introduce me as your friend."

Brad caught the snotty note in her tone and was irritated that she wasn't really letting this go. "Now hang on a minute. How was I supposed to introduce you? Are we even together? Is this a date? Or did you just ask me to dinner because all your friends were busy and you didn't want to eat alone?"

Lindsay's eyes went wide and she looked chastened, so Brad guessed he'd hit the mark.

God, why was he trying this hard? He was tired of her scraps. Ever since they'd reconnected, Lindsay kept showing she was interested in getting back together, but she was too stubborn to admit it. And she was doing it to him again now. If they had any hope of making this work, she had to meet him in the middle. He couldn't do all the work.

"*Is* this a date?"

"Do you want it to be a date?"

Brad let out a breath. He'd ordered an appetizer that was a plate of Irish cheddar with house-made crackers and a little tub of apricot jam, so he spread some jam on a cracker and tasted it. It was very good, probably also house-made. He glared at Lindsay, irritated now.

"What do you want, Linds? Because I've made my feelings pretty clear, I thought."

"You want it to be a date. You want us to be together."

"I've wanted you back since the moment you walked out of my life, that's true. But I also want you to trust me, and I want you to be willing to try to make this work. It can't just be me doing all the work and hoping you'll come around anymore. I'm... I'm tired of trying to prove myself to you, if I'm honest. Am I perfect? No. Will I fuck up sometimes? Probably. But you have to trust that at the end of the day, my priority is you—us."

Lindsay stared at her appetizer—a chopped salad with bacon and crispy chickpeas—and then said, "Oh."

"If we get back together, I'm going to talk to other women. And other men. And, yeah, I know a lot of chefs in this city. And probably I'll flirt with people in all of those categories sometimes. But you have to trust that I will always choose you, always come home to you, and always be faithful to *you*. If you don't trust that, then I guess we have nothing else to talk about."

He watched her wrestle with that, so at least he'd gotten through to her. He didn't want to bail on dinner—he really wanted to try that Yorkshire pudding now—but he was feeling pretty steamed.

Lindsay started eating her salad, so Brad dove into the cheese plate.

The rest of dinner was tense. Brad figured Lindsay was thinking through what she wanted while she ate, so he didn't push her. The Yorkshire pudding *was* good—fluffy and eggy and exactly what it was supposed to be—and the chicken sausage was a nice complement to it.

After a few minutes of silence, Brad said, "How's the bangers and mash?"

"Good. Really good pork sausage. Nice snap to the casing."

Brad laughed because it was so like a chef to comment on the snap of a sausage and not the taste.

They each ate a few bites off each other's plates. Brad was impressed by how creamy and well-seasoned Lindsay's potatoes were. Lindsay ate a bit of Yorkshire pudding and said, "Oh, right. I remember this now."

"There's kind of an art form to getting them right. They're sort of like a souffle in that way. If you nail it, they are fluffy and delicious like this. But if you do one thing wrong, the whole thing deflates into a flat, dense, flavorless hockey puck. I made you eat a lot of them because I was practicing."

"Sure. I remember now. Like how you made me eat a hundred éclairs while you were trying to master choux pastry."

"I don't recall you being that mad about it. Who can be mad about eating an éclair? Or five?"

"Not all of your early batches were good."

"True, but I make great éclairs now. I should make mini ones for the café, maybe."

"Are you going to try to make them feline in some way?"

He had a flash of making icing with stripes, like a striped cat. He might be the only one who thought stripes looked feline, though, so he filed it away to mull over later. He'd think of something. "I will certainly try."

Brad was pretty full by the time the waitress handed them dessert menus, but he agreed to split a slice of chocolate stout cake with Lindsay.

By the time they were sinking their forks into what turned out to be an excellent slice of cake, the tension between them had dissipated. When Michelle swung back out at the end of the meal to ask if everything met with their approval, Brad was polite but kept an eye on Lindsay, who still seemed irritated he'd torpedoed her review.

He thought about inviting her back to his place once they left the restaurant, but he was still annoyed, too, so he just said, "Well, this was fun."

She sighed. "Was it?"

"I will admit, arguing with you was not super fun. But, look, we know where we stand, I think."

She stood there on the sidewalk for a long moment with her lips pressed together.

"You invited me to dinner," said Brad. "I thought we were making progress. If this *wasn't* a date, what was it?"

"I don't know." Lindsay shook her head. "I need more time to think."

Brad didn't know why she'd need more time, but he nodded. "All right. Well, let me know when you decide something."

Lindsay hooked her thumb to point south, in the direction of her apartment. Brad's was a few blocks north. "I mean, do you want to come to my place for a cup of coffee or something."

"Not tonight. Gotta get up at four to make cat treats and all that."

"Right. Of course."

"And I don't think it's fair for us to…well, act on our physical feelings when we're still tied up mentally." He gave Lindsay what he hoped was a meaningful look, because his feelings were pretty well sorted out at this point.

"Makes sense," she murmured.

"Right. Good night, Lindsay. I'll see you sometime." There. Let that just be in the universe. He could only chase her for so long; she needed to come to him next.

"Of course. Good night, Brad."

Brad nodded and turned to walk home before he could change his mind.

CHAPTER 18

LINDSAY HADN'T STRETCHED HER CULINARY muscles in a while, but she was taking full advantage of Paige and Josh's kitchen. It was a little too small and simple to be categorized as a chef's kitchen, but it was double the size of the little kitchen in her own apartment. She'd never understood why so many Brooklyn landlords only put tiny kitchens in apartments. Did they think everyone used their ovens for storage like a *Sex and the City* character? If they were legally required to buy appliances anyway, would it really have put them out so much to build some dang counters? Lindsay's kitchen at least had a single square foot of counter space, but she'd seen some apartments in her day that were little more than a cube fridge and an Easy-Bake Oven.

So, yeah, she was jealous that Paige and Josh could afford a place with a kitchen this nice, especially since, given how clean everything was, they hardly ever cooked or else had a really good cleaning lady.

Paige's big, fluffy white cat sat on the counter, close enough to the platters Lindsay had set out that she was worried cat hair would get in the food. The other cat, George, was hanging out on the floor as if he expected Lindsay to drop food for him to eat.

"You are SOL, little guy," Lindsay told the cat.

"How's it going?" asked Paige from the sofa. The kitchen and living room were one large space in this apartment, so Paige was watching some home-renovation show while sitting in reserve in case Lindsay needed help.

"Fine. We've got artichoke dip with veggies, three kinds of sliders, salad, veggie slaw, and french fries. And I never want to chop another vegetable for the rest of my life. Also, your cats are trying to steal food."

Paige laughed and stood up. "All right, guys. You have to hang out in the bedroom for a bit." It took some work, but Paige managed to shoo both cats into the bedroom and shut the door. "There are chips in the cabinet next to the fridge, too."

"Cool." Lindsay had arranged the slider patties on a plate, ready to go on the griddle as soon as people started arriving. She'd made beef, turkey, and vegetarian patties. She'd wanted finger food that would fill people up.

"So tell me," Paige said, walking over to look at what Lindsay had laid out. "You invited Brad. Is he bringing dessert?"

"He said something about cookies."

"And how are things going between you?"

Lindsay shrugged. "Awkward. When I called to invite him tonight, he said no at first. I think he's mad at me."

"Why?"

Lindsay sighed. "We had a fight the other night. He wants me to put up or shut up."

"What does that mean?"

"He wants to get back together, but I haven't decided, and I think he's tired of waiting."

"Ah, okay." Paige nodded like she understood exactly what this situation was. "But he *is* coming, right? Because I didn't buy anything sweet, figuring he'd bring dessert."

Lindsay laughed. Paige had priorities. "Yes, he's coming. I convinced him by pointing out that the episode he won is airing right after mine. And he's mad at me, but he still likes the rest of you."

The party was a viewing party for Lindsay's first episode of *Mystery Meal.* Lindsay was not especially excited to see herself on TV, but her friends had insisted on this party. She figured if anything got too mortifying, she could busy herself in the kitchen.

Josh came out of the office holding two chairs. "Do we have enough seating?" he asked.

"People can sit on the floor," said Paige. "That rug is pretty soft."

Josh set up the chairs and stood back to look at the seating area. He and Paige had a sofa and a couple of armchairs, and he'd just added a couple of padded folding chairs that must have been in a closet.

"I'm gonna get those big throw pillows. Maybe people can sit on those." Josh turned to go into the bedroom.

"The cats are in there," said Paige.

Josh grimaced and then slowly opened the door. "No, no. Stay in there, Houdini," he said. Then he closed the door softly.

Paige grinned. "He's cute when he's fretting about an event."

"I thought that was your job."

"Normally it would be, but he insisted on planning this since I've been so preoccupied by the wedding. He thinks he's doing me a favor. I love planning events, but this is just people I like, so it's low stakes."

"Not much for him to mess up, in other words."

Paige shrugged. Her intercom buzzed, so Lindsay put her attention back on the party food while Paige went to answer the door. Lauren and Caleb arrived a moment later, with little Hannah in her stroller. With practiced ease, Caleb lifted the detachable baby seat out of the stroller and Lauren folded the stroller frame and shoved it out of the way in a corner.

Lindsay walked over to say hello and made baby noises at Hannah, which got her a big smile in response. That little girl was one cute baby, all big eyes and wispy hair.

Evan arrived with a flourish a few minutes later.

"It's done!" he said, plunking a bottle of wine on the kitchen counter. "Will and I are no more."

"Aw," said Lindsay. "I'm sorry."

"It's all right. The really sad thing is that he didn't seem heartbroken," said Evan. He flopped onto the sofa. "He seemed to expect it. So I guess I'm on the market again."

Lauren picked up Hannah and sat next to Evan on the sofa. "Other fish," she said.

"Oh, sure. You're a smug married now. Paige is going to have what I have no doubt will be the perfect wedding. Even Lindsay has an 'It's Complicated' with Brad. And here I am, all alone."

Lauren jostled Hannah in her lap and said, "I'm sorry you

broke up with Will. Breakups always suck. But you have a lot going for you, Ev. You're cute, you're successful, and you have excellent taste in friends. I have no doubt your Mr. Right is out there somewhere."

"You can always ask out Pablo," said Lindsay. "He's single again, remember?"

"You should understand by now that Pablo is a symbol," said Evan. "He's the living embodiment of everything I want but can't have. I can't ask him out now. I've been obsessing over him for so long that he will inevitably let me down."

"That's cheery," said Lauren. "But buck up, camper, because this is a party for Lindsay. We're celebrating tonight, not wallowing."

"If this is a party for Lindsay, why is she doing all the cooking?"

"Is there anyone else here who you'd prefer to have cook?" Lindsay asked.

Evan made a show of looking around. "Okay, fair point."

Lindsay got the first batch of sliders on the griddle and so didn't hear the intercom or know anyone had arrived until Brad was carrying a huge Tupperware bin full of cookies into the kitchen.

His arrival made Lindsay's pulse spike.

She decided to focus on her little hamburgers. The patties were small enough that they cooked superfast, so she had to keep an eye on them. As she flipped over the first batch, Brad said, "Hi, Linds."

"Hi."

"I didn't know how many people would be here, so I made three batches of cookies."

"Probably more than we need, but I'm sure we can find people to eat them. Probably Evan. He just broke up with Will, so he may be wanting to eat his feelings."

Brad turned toward Evan. "Sorry to hear that, man."

Evan waved his hand. "It's fine. I'll survive."

Brad tilted his head like he didn't understand that and then turned back to Lindsay. "You need help with anything?"

"Nah, go sit. I've got this under control."

She probably could have used another set of hands as she started placing little burger patties on the buns she'd already set out. But she didn't want Brad hovering around her, especially not with how things were between them right then. They'd hardly talked at all in two weeks. When she'd called to invite him, his tone was decidedly *I'm not mad, I'm just disappointed*, and Lindsay hated that she'd made Brad feel that way. He had every right to be mad, and she knew that.

"T-minus ten minutes," Paige said, turning on the TV and navigating to the Food Channel.

Lindsay set out a tray of sliders on the kitchen table with the other food she'd already prepared. "Help yourself, everyone."

She made a plate for herself after explaining which sliders were which, and then walked over to the living room area to find a seat.

Paige pointed to the center of the sofa. "I believe that's the captain's chair."

"I don't know if I really want to be front and center to watch myself on TV."

"Take one of the armchairs, then. You should at least have a comfortable seat after all that cooking."

And so, Evan, Lauren, and Caleb ended up on the couch,

Lindsay and Brad each got an armchair, and Josh insisted he and Paige could sit on the folding chairs since the guests should have had the comfortable seats.

The show came on shortly after everyone settled. Caleb and Lauren handed Hannah back and forth so they could take turns eating without an infant trying to steal their food, although Lindsay caught Caleb sneaking Hannah little bits of cheese.

Caleb was a good dad, Lindsay reflected as she tried not to see her face on the TV. Hannah wore a pink dress with ruffles, an interesting contrast to Caleb's rougher edges. He had on a blue T-shirt with his veterinary clinic logo and jeans, and Lauren was similarly dressed in mom attire of a purple tunic and leggings, but they looked perfectly content holding their baby.

She heard herself make a dumb joke about skirt steak on screen and shook her head.

Luckily, most of the episode focused on the chefs and what they were up to. The camera panned over the chefs chopping and blending and sautéing. Lindsay did actually find this kind of thing interesting; she still had enough of her culinary schooling in her to appreciate good knife work and nice plating.

At the commercial, she said, "I couldn't see most of this from where I was sitting. I mean, I could see that the chefs were working, but not close up like this."

"My French technique teacher would have some things to say about Chef Allen's knife skills," Brad said, gesturing at the TV.

"Yeah, his work is a little sloppy," said Lindsay. "Tasted good, though."

"I've always wanted to know what it would be like to judge

a show like this," said Caleb. "I don't really know anything more advanced than 'this tastes good' or 'this tastes bad,' so I probably wouldn't make good TV, but to taste a meal like that must be something."

"On your next anniversary," said Brad, "take Lauren to City Tavern on Essex on the Lower East Side. I know a chef there and can probably finagle a table for you to try the tasting menu. I promise you will not be disappointed. They do all kinds of experimental food there, but the executive chef is at the top of his game, and everything is delicious."

Lindsay was conscious of the fact that Brad was watching her, but she rolled her eyes anyway. "Brad knows everyone."

"What?" said Brad. "I mean, I do, but in this case, I worked with the pastry chef at Milk Bar, and she introduced me to the executive chef. City Tavern is basically new takes on very old dishes, but it's excellent."

"If you find me a reliable babysitter," Lauren said, "that sounds delightful."

The show came back on for the judging portion of the first round. Lindsay mostly looked at the floor because looking at the screen seemed to make every flaw apparent. She had one flyaway bit of hair the hairdresser had failed to tame. Her mascara was a little smudgy on her left eye. But that was fairly minor. Her voice was what grated on her. Did she really sound that nasal?

On screen, Ben Hawthorne said, "And the chefs moving to the next round are…" before the show crashed too commercial again.

"Hearing you talk about food is wild," said Josh. "I had no idea you were so knowledgeable."

"I *did* go to culinary school."

"The sliders are amazing, Linds," said Evan. "Even the veggie ones. Did you use that weird, pink fake-meat stuff?"

"I did. It cooks up quite nicely. No one will ever convince me it's beef, but I like using it for burgers. They're lighter tasting than beef burgers."

"What's in the sauce?" Brad asked.

"Trade secret."

Brad smirked and licked some sauce off the bun of one of his sliders. "Let's see. Mayo base, I think. Something sweet, probably honey. No, maple syrup. Some kind of spice blend that is heavy on black pepper and paprika. And it's got a bit of a kick, so...sriracha."

"You're just showing off," said Lindsay.

Brad grinned. "It's good sauce. I was asking for your recipe."

"The show's back on."

After the segment of chefs making their second-round dishes with heavy cream, Lindsay turned to Brad and asked, "All right, Mr. Pastry. What would you make?"

"With heavy cream?" He considered. "Tres leches cake."

"In a half hour?"

"Sure. If you make small cakes, they'll bake in twenty minutes or less. I might make little cakes in ramekins and have them bake while I make the rest of the components."

"Tres leches cake." How very Brad to think up something fairly complicated and hard to pull off in half an hour. Lindsay thought he'd be able to do it, though.

Brad shrugged. "First thing that popped into my head. Also, as we're about to see, I did win this damn show."

When the episode ended and finally put Lindsay out of her misery, her friends all clapped.

"It is supremely weird seeing yourself on television," Lindsay said.

"You did such a great job!" said Paige. "I'm not even just saying that. You sounded so smart. I don't know anything about flavor profiles or Spanish cuisine, and I still found what you said in the skirt-steak round interesting."

"Well, the second episode I judged airs in two weeks. You all can watch that one without me."

"Oh, here comes Brad," said Lauren.

Lindsay had seen the live feed of Brad's episode, not the edited version. There was a talking-head interview with him where he name-dropped the cat café twice—Paige pumped her fist and said, "Yeah, baby," each time he did—and then he made a lobster roll.

"I know it would kill Lindsay," said Lauren, "but if you ever want to make lobster rolls for the rest of us, I'm first in line."

"What was in the aioli?" Lindsay asked.

Brad winked. "Trade secret."

"I saw egg, garlic, olive oil...pepper?"

"I threw a dash of Old Bay in there, too."

After the commercial, they all watched Brad make the Mexican chocolate cupcakes.

"I can't believe you won with a cupcake," said Paige.

"I can't believe he made cupcakes in half an hour."

"The trick to this show seems to be timing," said Brad. "I

think that's what tripped up some of the eliminated chefs. They didn't manage their time well."

An old episode of *Champion Chef* came on after *Mystery Meal*, and everyone kept chatting while they polished off the rest of Lindsay's food.

Josh asked Paige, "Can we have sliders and french fries at the wedding?"

"No, darling. Seafood. The wedding is at a seafood restaurant."

"Oh, right. Well, this was great, Lindsay. I'd eat three more sliders if there were any left."

"There are still cookies," Brad said, standing. "Chocolate chip, butter shortbread, and cinnamon molasses."

"Oh, that last one sounds wonderful," said Lauren.

"I created the recipe. I'm sure I'm not the first person who thought to put both cinnamon and molasses in a cookie, but I've spent some time perfecting these."

"You can put those on the coffee table," Paige said.

Brad got up to get the cookies, and Josh got up to let the cats out of the bedroom. Both zoomed out, but then got a good look at the crowd in the living room and ran back to the bedroom.

Brad walked back into the living room area with his bin of cookies. When he peeled the top off the container, the scent of cinnamon and sugar hit Lindsay's nostrils.

In other words, Brad was hot, he was charming, and he knew how to make all kinds of confections. Lindsay had enough of a sweet tooth for this to make him an ideal mate. If she remembered correctly, he made a mean breakfast, too. Could they in some future live in an apartment with a big enough kitchen that they could spend weekend mornings eating his cream cheese–stuffed French toast at the island? Could they feed each other bacon and the latest of Brad's experimental muffins?

Why was she resisting him so much?

Everyone protested being full and then gorged themselves on cookies. Hannah fell asleep in her father's lap and he gently put her in her baby seat while he commandeered a plastic baggie to take even more of the cookies home.

It was a nice little family they'd all made. Caleb and Josh had been good additions to their friend group, both of them upstanding guys who clearly doted on their significant others. Caleb was serious and sometimes a little grouchy, but fatherhood had mellowed him out a little. Josh was upbeat and sometimes goofy, but he clearly thought Paige hung the moon. Would Brad do well with her friends, too? He'd fit right in so far.

The longer the night wore on, the harder it was to remember why she didn't want to be with Brad.

Lauren and Caleb left the party first so they could get Hannah home and to bed. Evan left shortly thereafter, saying he had to get some work done before he could sleep. That left Lindsay and Paige cleaning up the kitchen when Brad offered to help. So Lindsay let him do the dishes.

And then, when everything was tidy again, Brad and Lindsay left. On the elevator ride back to the lobby, Lindsay said. "So, uh. Can we talk?"

"Sure," said Brad, though he looked wary. "Where?"

"Let's get a car to my place."

Brad was not at all sure going home with Lindsay was a good idea, but he hadn't been able to bring himself to say no.

They were mostly silent in the car. It stopped in front of a nondescript brick building. Lindsay led him inside to her second-floor apartment, which was very pretty but very small. Lindsay had never struck him as excessively girlie, but the apartment had bright-white walls that she'd offset with pops of purple and pink in her furniture: purple throw pillows, pink curtains, and a big vase full of pink and purple gerbera daisies on the kitchen counter. The apartment wasn't much more than a studio with a little sleeping alcove, but Lindsay had organized the space well, with a desk near the kitchen—the only surface with any clutter and probably the place Lindsay spent the most time—a sofa facing the TV, and her bed with a purple bedspread in the alcove.

"This is nice," he said.

"It's small. I'm not exactly raking it in as a food writer, although the job at the *Forum* came with a very nice raise."

"Well, that's something."

A tuxedo cat who was on the small side trotted out to greet them. After the cat rubbed himself on Lindsay's shins, he gave Brad a once-over.

"Hello there, fine fellow," Brad said to the cat and immediately felt silly.

Lindsay didn't seem to notice. "That's Fred Astaire the cat."

"Right, of course." Brad knelt down to pat the cat's head. Fred Astaire let himself be petted but eyed Brad the whole time like he didn't trust him. Then he ran across the apartment and hopped up on Lindsay's bed.

Lindsay said, "Look, I feel bad about how we ended things two weeks ago."

Brad was suddenly exhausted. He was tired of trying to hash this out with her. He apparently couldn't resist her enough to say no to coming to her place tonight, but he didn't want to have the same fight again. So he decided to cut her off at the pass. "You trust me or you don't. It's that simple."

She looked at him for a long time. "I've missed talking to you the last couple of weeks. It turns out I kind of got used to having you back in my life."

"Lindsay..."

"I know, okay? I know what you need from me. You must realize now how hard that is. But I–I do trust you."

He wasn't sure he believed her. It felt a little strange for the tables to be turned in this way. Now she was telling him what he wanted to hear in order to get him to stay. But did she really mean it?

He sat on the sofa. His heart ached. He'd never been very good at being stoic or cutting off his emotions. He'd loved her fiercely once, he was falling in love with her again, and he wanted her in his life, but not if it was this fucking hard. "I don't want to argue with you anymore."

"I'm not arguing."

"What kind of future do we even have together? Say we do actually get back together. You're always going to have an eye on me. I love spending time with you, but we also both have lives apart from each other, and I need you to trust that I will always come home to you. And if I have your trust, I will never abuse it, but I'm going to live my life, too. I'm going to network and talk to people and, yes, probably flirt. And you need to know that it doesn't mean anything because you're the most important person in my life." He sighed, realizing what he'd just said. "Theoretically. And I'm going to fuck up and make mistakes, and you will too, but we can have adult conversations about those things rather than making assumptions based on old baggage and not on the reality in front of us."

Lindsay looked a little surprised. She nodded slowly. "I'm getting there."

"Okay. I want to get back together, but I'm tired of jumping through hoops for you."

"What hoops?"

"If you don't want to be with me, just say it, and I'll go home and stop bothering you."

"Brad, come on."

He sat up straight and looked at her. She sat beside him on the sofa and looked at the floor.

"You come on, Linds. I've been throwing myself at you for weeks. I told you I wanted to get back together. You keep saying it didn't work out before, so there's no reason it will now. You *don't* trust me, as illustrated by that night two weeks ago. So, fine, I'm done trying to get you back. You don't want me, I'll go."

Lindsay pressed her lips together. Brad was about to get up and leave when she said, "Of course I want you back. Of *course* I do. We were in love once, and I think we could easily fall back into that, but... Getting over you was so hard that I never fully did, and now that you're back in my life, I don't want to let you go again, but I have to guard my heart."

"Or you can open your heart and let me in again."

She took a deep breath. "I want to. I want to trust you. I *do* trust you. I know you'd never cheat on me. I spent years convincing myself that you cheated on me with Phoebe, even when I knew deep down that wasn't really true. But I needed you to be the bad guy because…if I walked away without that, I'd made the biggest mistake of my life."

"You can fix that mistake." Brad felt a small measure of hope. But it also felt precarious. There were still a lot of ways they could fuck this up.

Lindsay guarded her heart intensely. Being with Brad made her vulnerable because she had to push her guards aside. When she really did that, he knew they could find a way forward together, but he wasn't sure she was really there yet.

"You saved my job," Lindsay said. "You got me this great opportunity, and you told off a reporter in the process. You brought cupcakes to my office. How did I not see what you were doing?"

"I don't know. I thought I was being obvious."

She laughed softly. "That year we were together, we did have fun. I think that's the happiest I've ever been."

"We could have that again. But you gotta meet me halfway. I hate feeling like you're only with me because I finally wore you down."

"That's not what this is. I wanted you to come home with me tonight."

He was tired of talking. "I should probably go home." He stood.

"Brad, no. Don't you hear what I'm saying? Spend the night with me. Do you have to work tomorrow?"

"No, I have the day off."

"Then stay with me tonight."

"I don't know."

"Do *you* not trust *me*?"

He thought about it for a moment. "How do I know that you won't just change your mind again tomorrow?"

"I won't." She stood and faced him. "Do you regret anything you've done in the last few weeks?"

"No." And he didn't. If he had it to do over, he would have called Aaron about getting her on the show. He would have slept with her every time it had happened, too. He'd regret it if he walked away tonight, but maybe it was for the best, because he still didn't trust this and couldn't read her mind.

But then she was kissing him. He caught her as she launched herself at him and put his hands on her waist. He held her there and succumbed to it, opened his mouth to let her in.

He was so stupid. She could slip through his fingers at any second.

But he kept kissing her because he couldn't tear himself away.

She threaded her fingers through his hair and pulled him harder into the kiss. She pressed her body against his. She was ready to go, for sure, but was this a mistake?

Brad didn't know, but he did know he didn't want to stop kissing her.

"Stay with me tonight," she said.

"Okay."

He kissed her again and let her lead him to her bed, even while knowing this was probably the last time they'd ever be together.

———————

Brad's head rested on Lindsay's chest, and she ran her fingers through his soft hair and sighed happily.

They'd made love. That was the only way she could describe it. She'd tried to use her body to convey how she felt, because lord knew she kept making a hash of verbalizing it. He'd gazed into her eyes as he moved inside her, and there had definitely been a moment when she'd *felt* everything. When her heart felt full and when she knew without a doubt that Brad wanted her even if he didn't love her again...yet. She *did* trust him.

Because Brad had demonstrated, over and over again, that he wanted her, that he was willing to open his heart to her, that he was willing to risk everything blowing up again if only for sweet moments like tonight. It was Lindsay who kept herself closed off, who wasn't willing to open up, who felt like she didn't know how to trust another person with her heart.

She felt all in one amazing moment when their eyes met; she'd understood exactly how he felt and what he wanted from her. She wanted those same things from him. And it was on her now to prove it.

She knew her hold on this was not firm. As soon as the ecstasy was over, he'd seemed wary. And here they were, lying in her bed, and they hadn't spoken for five whole minutes. Lindsay knew

Brad was awake even though his face was turned away from hers. His breath was too erratic for sleep.

"Can I ask you something?" she said.

"Okay." There was wariness in his tone, like he expected not to like the question.

She sighed and considered how to word what she wanted to ask. "I understand full well that continuing to relive the past doesn't do any good for us in the present, and that things are different now. But I just want to say this one thing."

"Uh-huh. Okay."

"Back in culinary school, I used to have this fantasy of opening a restaurant. I didn't want to reinvent the wheel or anything, but I wanted to serve good food people liked and become one of those neighborhood places with regular customers. I mean, the kind of place that's like... Well, there's a bar up the street here and there's nothing unique about it. They have an above-average beer selection and make a decent hamburger, but the decor is very thrift store, and I always figured the lighting was dim to hide a few sins I don't want to know about. And, like, this bar has been there for twenty years, and it's always packed on the weekends. All these trendy bars and restaurants have popped up around it and opened and closed, but this place is a neighborhood staple. That's what I always wanted to create."

"That's a nice dream. It's what we used to talk about."

"Yeah. I used to imagine we owned this place together. And we were creative enough to put a few standout dishes on the menu to attract new guests. But I don't need to do fine dining. A midprice restaurant with reliably good food and, well, a killer dessert menu.

That's what I wanted. And I figured we'd be one of those power-house couples. Like, you know, Dean and Stacia?"

Brad was silent for a beat before he said, "Yeah."

Dean and Stacia Lang had become legends in the last decade for being a restaurant power couple. They'd each won TV chef competitions on their own. They'd owned a restaurant in Manhattan together for ten years and had recently started expanding to other cities. They had a dozen restaurants now. Plenty of people in culinary school had told Lindsay that there was no way two chefs could go into business together and also be together romantically. That was a lot of together time, wasn't it? Wasn't a couple like that bound to implode?

Not if they liked each other and had a solid business model.

She said, "Part of me thought we could be them. A solid couple who loved each other and loved the work they did together."

"I can see that. Again, it's a nice dream."

"Did you never see that in our future?"

He rolled and held his head up to look at her. "I mean, back in culinary school, I didn't think much past graduation. I assumed we'd be together, but I hadn't given much thought to the future beyond that. Like, sure, sure, the restaurant we talked about back then, I saw that as part of the ten-year plan—well, the twenty-year plan—but it all felt hypothetical and not like a real plan."

"And what about now?"

"Now, I don't know. The cat café gig is temporary. I love it, but it's not what I want to do forever. I mean, I wanted the opportunity to make my own menu, and I got that here, I proved to myself I could do it. Lauren's letting me have fun for now, but

I'm going to need to design a more regular menu. Once I've got all the recipes I want in place, there's no reason the assistants or another pastry chef couldn't come in and make those pastries. And then... I don't know."

"Do you want to open a bakery?"

"Not especially. Somehow, I miss French pastry. I'd been working up to executive pastry chef at a fine dining restaurant. That's what I really want to do. The kinds of people who come to a bakery want the basics. They want vanilla birthday cakes and chocolate chip cookies, and there's nothing wrong with those things, but they aren't really challenging to me in a satisfying way. Figuring out how to make cat treats was actually really fun for me because it was a weird challenge. I like the idea of using unexpected ingredients, doing something a little avant-garde."

As if he'd been summoned by Brad's cat-related talk, Fred Astaire ran into the alcove and hopped up on the bed. He settled at Lindsay's side and started purring, so Lindsay petted him.

"So you want to be innovative," Lindsay said.

"Yeah. Or at least have discretion over what I make. Like, say I worked at your midprice neighborhood establishment. I'd have to make some dessert staples. Cheesecake, chocolate cake, a brownie sundae, that kind of thing. But I could have a couple of oddball things on the menu, too. And some of them wouldn't even be that weird, because everyone watches those British baking shows on TV now."

"Well, like I said, at this imaginary restaurant, we'd have to have a couple of unusual things to attract customers. Like, sure, we'd have to put a burger on the menu."

"Or those sliders from tonight. Those were good. Did you use a recipe?"

"No. I just decided to make sliders and figured I'd have to do beef, turkey, and veggie and then flavored the meat accordingly. But you're right. I could do a pork-belly slider and serve it Filipino style with some kind of salty-sweet sauce."

"Filipino style?"

"Yeah. When I was in San Francisco last year, I ate at this Filipino fast food place that is apparently a California chain, but it was so good I went back twice. The trick is to combine flavors that shouldn't go together but totally do, like taking something salty like fish sauce and combining it with something sweet like mango."

"That does actually sound good."

"Or, like, I want to try to re-create the cream sauce for seafood that the one chef used on the show tonight, because that tasted incredible."

"So you'd have staples, but you'd apply your wide culinary knowledge to putting a spin on old classics, basically," Brad said.

"Sure. And again, there are some things the masses want to see on the menu, and you include a few options for various diets. Put some vegan options on the menu, some gluten-free options. But don't just put a salad or a vegan burger on there; figure out how to make something tasty that happens to be vegan."

"You've given this a lot of thought."

"I have."

"Then why did you stop cooking?"

That was the question, wasn't it? "Part of it was what we've talked about. I left school and couldn't quite find a place that fit me. There weren't a ton of jobs available, so I was working as a line cook, figuring I'd pay my dues and work my way up. But I hated the drudgery of firing the same dishes over and over."

"Where were you working?"

"An upscale pub off Times Square. We made a lot of meals for tourists, so it had to be kind of bland and predictable. There was no creativity involved. Zillions of burgers and grilled chicken sandwiches because those were the cheapest things on the menu."

"Sure."

"I hated it. I hated coming home smelling like grease. I hated that I had to follow the executive chef's recipes, because he had some weird ideas about seasoning. So that was part of it."

"Everyone has to pay their dues."

"Yeah, sure, Milk Bar."

"I was making another chef's recipes there, too. It wasn't that different."

Lindsay sighed. The truth was that she'd stopped dreaming after she broke up with Brad. The whole point of that plan had been to open the place together. And she hadn't seen much value in paying her dues at a job that genuinely made her miserable if she wasn't going to open that dream restaurant. The future she'd planned for herself had evaporated. So she'd carved out a new niche for herself.

She'd blamed Brad for that for a long time, because she hadn't been able to face her own failings. But, of course, it hadn't been Brad who had ended their relationship, and it hadn't been Brad who had made her slave away in a hot kitchen she hated, and it hadn't been Brad who'd quit cooking.

No, she'd sabotaged herself. She'd been so afraid of risking her heart that she hadn't opened herself up to possibilities. Brad had opened her up just enough to let her dream, but she'd never invited him into her soul, not all the way.

But in the time that Brad had come back into her life recently, she'd started to dream again. And she understood now that she had to let him in all the way or this wasn't worth doing. Anything less than that would just lead them back to heartache.

She wasn't ready to say all that aloud, so she said, "I just didn't feel the same joy for cooking that I had in culinary school. So I decided to do something else."

"Okay."

"I was just curious if you had any ideas for how you wanted your career to go now."

Brad took a deep breath and lay on his back. "I guess I figured I'd work at the cat café another year or two. Probably stay on as executive pastry chef but in more of a consultant role while I baked somewhere else. I don't know if I see myself in my own place, but I'd love to work in a restaurant where I had free rein over the dessert menu."

"Okay. Just curious."

"Are you going to stay a food editor?"

"For now. I really like this job. But the *Forum* is hanging on by a thread financially, so I don't know how long I'll have it."

"You think you'll ever cook again?"

Cooking for her friends always reminded her how much she loved to cook. So, yeah, she wanted to cook in a restaurant again. She wanted to create recipes. She hadn't realized how much she'd missed that dream until she started thinking about it again. How she cooked, she wasn't sure yet. Should she go back to a restaurant? Should she just make a YouTube channel?

She petted Fred Astaire and said, "I might cook again. But I'd probably have to start over if I went back into the industry. I haven't cooked in a restaurant in four years."

"Maybe," said Brad. "I dunno. I worked with a guy two jobs ago who was a great chef but didn't even go to culinary school. Working in restaurants seems to be half talent and half who you know."

"Hmm."

"I'm just saying. And if you opened your own place, there are no rules."

"That's a lot of pressure, though."

Brad nodded. "I'd rather have a regular paycheck myself."

"It sounds like you have given your future some thought."

"Sure. I have."

Lindsay wanted to ask if his future involved a wife working at his side, but she didn't want to know the answer. If he saw himself with a wife who wasn't her, it would break her heart, not that she thought he'd say that directly.

"Was that what you wanted to ask?" he said. "What I thought about the future?"

"Yeah, basically. I was just curious."

"Right."

So, basically, they were still at an impasse. He didn't trust that she wouldn't freak out and dump him the next day. Lindsay did trust him, though. This time they'd spent together had shown her that Brad was worth trusting, and the reason things hadn't worked out the first time was mostly on her. She'd pushed him away because of her own garbage. Now he was back and giving her a second chance she probably didn't deserve. She wasn't going to push him away this time, though. He'd proved himself to her. Now she'd have to prove herself to him.

CHAPTER 19

WHEN BRAD GOT READY TO leave the café a few afternoons later, Diane breezed in.

Brad was standing near the front counter with Lauren, doing one last check that they had enough snacks for customers for the rest of the day.

"Serves them right," said Diane, although her grouchy tone was somewhat belied by the sparkly purple headband that kept her hair away from her face and the wispy pink tunic she had on over capri jeans.

Brad hadn't talked to Diane since the *Times* interview had imploded, though, and he looked around to see if there was any way he could hide his big frame behind the counter. Looked like he'd be out of luck.

"What's going on?" asked Lauren.

Diane turned the scowl on her face into a wide smile, as if by magic. "Our real estate developers across the street seem to be struggling."

"What?" asked Brad, not understanding Diane's glee.

Lauren waved her hand as if it were nothing. "There's a developer snatching up property in the neighborhood. He bought the building across the street. The first floor used to house this really great coffee shop, but he shut it down to get a higher-paying tenant. He *tried* to buy this building, but Diane wasn't having it."

"This building has been here for a hundred years, and it's my retirement project," said Diane. "No one is taking it from me."

"Did something happen across the street, Diane?" asked Lauren.

"Well, our friend found a sucker in the form of a former boy-band singer to finance a restaurant. I guess you guys already know that. I saw Lindsay's review. But this boy-band kid is an outsider who doesn't know the neighborhood. So he opened this stupid restaurant that serves bland food, and of course it failed."

"It failed?" asked Brad. "You mean, it's closed permanently?"

"It sure looks like it has gone out of business to me," said Diane.

Lauren frowned. "Already?"

"This neighborhood doesn't want chain stores and restaurants, and it certainly doesn't want novelty restaurants owned by celebrities that belong in Midtown, not Brooklyn."

"I never ate there," said Brad, mostly for something to say because his head was spinning.

"The chef didn't seem to know what salt is," said Lauren.

"Agreed," said Diane. "I got some takeout from there. Totally flavorless."

A few minutes later, Brad closed down the kitchen for the

day, and when he came back out front to say goodbye, Diane and Lauren were still chatting.

"Brad, did you make any of those carrot muffins today?" Diane asked.

"I did." Brad scanned the display case and pointed. "Looks like there's one left."

"Oh, goodie. Are these the ones with the cream cheese filling?"

"They are."

"So delicious. Hiring you was the best decision I've made yet." Diane patted his shoulder.

"I'm glad you think so. I'll admit, I was worried when that interview with your friend at the *Times* went south."

Diane nodded. "Yes, sorry about that. She said you had some contact she wanted to use. I honestly did not expect that to happen."

"She almost seemed more interested in my friend at the Food Channel than me."

Diane sighed. "Yes, well. Heather is more relative than friend. She is my late wife's niece. She's been working her way up toward being a food reviewer at the *Times*, but after Mr. Russo was a judge on *Champion Chef*, she's been kind of obsessive about following in his footsteps. Of course, she also gave one of Billy Watts's restaurants a bad review."

"Yeah, I heard. First rule of making friends at the Food Channel is not to say anything bad about their talent."

"Right, precisely. She wants to be a big name in food journalism. If she were smart, she would have done the feature story on the café, just a nice fluffy piece about the new chef doing creative things with cat treats and human treats, and called it a day. Alas."

"So you're not mad at me."

Diane patted his arm. "Nope. Plus I saw that Lindsay *did* get on TV and figured you had something to do with that. Lindsay deserves good things."

Brad was surprised Diane knew Lindsay well enough to say something like that considering she didn't work here, but Diane and Lauren were close. Diane seemed like more of a mom than a boss.

"Anyway, Bradley, I did want you to know, I genuinely appreciate everything you do for the café. I heard you adopted one of our cats, too."

"Yes, Hamilton. He seems to have made himself at home in my apartment."

Diane grinned. "Yeah, cats do that."

Lauren cleared her throat. She'd put Diane's carrot muffin on a plate, and beside it sat Diane's travel mug with the tag from a new tea bag hanging out of it.

"Oh, delightful. I'm looking forward to this. That zucchini thing you made last week was delicious, too, Bradley. Have Lauren text me the next time you make some of those."

"Okay, I will," said Brad, feeling relieved.

When Brad walked outside a few minutes later, he looked across the street and saw that Pepper was indeed closed. Curious, he crossed the street. He gazed through the glass storefront. The furniture was all there, though the chairs were up on the tables. No one was inside.

Brad called Aaron, who seemed to know everything happening in the New York City food world. After they greeted each other, Brad said, "Do you know anything about the restaurant Pepper in Brooklyn? It's the new restaurant owned by some boy-band guy."

"Oh, yeah, Joey Maguire."

Brad laughed. "You know his name?"

"My sister was really into the Bayside Boys when she was a tween. They had that song 'Can't Stop My Heart.'"

"That must have been during my angry-rock phase." Brad had read Lindsay's review but wouldn't have been able to pick Joey Maguire out of a lineup.

Aaron laughed. "Anyway, I heard he opened a restaurant in Brooklyn. I heard this from my sister, by the way, and she squealed at me as she told me."

"It's the restaurant Lindsay reviewed that got her the job at the *Forum*."

"Yes, I read that review. And I heard yesterday that the restaurant had already gone out of business."

"Wow. It's only been open, like, two months. Did Lindsay kill it?"

"No, no. Actually, I think she prolonged its misery. Novelty restaurants don't generally do that well outside of Manhattan. But that place got so much press that people went there to check it out. You know how sometimes people hate-watch a bad TV show or movie just to bag on it? I think people were doing the gastronomic equivalent of that."

"So it's closed for good?"

"Yeah, that's what I've heard. Why do you ask?"

"I work across the street. I'm standing in front of it now, and there are no signs or anything, but it's closed right now."

"It happens. Especially if the food isn't good enough to build a regular customer base. There's only so long you can coast on novelty."

Brad got off the phone a few minutes later. It was a nice day, so he decided to walk home.

As he walked, he fantasized about what it might be like to run a restaurant. It wasn't something he'd thought much about before, but Lindsay had planted that idea in his brain. She'd said all those things about her dream of them opening a restaurant together, and he'd been thinking about it ever since. What would it be like? Would they plan menus together? Interview staff? Choose the theme and the decorations? It would be a lot of hard work, but wouldn't it be fun to have a space that was theirs, where they could use everything they knew about food to create a wonderful experience and build a regular customer base?

Of course, this was all extremely hypothetical. They were just barely back together, if they even were, and restaurants were extremely risky ventures. He'd just stared at the evidence of that. Still, it was hard not to imagine.

There was an Italian restaurant on the same block as Pepper that was upscale but very good. Brad had gotten lunch from it a few times. So the block didn't need another upscale restaurant, but the kind of place Lindsay had talked about—a midprice family restaurant with a diverse menu—might do quite well here. The neighborhood had a lot of young families, but also a lot of young working people. Given the crowd at places like Pop, this was a neighborhood with people who had some money to spend but wanted casual, not upscale.

And if he could design the dessert menu? That would be perfect. Not the same defrosted cheesecake every family restaurant served, but a fresh cheesecake with different fruit compotes depending on the season. Not just chocolate layer cake, but a Brooklyn blackout cake—chocolate cake with chocolate pudding filling and chocolate cookie crumbs on top for a textural crunch. He could do a bread pudding, a cookie plate, and then maybe a special dessert. He could make fresh bread for the restaurant.

And working beside Lindsay would be a dream. He'd been feeling conflicted about how things were going between them, but if they could find some way to build a real relationship, and then they worked together to build a successful restaurant? Well, that was a dream worth building.

Sure, he'd heard about couples who went into business together and ended up divorcing. But he knew couples who owned successful restaurants, too.

And, sure, in the back of his mind, he thought maybe his father would think owning a restaurant was a more noble profession than baking cookies for cats, although Brad wouldn't hold his breath. He couldn't live his life based on what his father thought. He had to do what made him happy.

As Brad approached Flatbush Avenue to cross into his neighborhood, he realized that it was only a dream. He didn't have the capital to open a restaurant. Things with Lindsay still felt precarious. It was a nice idea, but a dream was all it could be.

He shook his head and crossed the street. Running a restaurant felt like as much a dream as actually making a relationship work with Lindsay, something he was losing hope would ever really happen as the days went on.

———————

Lindsay went to the cat café the next afternoon.

She'd been shut up in her apartment too much the last few days. She was working at home this week while the upper management at the *Forum* had company meetings. Erica had seemed concerned when she'd called to tell Lindsay to work from home, like perhaps this was at last a harbinger of the layoffs everyone had been expecting. It seemed likely the owners would do some reorganizing or would try to streamline the office to decrease costs. Lindsay didn't know, but Erica had assured her that as long as Erica had a job, Lindsay would have a job, too.

That was reassuring, but Lindsay had spent too much time wondering what would happen if Erica no longer had a job.

So she needed a change of scenery. Evan liked to work in the cat room at the café on some afternoons, and indeed, Lindsay found him and Paige sitting together at a table in the corner.

"Ah, hello, stranger," Evan said as Lindsay sat.

"I saw you a week ago," said Lindsay.

Evan laughed. "You never come here anymore was what I meant."

"I'm not avoiding Brad anymore." That was only partially true, though. They'd texted a few times over the last few days, but Brad's responses had mostly been monosyllabic and noncommittal.

And, of course, after months of Brad trying to win her over, now that he was giving up, she'd realized that she wanted him back. The trick now would be to convince him that she was serious about it, that she trusted him, and that she wouldn't bail this time.

"Is he here?" she asked now.

"Yeah, in the back," said Paige. "The lunch rush was a little nutty today. Apparently a magazine moved into the office space across the street, and their staff just learned we serve lunch. So they've been coming over here and invading our space between about noon and one a day or two per week. So Brad has had to make more sandwiches than usual."

"They sit with the cats?"

"Yep," said Paige. "I think they like having the break."

Brad walked into the room then. When he saw Lindsay, his eyes went wide. "Hi."

"Hi."

He rubbed his forehead. "I'm done for the day. Those office workers ate all my rolls."

"You have a few minutes to hang out before you go?" asked Paige.

Brad glanced at Lindsay and shrugged. "All right."

"I just came here to work outside of my house today," said Lindsay. "Corporate meetings at the *Forum* all week, so they're using the work area for that."

Brad sat in the chair next to Lindsay. "What are you working on?"

"I'm editing reviews from the freelancers who work for me. A ton of new restaurants have opened this summer."

"Anything exciting?"

Lindsay pointed at her laptop. "There's a new place on Montague near the courthouses in Brooklyn Heights that my reviewer says is wonderful. Modern Thai food. And the reviewer is good. Her descriptions of noodles and curry made my mouth water."

A small calico cat wandered over to the table and rubbed against Brad's leg. "Don't get any ideas, cat," said Brad. He leaned down to pet the cat's head. "I already have one of you at home."

"That's Jane," said Paige. "She's a package deal with Rochester over there." She pointed to a black cat who was lounging on the arm of one of the couches, his eyes narrowed to slits as he stared at their table. "They seem to have bonded."

"I see what you did there with the names," said Brad.

"We got Jane, Rochester, St. John, and Mrs. Fairfax from a shelter about three weeks ago."

Brad laughed. "Clever."

"I try."

"You've read *Jane Eyre*?" Lindsay asked.

"I've seen the movie with Michael Fassbender." Brad shrugged. "So... I assume you heard Pepper closed."

"I did," said Lindsay. "I felt a little guilty about it. But one of the chefs who filmed *Mystery Meal* with me pointed out that celebrity restaurants tend not to do very well in the boroughs. Although he gave Pepper six months, and it ended up being two."

Brad gave her a long look. "Just yesterday, I was thinking about what I'd do with the space."

That surprised Lindsay, but she was conscious of Paige and Evan sitting there, so she just said, "What would you do?"

Brad smiled. "I looked in the window. It's a pretty big dining area. That gray they painted everything is not very warm or inviting, so I'd redecorate, obviously. Then make it a midprice family restaurant to appeal to the stroller crowd."

Lindsay laughed. "How fun would it be to design a kids' menu?"

"Josh and I went out for sushi the other night," said Paige, "and there was a family with a toddler sitting at the next table. The kid ate California rolls like they were a thing kids normally eat. It was wild."

Kid-friendly sushi rolls would be a fun challenge. Maybe grilled shrimp or tuna with tempura flakes. Things with texture and flavor but not spice.

Lindsay's brain hadn't run with ideas like this in a while. It was fun to engage with it again.

"I see the wheels turning," said Evan. "You're imagining what *you* would do with the space, aren't you, Lindsay?"

"Yes. Brad's on the money with a family restaurant. I was just trying to decide what I'd put on the menu. You could have something eclectic. Classic American stuff like burgers and mac and cheese, but then maybe you add fish tacos and sushi rolls and pot stickers and integrate everything so there are lot of options but maybe similar flavor profiles. Not, like, ten pages of diner menu options, but a dozen or so entrées that would appeal to a lot of diners."

"You *have* given this a lot of thought," said Brad.

"Some, yeah."

"Too bad we don't have the money to buy the space."

Lindsay couldn't tell if he was being serious. Given that she was a writer who until a couple of months ago had been making a living by the word, no, she didn't have the money to finance a restaurant. Nor was she that confident in her abilities to run one. She could cook, but a lot of her restaurant experience was more theoretical than practical. So she'd been thinking about it, but it was a fantasy, not something real.

Had Brad been thinking about it? Did *he* think this was real?

Did Pepper need a new chef?

No, that was crazy. She and Brad were in a strange, unsteady place, first of all, and restaurants were terrible investments. Pepper proved that just as many restaurants closed in New York City every year as opened, and even then, a lot of them operated on thin margins.

So, fine, she and Brad would not be running a restaurant together. He could have played along with the fantasy a little longer, though.

"If it were me," said Evan, "I'd totally redesign the space. Warm, welcoming colors. Nothing too bright and scary, but get rid of the gray, for sure. Better chairs, because the ones at Pepper were both hideous and uncomfortable."

"Maybe they were trying to encourage turnover," said Paige. "No one was going to linger in chairs that uncomfortable."

Evan grimaced. "Such bad design. Well, no, it wasn't terrible. The gray they picked for the walls is super trendy right now. And it was cohesive at least, even if the pepper-shaker prints were obvious. But for a restaurant, it felt kind of sterile."

"The designer always has opinions on design."

Evan shrugged. "I mean, they obviously hired someone and

said, 'The theme is pepper,' and the designer ran with it. Maybe the real issue was with a theme."

"Maybe they'll open a new restaurant called Salt," said Paige. "Do you have opinions on food?"

"What Lindsay said sounds good. If it tastes good, I'll eat it."

Lauren and Caleb walked through the room then, each carrying a huge bag of cat food. They must have just gotten a delivery. When they came back out, Caleb kissed Lauren's cheek and said something about having to get back to work.

"You guys live on this block," said Lindsay. Lauren and Caleb had an apartment in the same building as the cat café and the vet clinic next door. "What kind of restaurant do you think Pepper should become?"

Lauren tilted her head and considered it for a minute. "It'd be nice to have a place I could bring Hannah without people judgmentally staring at us. Caleb and I ate at a place a few blocks from here, and the couple at the next table actually complained to the waitstaff that we'd brought a baby. She wasn't even crying! She was just babbling in the way babies do."

"Really? They complained?"

"Yeah. Then they left in disgust. Our waiter gave us a free dessert for our trouble, because they also thought this couple was terrible. But still, if the *expectation* was that families were welcome, maybe people would not be such dicks. If they want fine dining, they can go to Elizabeth's down the block. If we're just at the diner on Hoyt, absolute silence is unreasonable."

Lindsay glanced at Brad. It was interesting to know that they'd landed on a good idea that they couldn't do anything with.

But then Lindsay thought about that empty restaurant across the street and got an idea. Maybe she didn't have the resources to run a dream restaurant with Brad, but she knew who she could talk to about bringing a great restaurant to the neighborhood.

CHAPTER 20

A TINY PART OF LINDSAY couldn't believe she was here again.

Talking to Brad about what they could potentially do with Pepper prompted her to try calling Joey Maguire. Well, one of the PR people at the *Forum* had set it up, but Joey had let it leak to the media that he was interested in opening another restaurant, so on the pretense of wanting to interview him about what was next for her column, Lindsay went to Pepper.

Joey met her at the front door and let her in.

He was mesmerizing in a way. Lindsay had met a couple of celebrities in her time, but Joey Maguire was on a different level. He was a year or two younger than Lindsay, although much taller; the "little" moniker was mostly because he was the baby of the group, not the smallest guy. He had a beautiful face: big blue eyes, a narrow nose, surprisingly plump lips for a man. He had some Hollywood affectations, too; his tan looked sprayed on and his blond hair likely came from a bottle. The Bayside Boys had been a California-based boy band whose heyday occurred around the time Lindsay had been in undergrad. The band had since split up to do other things, and Joey had released a solo album a couple of years before that had gotten a lot of critical acclaim and gone platinum, but apparently restaurants were what he was doing now.

"Thanks so much for meeting with me," she said.

"You're welcome. Come on in." Joey's voice was a reminder that he was originally from the South, despite being in a band from California. He'd never shaken his twang.

Lindsay followed him into the restaurant. Most of Pepper's decor was still up exactly as it had been when Lindsay and her friends had eaten here. Joey Maguire led Lindsay over to a table in the center of the restaurant. He offered her a seat.

Once they were seated, Lindsay asked, "You mind if I record?"

"That's fine. Welcome to my restaurant."

"You're more gracious than I would be. I was not kind in my review of this restaurant."

"I think you did me a favor." Joey smiled. "I will admit, I didn't know a lot about food when I first got into this. But I liked the idea of running a restaurant. One of my investors suggested I do something that lined up with my public persona, so I picked southern cuisine, but the chef I hired… He wasn't very good."

"I noticed," Lindsay said with a smile.

"I didn't know enough to judge," Joey said with a shrug. "I'm not used to failing. But I guess I could only coast on my name for so long. So I closed the restaurant before I dug too big a hole for myself."

"So what's next for you?"

"Well, my hope is to rebrand and reopen. I figured I could start by picking a better chef. You know anyone?"

Lindsay laughed, not sure if he was kidding. She mumbled something about the name of her culinary school and still being in touch with several graduates.

"That's a great school," Joey said. "I, uh, have done a lot of research in the last couple of weeks."

"That's a good first step. And it's not that I want restaurants to fail. I just want them to be good."

"If you were in charge, what would you do here?"

Lindsay balked, surprised to be confronted with this question again. But she was honest. "Well, since we found out Pepper closed, my friends and I have been talking about what we'd do to replace it." That sounded like a more significant investment than was warranted, so Lindsay added, "One of my best friends manages the cat café across the street, so she keeps tabs on what's going on in the neighborhood."

"Oh, sure. Wow, that's cool. Is it really a café with cats? I haven't had the chance to stop in yet."

"Yeah. One of my friends from culinary school is the pastry chef, actually. So you can go there for breakfast or lunch takeout, or you can get a scone and a latte and hang out in a room with the cats. There are usually about a dozen cats in the café at a time."

"I'll have to check it out sometime. That sounds really cool." Joey grinned. His teeth were unnaturally white and straight.

"Anyway, we thought what the neighborhood needed was a kid-friendly family restaurant in the midprice range. We've got plenty of casual places, and there's a fine-dining restaurant a couple of doors down, but there are not many places where all the families in this part of Brooklyn can bring their kids and sit down for a meal."

Joey nodded slowly. "That's not the kind of thing I would have imagined investing in, but that's a really good point. Cater to what the neighborhood needs."

"Brooklyn is not Manhattan."

"That's true. This part of Brooklyn has been developing so much that I imagined it would have a vibe more similar to Manhattan than anything else, but I was definitely wrong about that. At least I got a good deal on this space."

Lindsay actually kind of doubted that. Lauren had encountered the real estate developer who owned the building a couple of years before, so Lindsay had heard he was ruthless. Joey had probably gotten swindled. He struck Lindsay as being a little naive.

"Anyway," Joey said. "I'm glad you came by today. I wanted you to know that I bear you no ill will. In fact, ever since you called, I've been wondering if *you* wanted to cook here."

"Me?" Well, that seemed crazy. Sure, Lindsay had been fantasizing about running a restaurant, but she hadn't expected anyone to offer her a job.

"Sure. You have a culinary school degree and some restaurant experience, right?"

"A little."

"And I saw you judge that show on the Food Channel. You clearly know what you're talking about."

"Sure, but that doesn't mean I can cook restaurant-quality food."

"Only one way to find that out."

Lindsay stared at Joey for a long moment, trying to work out if he was serious. "Are you…"

"Cook me something."

Lindsay's heart pounded. This was really happening. "Uh, what should I cook?"

"Can you cook a steak?"

"Sure."

Joey sat there looking at her expectantly. "Cook a steak. The kitchen is fully stocked. Make something with whatever you find there."

This was definitely the weirdest interview Lindsay had ever conducted. Still, she got up and went into the kitchen. She looked around and managed to find the refrigerator. She could at least say for the previous chef that he was neat; the kitchen was clean, and the walk-in fridge was well organized. There was a clean apron hanging from a hook near the door, so Lindsay put it on and then raided the walk-in. She found a beef tenderloin and a bunch of asparagus, which would probably get the job done.

The first thing she did was turn on the stove. She found a cast-iron skillet and put it in the oven to get it to heat up. Then she sliced the tenderloin into filets. It had been a while since she'd done this, but the memory for how to cook a steak was still rattling around in her head. She liberally salted and peppered two filets, then moved the skillet to the stovetop. She dropped both fillets on the hot skillet while she decided what to do with the asparagus.

What the hell was she doing? Why was she cooking for Joey Maguire? This wasn't how the world worked. Chefs worked for decades for an opportunity like this, and she had all of one year of restaurant experience under her belt. Joey Maguire was delusional if he thought she could do this. Or was he? She *could* cook a steak.

But was this a job she even wanted? She felt like she'd lost control somewhere. But maybe that was a good thing. She'd never been completely risk averse in her career—freelance food writing wasn't the most stable or lucrative occupation—but she was generally a person who tended to stay in her own comfort zone. But wasn't that what had gone awry with Brad? She hadn't been willing to put her heart on the line.

She couldn't think about that right now, though; she had to focus, because suddenly she wanted to impress Joey Maguire.

About fifteen minutes later, she brought two plates out to Joey, who was still sitting at the same table, reading a book. She put one plate in front of Joey and the other in front of the empty chair she planned to sit in.

"And asparagus!" Joey said, sounding delighted. "That is one of my favorite vegetables."

"Oh. I didn't even know that. It was the first vegetable I saw in the fridge."

She'd opted to quickly blanch the asparagus and then grill it with olive oil and garlic. She felt better about her choices now that Joey was slicing into his steak. Since Lindsay had made a plate for herself, she sliced hers, too, and was glad to see she'd achieved a perfect medium rare. Any further cooking would have been a crime against filet mignon.

"Oh, that's good," Joey said with his mouth full. "So tender. Like butter."

"I'm glad you like it."

"This is ten times better than anything my old chef made. I knew he wasn't really up to snuff after the first week, but he had such an impressive résumé, and he brought a rack of ribs to his interview that were really delicious. Turns out that was all he really knew how to make."

"If a chef can't do the basics, he's not much of a chef."

"Look, I signed a five-year lease on this space. I could break it and pay the fee and walk away, or I could open a new restaurant with a competent executive chef this time. This is amazing." Joey took another bite. "Oh, so good. So look, job is yours if you want it."

Lindsay was gratified by his faith in her and how much he liked her cooking. But becoming a chef was a big career change, and she liked the job she had a lot. This was a leap she wasn't quite ready for, no matter how much she'd discussed it with Brad in the abstract.

"This is one dish," she said.

"True, but it's not the rack-of-ribs situation again. You didn't know you'd be cooking a steak when you walked in here, and you still did it flawlessly. You've got the chops. I have faith."

So he'd learned nothing from his previous venture. "Are you sure about this? Steak could be the only thing *I* know how to cook."

"Is it?"

"No. But I barely have any restaurant experience."

"Doesn't matter. My previous chef had almost twenty years of restaurant experience, and look how that turned out."

Lindsay sat back in her chair and stared at Joey. She couldn't make her brain process this offer. On the one hand, she already had a job she liked and didn't want to quit it for a job that might not last two months. On the other hand, this was the dream, wasn't it? This was the very thing she'd been fantasizing since she decided to accept Brad back into her life.

"I'd give you a lot of control," Joey said. "There are a couple of things I'd want to keep on the menu, but you're the expert. And I can pay you a pretty good rate."

He reached into his pocket and pulled out a pen and a little pad of paper. He wrote something on the paper and handed it to Lindsay. It showed…a very big number.

"Executive chef salary," said Joey. "I'm told that's close to the average."

"This is…good, yes." And so much more than what she was currently making. Lindsay told herself to focus. "Uh, out of curiosity, what dishes would you keep on the menu?"

"A couple of the staples from my childhood. Mac and cheese, corn bread, that kind of thing. My granny used to make fried okra that was actually good and not slimy, and I wanted to add that to the menu, but the old chef refused. But southern dishes like that, or modern takes on them."

Lindsay nodded. "Sure, that makes sense." *Focus, Linds.* "But I already have a job."

"I know, but… I can tack on an extra ten thousand a year if that sweetens the pot."

What was even happening right now? Had Lindsay walked into some bizarre parallel universe? "I'd be lying if I said I wasn't intrigued by this offer, but this is completely unexpected. I didn't think I was coming here today for a job interview. I thought *I* would be interviewing *you*. Can I have some time to think about it?"

"Absolutely. Not too long, because the longer this place sits empty, the more money I lose. I want to have a concept for the rebrand rolling by next week, and I don't want to be closed longer than a month. So I need an answer by...Monday, say?"

"Yes, okay. Monday. And I will definitely consider this. I'll give it *a lot* of thought. I just need to think it over for a bit."

"Good, good." Joey stood, so Lindsay grabbed her handbag and followed him back to the front door. "I hope you do come work for this restaurant. I think we could build something great together."

"Yeah... Thank you. Sincerely. I've never had an opportunity like this before."

"I hope to hear from you by Monday!"

———————

Brad walked out of the café after his shift for the day and saw Lindsay walk out of Pepper and shake hands with some blond guy. Curious, Brad crossed the street and caught Lindsay as she turned to walk away from the building.

"What are you doing here?" she asked.

"I'm just leaving the café for the day. Walk with me?"

"Yeah, okay."

After they walked a few steps, Brad asked, "So why were you at Pepper?"

"I was interviewing Joey Maguire for the *Forum* about what he plans to do next with the restaurant."

"Ah, okay. And what does he plan to do?"

"He's not totally sure yet. I'm not sure I got much that will be useful for an article."

Brad laughed. "Is he dreamy? I only saw the side of his face."

"I mean...sure. He's a good-looking guy." Lindsay shot Brad a sidelong glance. "Okay, if I'm honest, he's *very* good-looking."

"I was just curious. I talked to my sister last night, and when I mentioned the restaurant had closed, she said she was *obsessed* with Little Joey Maguire. Had a huge poster of him on her bedroom wall, which I hadn't remembered. She wanted to know how the food was, so I sent her your review. So Joey still owns this space?"

Lindsay laughed. "Yup. You can take your sister to whatever he opens next."

"Hopefully it'll be a lot better than Pepper when she visits."

They walked a block in relative silence. Lindsay seemed to be thinking hard about something.

"Are you mentally writing your article?" Brad asked.

"What? Oh, no. Just thinking."

"About?"

Lindsay hesitated, but she said, "You know how we were talking about what we'd do with the Pepper space if we ran a restaurant together? Obviously we can't afford that, but I was just thinking, what if Joey were still financing it and let us do whatever we wanted with the space? Hypothetically."

Brad figured this idea had come from speaking to Joey just now, so he decided to play along. "I don't think much would change from what we've already talked about. I'd try to talk him into a family restaurant kinda place with a few upscale dishes and a killer dessert menu." Brad shrugged. "We've already discussed this at length. The only difference is that you'd have a guy financing it instead of us as owners. Which means we probably wouldn't have complete creative control."

"Yeah, Joey said he had a few dishes he'd want to keep on any menu."

"Out of curiosity, did he specify?"

"Mac and cheese, some of the southern stuff. I am actually not certain he knows, exactly, but he's a southern boy and wants southern food on the menu of his restaurant. I can see him being the kind of owner who *says* you have complete creative control but still meddles. He said something about fried okra."

"Oh, yuck."

"He swears his granny's recipe is tasty and not slimy. To me, that sounds like a challenge I'd want to take on." Lindsay laughed. "They should do an okra round on *Mystery Meal*."

They walked another few feet in silence, and then Brad said, "You keep bringing up this restaurant hypothetically. How serious are you about it?"

Lindsay waited a moment before she said, "All right, I'm thinking a little about getting back into restaurant work. But I really don't know."

"Interesting." And also great. Brad knew Lindsay was a great chef and would have liked to see her living up to her potential there, although it was of course her decision. If they were a couple, he'd support whatever decision she made as long as it made her happy.

"I'm struggling to decide, though. I mean, a full-time chef job would be a lot of work. Right now, I have a good paycheck and flexible hours and I still get to write about food all the time. But I miss cooking. I just don't know."

"There's no rush to decide, is there?" Brad asked.

Lindsay gave him a sidelong look. "I guess not."

"But you're serious. You're thinking about restaurant work."

"Yeah. Would you consider switching jobs? I mean, say, hypothetically, I talked Joey Maguire into hiring me, would you want to work with me?"

"Sure," said Brad. And he would. The idea of running a restaurant with Lindsay had been growing on him. And it wasn't unusual for executive chefs to have their fingers in multiple projects, so he could still oversee things at the cat café if he got another restaurant job.

But this was all hypothetical. A thought exercise it was fun to talk about with Lindsay. But he wondered how serious she was now.

Then she shrugged. "Well. How was your day?"

"Uneventful. I made zucchini bread."

Lindsay laughed. "That seems good. I love zucchini bread."

"My mom's recipe, actually. I think it turned out pretty well. I got a good deal on zucchini from the farmers market yesterday."

Small talk was all well and good, but Brad didn't know what to say. He felt like he was still on shaky ground with Lindsay. Were they friends? Were they dating? He didn't want to question her being nice to him and cause her to fight with him, so he figured he'd savor this.

They chatted about recipes on the rest of the walk until they got to the spot near where they'd have to part ways to go to their respective homes. Brad lived closer to the café than Lindsay did, so he contemplated asking her to come with him, but he thought better of it. Lindsay was right; sex had never been their problem, and if they got back together, they'd have a lifetime to get even better at it. Trust was their problem. Did they have it? Brad wasn't sure, which was probably a no.

"I, uh, gotta work," Lindsay said, hooking her thumb in the direction of her apartment.

"Of course. I'm pretty tired from making muffins and sandwiches and zucchini bread."

Lindsay stepped closer and kissed Brad's cheek. "Have a good evening. I'll catch you later, okay?"

So...okay. Maybe this was a thing. "Yeah, sure," said Brad. "See you soon."

CHAPTER 21

PAIGE WALKED INTO POP WITH a big grin on her face. As she sat across from Lindsay, she said, "We got two new kittens today, and they are the *cutest*."

"I didn't know you kept kittens at the cat café," said Lindsay.

Paige got out her phone and started tapping on the screen. "We don't normally, but someone dumped these at the vet clinic, who offered them to us once they had all their shots. Look at this!"

Paige showed Lindsay a photo of two gray-and-black-striped kittens with big eyes and noses, sitting beside each other and tilting their heads at the camera.

"Okay, these guys are darling."

"I am certain they will be adopted in sixty seconds because everyone loves kittens, but until then, they are my babies."

"You have names for them?"

"Not yet. I've been thinking about famous siblings. Hansel and Gretel?"

"Castor and Pollux? What gender are they?"

"One's a girl and one's a boy. Jake and Maggie, like the Gyllenhaals."

"Ooh, what about Shirley MacLaine and Warren Beatty?"

"They're siblings?"

"Yeah. You didn't know that?"

Paige shrugged. "No, but I think we have a winner. I love them more already."

"Are you going to bring them home?"

Paige laughed. "We have two cats at home already. They'd never forgive me."

"Or Josh would never forgive you."

"That too. We don't need any new cats, and kittens can be hard to manage. But how cute are these guys?"

Evan walked in then. "Is Paige showing you the kitten photos? She's already texted me a half dozen."

"Itty-bitty kitties," Paige cooed at her phone.

Evan rolled his eyes. "Good evening, ladies. Is Lauren coming?"

"I think it's just us," said Paige. "Caleb's working tonight, so Lauren is taking care of Hannah."

"Good. I can have single solidarity with Lindsay and be in the majority for once."

Lindsay laughed. "Well…"

"Nope. You and Brad are not back together."

"Not officially, no."

"Sisters before misters." Evan held up his fist, so Lindsay bumped it. "At least pretend to be single until we leave the bar so I don't feel so pathetic."

After they ordered cocktails, Lindsay said, "I actually do have some news that I'd love to get your take on."

"Shoot," said Evan.

"So, I went back to Pepper to meet Joey Maguire. I was planning to do an interview with him for the *Forum*."

"Oh my god, you did! You met him! Is he the cutest?" said Paige.

"I mean, he's a good-looking guy, yes. That's not even the point of this story."

"Oh, no," said Evan. "You can't just drop on us that you interviewed Joey Maguire and not talk about him. He's so flipping cute."

Lindsay laughed. "All right, yes, he's very easy on the eyes. Super-nice guy, too. But again, not the point."

"What is the point?" asked Evan.

"So, I went to interview him to see what he planned to do with the restaurant space next, but really to find out what Pepper would become now that it's closed. And then he suggested that maybe I should be the chef at his restaurant, and I told him that was crazy, because I have never been a head chef nor do I have much restaurant experience. But then he told me to cook a steak, so I did, and he loved it so much he offered me a job."

"What?" said Paige.

Lindsay was still struggling to make sense of what had happened, but she'd been thinking about it for a full day and was no closer to a decision. "He wants me as executive chef of Pepper 2.0, whatever that ends up being. Probably a midrange family restaurant with an eclectic menu. That I'd design. Because I'd be executive chef."

"Wow!" said Paige. "That's amazing. Are you going to do it?"

"I don't know. I can't decide. I feel... Well, I feel really unqualified."

"Oh my god," said Evan. "This is just like on *Friends* when Monica gives that restaurant a bad review and the owner offers her a job."

"It's not... Well, okay, it is exactly like that. But this is not an episode of *Friends*."

"You're not allowed to watch *Friends* anymore," Paige told Evan.

"Okay, fine," said Evan, "but what an incredible opportunity. And you're a great chef, Linds. You'll kick ass at this."

"It's not just about making good food. Running a restaurant means managing people and logistics and all that." There was so much to this job that overwhelmed Lindsay. Sure, she could cook a meal, but she'd have to cook a few hundred every night, or coordinate a kitchen staff to cook them. And they'd have to get done in a timely manner, and they'd have to be consistent, and they'd have to go out to the right tables. She'd have to manage supplies and order food and troubleshoot and problem solve. She had just enough restaurant experience to know how chaotic a busy kitchen could be. It hadn't occurred to her until she'd left Pepper that the challenge was not cooking, but everything else that came with running a restaurant.

She was not at all confident she could do this job.

But what if she had an ally like Brad at her side? What if he were the executive pastry chef and they ran the kitchen together? He had more experience with the executive part of the executive chef job.

"I just don't know. It was a very nice offer, but I don't know if I can do it."

"I know it would be a lot of work." Evan tilted his head as if he were thinking. "I mean, I don't know anything about how restaurants are run, but you're smart and talented and you can figure it out. And it's not like it would be just you in the kitchen, right? You'd have other chefs working for you, right?"

"Yeah, I assume there would be a team of people in the kitchen. That's actually the part I'm worried about."

"Why did you quit working in restaurants, anyway?" Paige asked.

Lindsay frowned. Her stock answer was that she'd hated being a line cook and flipping hamburgers. The monotonous work of her first job wasn't great, but she could have stuck it out and then started working her way up the ranks of the city's best kitchens, the way Brad had. She had culinary school friends who were doing great things now, working in fine restaurants, building their own spaces. That could have been her.

She'd pushed a lot of that aside because she knew it wasn't fair to blame Brad for her bad choices. She was a smart, independent woman who had been living and working and making her own way in New York City for a long time. And yet, at some point, she'd decided that if she couldn't have the future she wanted, she just wouldn't cook at all.

But what if she could have that future now?

"Does it make me a bad feminist if I say that when Brad and I broke up, some of the magic went out of cooking? Our relationship was over and I just…didn't want to cook anymore."

"No," said Paige. "I think it means you really loved him."

Lindsay sighed.

"So now that he's back, you want to cook again?" asked Evan.

"It's not even that. I was in that kitchen at Pepper cooking a couple of steaks, and I realized at one point as I was putting together the meal and picking out the sides and getting just the right sear on the steaks that I was really enjoying what I was doing. The mechanics of cooking and thinking about how to make a complete meal were *fun*. And I'm *good* at this. So, yeah, even though it terrifies me, the offer is kind of tempting."

"I think you should go for it," said Paige.

"Yeah?"

"Yeah. When are you ever going to get another opportunity like this? And then you could probably talk to Lauren about managing people, because she's the best boss I've ever worked for. I'm not just saying that. She'll tell you straight when you're doing something wrong, but she also leaves you with the sense that she'll defend you to the death if anyone else tells you you're doing something wrong." Paige smiled. "Like, the other day, this customer came in to complain about Monique. He'd ordered a latte and had neglected to tell Monique he needed it to be soy, and he actually came back to complain about his stomachache because he was lactose intolerant, and *then* he tried to claim that Monique was angry and yelled at him when he'd ordered soy."

"And Lauren listened to this whole screed but because obviously Monique is the calmest, most mild-mannered person who works in the whole café, Lauren asked her if the man had ordered a soy latte. Monique asserted that he had not. I was working at the counter and can verify that he just asked for a latte. And Lauren just turned to this guy and said he was a racist and he could leave and never come back."

"Yeah, the old 'angry Black woman' stereotype does not fit Monique at all, except for the 'Black woman' part," said Evan. "I've never heard her lose her temper with anyone."

"I didn't know people in New York City could be so blatantly racist," said Paige.

"Oh, you sweet honey child," said Evan. "A man on the street called me a faggot yesterday, merely because I was walking down the street while gay. If you think there are no bigots in this city, you are sadly mistaken."

Paige sighed. "Anyway, I was just trying to say, Lindsay, that I think you should take the job. It'll be really hard, I'm sure, but also really rewarding."

"Paige is right," said Evan. "Normally, I would say, only take the job if you really want it, because I know you also love your job at the *Forum*. But the way you just talked about cooking a steak convinced me this is what you really want. So, yeah, I think you should take the job."

Lindsay was still not at all confident she could do the job, but she was touched that her friends were so encouraging. "I'm definitely considering it. I have to give Joey an answer by Monday."

Evan laughed. "So you and Little Joey Maguire are on a first-name basis?"

Lindsay shrugged. "What can I say? I'm very charming."

"Are you gonna hit that?" asked Evan.

"What? No. First of all, if I take the job, he'd be my boss. Second of all, I'm trying to get back together with Brad."

"And how's that going?"

Lindsay took a fortifying sip of her martini. "Not the best."

"What's going on?" asked Paige.

"He's being sincere now. He tried to win me over and I wasn't hearing it because I was so tied up in my own nonsense, but once I realized that I still have feelings for him and that, actually, I do trust him, too much time had passed, and he stopped believing I'd come around and decided I wasn't worth the trouble. So now we're at some kind of truce, but also an impasse. I can't just tell him I trust him because he won't believe me, so I have to find a way to show him."

Evan and Paige both nodded slowly. "You don't trust anyone," Paige said. "Except us, I mean."

"Brad said the same thing. It's...hard."

"Trust is hard," said Paige. "But love is amazing. I think if you and Brad can find a way to love and trust each other, you'll be very happy together."

"I think so, too," Lindsay said quietly.

"When Lauren told me she'd hired him, I was really expecting this monster to come work at the café. But he's actually pretty great. He's creative, he's got a good sense of humor, and he's good with the customers."

"That's because the customers are all trying to get in his pants," said Evan.

"Well, hopefully soon, I'll be the only one who gets in his pants," said Lindsay.

"I'll drink to that." Evan raised his glass. "Although, I swear to god, if you get married and leave me as the only single one, you're dead to me."

"Aw." Lindsay clinked her glass against Evan's. "I love you too, Ev. And your Mr. Right is out there somewhere."

"Wish he'd show up sooner."

———————

Brad's two assistant pastry chefs, Stephanie and Dan, were both fairly recent culinary school grads, but they were also both very good. Dan viewed baking as a science and got nervous when asked to improvise, but if Brad gave him a recipe, he followed it precisely. Stephanie was more laid-back and creative, but she also mostly stuck to the menus Brad had made.

The goal was for one of them to be in the kitchen at the cat café each day, sometimes both, with Brad only working on high-traffic weekdays. Brad was looking to get his schedule down to four days a week, because he could feel himself burning out after the zany hours of his first couple of months at this job. Lauren was being very accommodating, basically letting him set his own hours and run the kitchen however he saw fit as long as they had enough pastries to feed the masses.

All three of them were in the kitchen one morning, though, while Brad did some frosting-decoration training.

Dan prized taste over decoration, so he seemed pretty skeptical of making cupcakes look like cats. He gamely held up a piping bag, though, and moved as Brad directed. Once he'd drawn a passable orange cat in frosting, Stephanie took a turn and nailed it.

"Not every pastry chef is good at this kind of thing," said Brad. "Most days, Dan, you can stick to danishes and muffins. And the cat treats, obviously. But when I designed the menu, I was thinking about how the main theme of this place is cuteness. People come to hang out with the cats, so we should have some cat-themed pastries."

Dan nodded. "I totally understand. I'll practice and get better."

Brad nodded and then moved to take a tray of tuna cat cookies out of the oven. The cat treats themselves were small rectangles, sometimes a little irregularly cut, because Brad's technique was to make the dough, roll it out to quarter-inch thickness, and then use a spiral cutter to slice it up into treats. They were small enough he could bake a few dozen treats on one tray. Brad had coached Dan and Stephanie through making this particular batch, and as soon as they were cool, he planned to have everyone taste test them so they'd know when they got things right. These tuna treats were actually a little gross—they were the same texture as a ginger snap but tasted like fish—but Brad had studied feline nutrition to make sure he only used safe ingredients, and the café cats gobbled them up.

When Dan and Stephanie had finished frosting a dozen cupcakes, Brad put them all on a tray and carried them out to the counter.

Monique looked grateful. "There's a little girl in the cat room who was *very* disappointed we didn't have any cupcakes today. I told her our baker was making some more right now."

"Sorry about that. We did cake-decorator training today, so these took longer than usual." Brad walked around the counter and slid the tray into the empty spot in the display case. "You want me to go tell her there are cupcakes now?"

"Sure. Black girl with braided hair in a pink dress."

"Gotcha."

Brad walked into the cat room and immediately spotted the girl in question, sitting on the floor with her mom as three of the cats sniffed her and she giggled. The tableau made Brad's heart swell a little from the cuteness.

He was surprised to see Lindsay sitting in the room, too. She sipped from a mug and gave him a meaningful look. He held up a finger, hoping to convey that he'd be with her shortly.

He walked over to the little girl. "Hi," he said, kneeling. "I'm Brad, I'm the baker here. Monique up front told me that you wanted a cupcake."

The girl's whole face lit up. "Are they ready?"

"They are! Would you like me to help you get one?"

The girl was on her feet immediately. She looked like she was maybe four or five, and her mom smiled at her indulgently as Brad led them back up front. When he pointed out the cupcakes in the case, the girl said, "Mama, those cupcakes look like cats!"

"I know, honey pie." The mom turned to Monique and handed her a few dollars. "Can you put one of those cupcakes on a plate and give me a couple of forks?"

"Not a problem," said Monique.

"What's your name again?" the little girl asked Brad.

"Brad."

"Brad the baker!" The girl giggled. "I'm Tanisha."

"It's very nice to meet you, Tanisha."

"Did you make those cupcakes?"

"I did."

"Why did you make them look like cats?"

"Well, we're in a cat café, aren't we?"

The girl giggled again. "Yes."

Mom had her cupcake in hand and held out a hand for Tanisha. "Come along, honey. Let's go eat this." She turned to Brad. "Thanks for letting us know."

Brad turned to Monique as the mom and daughter walked back into the cat room. "I was a little worried the mom would yell at me for plying her daughter with sweets."

"No, she was disappointed we were out of cupcakes. That's why I sent you back there. I knew we'd get the sale."

Brad tapped his temple. "Smart." He took a deep breath. "Did you know Lindsay was back there?"

Monique shrugged.

Brad sighed and walked back into the cat room and sat at the table with Lindsay. "I'm still on the clock, but I can take a few minutes."

"Sorry. I did want to talk to you about something, but we don't have to right now."

"I'm gonna wonder about it if you don't give me a preview."

Lindsay smiled. "I'm actually just working here."

"Oh, well, then—"

"Well, I've got a potential opportunity to go back into restaurant work, and I'm seriously considering taking it. And I was wondering if you'd be interested in coming with me. Like, if I take this job as executive chef, would you be interested in executive pastry chef?"

"I mean...sure, in theory. I'm training my assistants today in an effort to have them take over more of the daily work so I can take more time off. I worked seven days a week the first month I was here, did you know that?"

Lindsay nodded. "I did know that. Burnout catching up with you?"

"That's an understatement," said Brad. "The new assistants are both fresh out of school, but they're very good."

"So, in theory, you could straddle both jobs."

"I mean...I guess. Not tomorrow, but in another month or so, yeah, I think the assistants will be ready to work without training wheels. But I'd only take a new job if I had creative control."

"Of course. I still haven't decided if I'm taking the job. I just figured, if you were interested in restaurant work again, I'd toss your name in the pot for pastry chef."

"So, wait, you got offered a restaurant job?"

"Yes, but it's a long story." Lindsay waved her hand. "I don't really think I can do it. I have zero executive chef experience."

"Sure, but every executive chef had a first executive chef job."

Lindsay frowned. "I guess. It's overwhelming. Or, I don't know, it's just a crazy idea. I have a job I really like. I don't know if I really want to take a risky, overwhelming, stressful job just because it would get me back in a kitchen."

"Okay." But Brad liked the idea of Lindsay cooking again. He wasn't totally sure why. Part of it was guilt over possibly being the reason she'd quit. But part of it was that he knew how passionate she was about food. She deserved a good job where she could use that passion.

"Is this a new restaurant?" Brad asked.

"Yes. And that's the other thing. It seems insane to me to quit a steady job to go work in a restaurant that might close in three months. Like, remember that place near school, the restaurant run by one of the *Top Chef* winners?"

Brad totally remembered that place. It had served the best chicken wings he'd ever eaten. "I still have dreams about those hot wings."

Lindsay laughed. "Right? The reviews were glowing, the chef was famous, and yet the restaurant only lasted six months."

"It's a tough industry." Brad tried to read what she was saying between the lines. This *was* a tough industry. So Lindsay would have to take a risk. Lindsay, the most risk-averse person Brad knew, would have to put everything on the line if she really wanted to follow this dream.

"So, yeah," Lindsay said, staring at the table. "Still trying to decide if I want this job."

"I'm starting to see why some chefs have their fingers in so many pots."

"Yeah." She sighed. "I'll let you get back to work."

"You didn't come here to talk to me, did you?"

"Nope. I was working at home, but they're replacing the water main on my block, and the jackhammering was getting to me. You were just a happy bonus. Although I did want to ask you about this, just to see. Like, I could pitch you to this restaurateur anyway and see what he says."

Brad smiled. "Sure. Can't hurt."

He thought about giving Lindsay a quick kiss, but he was

aware that little Tanisha still had an eye on him. Instead, he patted Lindsay's hand where it rested on the table, then made himself get up.

He spent the walk back to the kitchen wondering what all that was about.

When he got back to the kitchen, Stephanie asked, "Are there a lot of customers?"

"No, but someone I know was sitting in the cat room. Sorry to take so long. Those cat treats are probably close to ready to bag. You want to taste a few before we do?"

CHAPTER 22

SOME HIGHLY UNPLEASANT SUMMER COLD had moved through the café staff, so when Brad wrapped up work in the kitchen for the day on Saturday, Lauren all but got on her knees and begged him to help out at the counter. Brad was tired but couldn't in good conscience leave Lauren in the lurch, so he agreed. Monique, who looked a little the worse for wear after being out sick the last couple of days, rang up purchases and ran the espresso machine while Brad bagged pastries and poured regular coffee and hot water.

"It's not fair that you're not sick," Monique said during a lull.

"I've been chewing on immune-support gummies ever since the first one of you was felled by this virus. And I'll thank you to keep a wide radius." He winked to show he was kidding.

Monique shook her head. "This thing knocked me on my ass. I couldn't get out of bed for two days. Thank god for my boyfriend or I wouldn't have eaten. Although, now he's sick, so as soon as my shift is over, I gotta go home and feed him soup." Monique grabbed a napkin from the dispenser on the counter and blew her nose. "Ugh. Having a cold in the summer is the *worst*. Is it really hot in here, or is it just me?"

"It's a little warm, but after years of working in kitchens, I'm kind of impervious."

As soon as Lauren flipped the *Closed* sign on the front door, Monique hightailed it out of the café.

As Brad cleaned the counter and Lauren tallied up the cash in the register, Lauren said, "Paige and I are headed to Pop when we're done. You want to come with?"

Brad was tired, but suddenly the prospect of a cocktail was tempting. "Sure."

"The whole gang is going to be there. Lindsay, too. I don't know what your deal is with Lindsay, but just so you forewarned."

"That's okay. Things are a little ambiguous, but I'd like to see her. And I'm, like, 89 percent sure she doesn't want to stab me anymore."

Lauren smiled. "Cool."

When they left about a half hour later, Brad was struck by how chummy and normal this all felt, like he'd been incorporated right into the friend group. Lauren and Paige were clearly close friends, but they didn't fraternize with the rest of the café staff in the same way. And now they were headed for a post-work drink, but in a way that felt like Brad had been invited to the adults' table. He wasn't entirely sure what to make of it. Did this mean Lindsay's friends accepted him?

He decided to just roll with it as they walked into the bar and saw Lindsay, Evan, and Caleb already seated. Brad opted to sit next to Lindsay, who greeted him with a smile.

"And how is everyone?" said Evan once they were settled in their seats.

"My mother is going to be my undoing," said Paige. She turned to Lauren. "You were smart to have a small wedding. If my mother calls one more time to offer an opinion about flowers or colors, I'm going to scream." As if on cue, Paige's phone lit up from where it sat on the table. The display said "Mom" was calling. Paige crossed her arms. "I'm not answering that."

Josh walked in then, clad in a suit. He'd probably come straight from work; if Brad's memory served, Josh worked for the Brooklyn DA's office. He slumped into the seat next to Paige and looked at her face, then the phone. "Your mother calling?"

"You were right. We should have just gone to city hall."

Josh kissed Paige's cheek. "Only a month to go. By the way, *my* mother has decided to fly out a week early to 'help out,' so we're going to have to get skilled at the art of deflection. I plan to use Hannah. Like, look, Mom, grandchild."

"Hey!" said Lauren.

"Sorry about it, but this is a dire situation."

Brad followed this conversation for a few minutes. He understood the basics of the relationships between these people. Evan, Lindsay, and Lauren had gone to undergrad together. Josh and Lauren were siblings. Lauren and Paige had met somewhere work-related. Brad, of course, had his own friends, but he was touched that Lindsay's had brought him into their circle with open arms. Being with Lindsay likely meant a lot of nights just like this. Brad looked forward to that, assuming this all worked out.

Lindsay patted his knee and smiled at him before turning back to the conversation.

And Brad thought, yeah, *this* for the foreseeable future? This he liked.

Once everyone had cocktails and an assortment of small plates were strewn across the table, Evan said, "Guys, I have major breaking news."

"Why didn't you say something sooner?" asked Lauren.

"I was waiting for you all to settle in, because this is going to blow the tops of your heads right off."

Everyone turned their attention to Evan.

Now that he had the full court, he grinned. "So, okay, most of you know the last couple of years have been a bit of a trial for me romantically. There were a lot of bad first dates, there was an ill-conceived reunion with an ex, and then there was Will. Poor, sweet Will, who was a perfectly nice fellow but didn't ignite my loins."

Lindsay leaned toward Lauren. "Is this a speech? Is he giving a speech?"

Lauren shushed her.

Evan went on. "So, two days ago, I was headed home from the café after doing some work there, and on a whim, I dropped into the bookstore. And, of course, who should be working there but Pablo."

Lindsay leaned over to Brad. "Did you hear this whole story? Pablo is the love of Evan's life."

"Yeah. The bookstore guy, right?" Brad whispered back.

Lindsay nodded.

Evan went on. "So, I decided to browse the new releases and picked up a new biography of Andy Warhol, and Pablo walks over and tells me how great the book is. Like, he's doing the hand sell thing very well. Most of the time you can't even hear his accent, but he's got a little bit of the Bronx in his voice, just the way he says certain vowels, and when it's quiet, you can hear it and it's magical."

"Does this story have a point?" asked Lindsay, but she didn't sound angry or impatient.

"I'm getting there. I'm trying to set the scene. See, we're talking, and it popped into my head that Paige had mentioned he was single again, so I said something dorky about how my boyfriend and I had broken up a few weeks ago and I was filling the void with streaming movies and books about queer people— you know, laying it on pretty thick—and Pablo goes, 'Yeah, I went through a breakup recently, too. It sucks.'"

Brad had a sense of where this story was going, but Evan was sure taking his sweet time getting there.

As if she felt the same, Lauren said, "If this story doesn't end with you asking him out, I'm going to be really disappointed."

"Well, if you must know, our eyes met, we had a moment where the whole world stopped, and then I said, 'We should go out sometime.' I can't believe I finally said that."

"It only took two years," said Lindsay.

"Well, it felt weird asking him out when he worked at the coffee shop because I was a customer and I couldn't tell if he was being nice to me because he was nice to everyone or if he genuinely liked me. And then he went to work for the bookstore, and I bought so many books from him that he *must* have known I either really liked him or really hate trees. And *then* he was dating that beardy guy."

"Wait, you finally asked him out?" said Paige. "What did he say?"

Evan grinned. "He said yes! We're going to dinner Tuesday night."

There were enthusiastic congratulations from everyone at the table. Feeling like part of the family, Brad patted Evan's shoulder and said, "Good job, man."

"Guys, what should I wear?" Evan asked.

Brad started to laugh but then realized Evan was serious. The women at the table picked apart what they knew of Evan's closet and helped him decide on an outfit for his big date.

Brad ordered another drink and folded himself into the conversation, which turned next to pop culture stuff. Lindsay and Evan were apparently both streaming some show about British teenagers and were both obsessed with one of the characters, and Brad enjoyed watching them dork out about the show.

"He is so cute," said Lindsay. "I'm rooting for him to hook up with Timothy."

"Nah," said Evan. "Timothy is not even gay. But Cooper is totally going to hook up with Dan."

"With *Dan*? But he's the bully!"

Evan tapped his nose.

This went on at length, during which Josh and Caleb had a conversation about some scandal with the Brooklyn Borough president and other conversations floated and started around Brad.

Paige asked Brad's opinion about food at the wedding venue. They'd settled on entrées but needed to make final decisions about what appetizers would circulate during the cocktail hour. He suggested things that could be eaten in one bite, because once utensils got involved, it got more complicated. Paige nodded, but then said, "I don't know if there's going to be enough food." Given Paige's stress level about her wedding, Brad made a mental note to keep his own hypothetical wedding small.

Would that wedding be to Lindsay? Brad glanced at her, and she smiled back. So he decided, yeah, maybe it would be. Or, who knew, maybe they'd develop some kind of romantic and professional partnership where they cooked together and lived together and that was really what he wanted more than a wedding.

Brad chatted with Evan about books they'd read—although Brad hadn't had a lot of time for reading lately—and with Josh about a court case that was getting a lot of headlines. Caleb told a funny story about a dog who had come into the vet clinic that day. Lauren said that her cat Molly had still not warmed to Hannah but did like to nap in the crib whenever Hannah was not in it.

And Brad sat back and smiled, grateful for this group of people who were loving and friendly and like family to each other. And when he kissed Lindsay's cheek, she nudged him with her elbow.

This was something that had been missing from his life. This was casual and easy. Brad wanted it. He wanted Lindsay, he wanted them to be together, but he wanted the whole package. He wanted her friends and the cats and after-work cocktails. He wanted to make love at night and kiss each other in the morning and work together to build something professionally. He wanted that smile of hers aimed at him, he wanted to make jokes with her friends, and he wanted *her* and everything that came with her, for the rest of his life.

Brad was tired but having too much fun to let that bother him, so he ordered another cocktail.

CHAPTER 23

LINDSAY WOKE UP AWARE THAT she wasn't alone.

The snorer beside her was clearly Brad—well, and Fred Astaire the cat, who was also snoring softly near Lindsay's head—but she was trying to remember how they'd gotten here.

Well, he'd come by Pop the night before. The whole gang and their significant others had all been there. Brad had just shown up, but it was probably Lauren or Paige who had invited him. He'd been stuck working late at the café because most of the baristas were out sick, but he hadn't seemed resentful at all.

They'd had a lot of cocktails, though. Lindsay knew that much. She had, anyway. She'd taken advantage of Pop's two-for-one martini happy hour. Not for any real reason besides that she was in a good mood and everyone else was in a good mood and they'd laughed and chatted and the waitress kept the refills coming.

And then around the time Lauren and Caleb left to relieve their babysitter, Brad had complained of being tired on account of being up since four in the morning, and Lindsay had said something provocative, and now here they were, in her apartment, in her bed.

Probably it was time for both of them to admit that they were in a relationship.

Lindsay's throat was dry and her head throbbed, sure signs she'd overdone it on the martinis, so she got out of bed to get a glass of water and whatever headache pills were in her medicine cabinet. When she climbed back into bed, Brad stirred. His eyes shot open, and he looked around before his gaze landed on Lindsay and he seemed to understand.

"I wasn't going to sleep with you again until we had a serious talk," he said. "Whoops."

"I can't help it if I'm irresistible."

"I wish you understood how true that was." Brad yawned. "I had this whole plan for us to talk *before* we had sex again, but then I had too many manhattans."

"What did you want to talk about?"

"What? Here? Now?"

Lindsay didn't want to talk, but she wanted to get whatever he was going to say over with. She was tired of talking. She wanted to just…be in this relationship. She knew relationships took work and hard conversations sometimes, but she was tired of dancing around Brad, of trying to work out the getting-back-together choreography.

Well, she knew they had to have a serious conversation. She just didn't want the bubble to pop.

She ran a hand over Brad's bare chest. "We can do something else if you want."

Brad frowned. He put a hand over hers where it rested between his pecs, right next to the sun tattoo. "All right. Let me just ask you this, though. Are we back together?"

"I want to be, yes. You wore me down."

That only made his frown deepen. "I didn't mean to 'wear you down.'"

"Come on, Brad, I was kidding." Lindsay took her hand back and lay on her back. "What I actually mean is that I have come to realize I made a mistake in leaving you the first time, and I want to get back together because we're good together. And I trust you, which believe me, is not something I say to anyone, really. But it is truly, honestly how I feel."

"I know." Brad rubbed his eyes. "Fuck."

"What?"

"You know what the real kick in the teeth is in this situation?"

"Tell me."

"I love you, Linds. I do. I did five years ago and I do now. You were always the one who got away. And hearing you say you want to be together again should be exactly what I want to hear, but... it isn't."

Brad delivered this entire monologue with one arm thrown over his eyes, not looking at Lindsay. It was like he was just talking to a room.

Still, he loved her. He *loved* her.

That was big. Lindsay understood it was a big deal. This was the thing he'd been trying to tell her all along, wasn't it? Since the first moment they set eyes on each other a couple of months before, he'd been trying to tell her that he loved her and she was the one for him, and she hadn't wanted to hear it. She was his *one who got away*.

Well, that was true for her, too. Her friends were right. She'd had kind of an unhealthy fixation on Brad. She'd never been able to let go of him. But love? Did she love him?

She cared about him, yes. She trusted him. But love?

"I should have trusted you then. I didn't. I've learned that lesson now. You're worthy of my trust."

He lifted his arm and looked up at her.

She took a deep breath. He needed more. "I never opened my heart to you, not really. I kept it guarded, and I waited for something to go wrong. You were 100 percent right about me. And the fact that you know me so well should probably have told me something. So I'm telling you now that I trust you. I hope you believe me when I tell you that."

He sighed. "I do, it's just… Did you ever spend time imagining what it would be like when we got back together?"

"Sure."

"What did you imagine our reunion would be like?"

Lindsay turned her head to look at him and found he'd moved his arm away from his face and was looking at her now. She took a deep breath. "Well, if I'm honest, in the time we were apart, I put a lot of energy into convincing myself that I hated you. We probably could have run into each other sooner than we did if I weren't trying so hard to avoid you."

"Really?"

"Yeah. I… Well, I canceled going to a few events because I thought you might be there. I kept tabs on your career in part so I wouldn't accidentally eat in one of your restaurants."

A smile played on Brad's lips, which was nice to see considering how unhappy he'd looked for most of this conversation. "That does seem in character for you."

"Don't you see how insane that is? My friends all teased me about it. Evan accused me more than once of being obsessed with you. I of course denied it, but... You don't put that much effort into avoiding someone unless you're worried about what will happen if you see them again."

"And what were you worried would happen?"

It had taken some work for Lindsay to get over herself and her own carefully constructed walls to recognize the truth. She had to open herself up and let him in and put her soul in his hands and trust him to take care of that. She wanted to take a real risk, to show that she could put it all on the line, but only for one very special person. She'd never done that before. She wanted to now. "I worried I'd take one look at you and forget why I hated you and fall in love with you all over again."

He nodded. "I mean, I knew that's what would happen."

"What did you imagine?"

"That I'd know the exact right thing to say and charm your socks off and you'd forgive me for everything."

Lindsay laughed. "Uh-huh. I'm sure that would have worked."

Brad laughed with her. "Yes. That was the fantasy version. I knew that in real life there'd be a fight. Because I know *you*. I know how you operate." He sighed. "Pretty sure we were meant to be together, Linds."

"I know. It's so stupid."

He barked out a surprised laugh. "Well, yeah, it is that. And if all that's true, I can't get over that we wasted five years apart."

"Well, maybe you could see those five years as the time I needed to get over myself."

He put an arm around her and she thought they might have reached an understanding, but something he'd said still nagged at her. "What is it that you want to hear?"

"What?"

"Before, you said me trusting you should have been the thing you wanted to hear, but it wasn't."

What did Brad want to hear? Well, he wanted her to tell him she loved him. But he wanted her to get there on her own. He never wanted to feel like she was anything but completely, enthusiastically with him.

He held her now and enjoyed the press of her naked body against his in her pink and purple apartment. Since the last time he'd been here, she'd replaced her duvet with a crisp white one with a swirly black floral pattern on it—not any less feminine, but it felt more adult and less teenage girl. He wasn't sure why he cared, except that he was surprised that Lindsay would decorate her apartment like the inside of Barbie's Dreamhouse.

But that was beside the point.

"I don't know what I want," he said after what he knew had been an unacceptably long silence.

"I don't think you have to know right this minute," said Lindsay.

"Sure, but... Don't you think about what our future will be?"

Lindsay rolled slightly and Brad copied her movement so that they both lay facing each other. Lindsay said, "So you pictured our reunion as a fight, huh?"

"I always figured it would be, well, not very different from what happened, actually. I figured you'd still be mad but I could charm you into falling in love with me again." He grinned.

But the truth was, he'd never imagined it would be this hard. He knew he'd have to persuade Lindsay to give him another chance, that he'd have to explain what had happened all those years ago that made her leave. He'd thought Lindsay would be quicker to forgive him. He hadn't realized that the core of their issue was trust. She said she trusted him now and he believed her, mostly. But the longer this reunion, if that's what it was, dragged on, the less faith he had that everything would work out.

Lindsay stared at him for a long moment. "So, okay, where do you see us in the future?"

He closed his eyes and thought for a moment. "Well, you and I will live together in an apartment with a big kitchen. I don't want to bake cat treats forever, so I figure I'll get a new job once I've got the assistants fully trained. I'll probably still bake the cat treats myself, though. We're not selling enough that I need to have a big production machine going or anything, and I think people like the novelty of small batches anyway. I could make them and then work out some kind of arrangement with the cat café where I get a cut of the profits. But I'm rambling." He sighed. "I don't know. What is my dream job? I don't think running a bakery because there's no real challenge in making cupcakes all day, but doing patisserie at a high-end restaurant could be really fun."

"Sure. But that's your job. That's not us."

Brad opened his eyes and looked at her. Lindsay's expression was wide-eyed and earnest, vulnerable maybe. "Well," he said. "Like I said, we'll live together."

"Would we get married?"

"If you want."

"Do you want to?"

Brad was starting to hate this line of questioning. He understood that she was trying to ascertain if he had any future plans beyond his career. Did he want to get married? He was ambivalent. Did he want kids? Lauren's daughter, Hannah, was pretty dang cute, but Brad wasn't sure about that, either. Not right now, definitely. But he said, "I want to be with you. I want to live with you. I don't feel like we're on solid enough ground to get married tomorrow, but that could be in the cards someday if it was something we both wanted. Do you want kids?"

"I don't think so. Not right now, anyway."

"Sounds like we're on the same page there. And what about this potential restaurant job?"

Lindsay let out a long breath. "I have to let the guy know by Monday, and I'm still not sure. You know what I picture, though, with us? Yes, living together. Your apartment is big but needs someone to decorate it, and I'd be happy to take that on."

Brad laughed. "Your taste seems very girlie."

"I like purple. So sue me." She let out a breath. "I'm just saying, I'm still kind of stuck on this fantasy of us running a restaurant together someday, and it was something I didn't even know I wanted until you showed up back in my life."

"I'd like working with you."

"Yeah?"

"Yeah. We'd have fun."

Lindsay smiled. "The idea first popped into my head when you and I hosted that dinner party to celebrate your deciding to switch to pastry. You remember that?"

He did remember. It was almost a silly question to ask if he remembered any particular moment with Lindsay because they were all etched clearly on his memory. "I remember my souffles didn't work because I got a little big for my britches."

Lindsay laughed. "You had those cookies as backup."

"I did, but I was so embarrassed."

"I wasn't."

"Well, sure. You made a beautiful dinner for everyone."

"No, I mean... That night was so much fun. Sharing a kitchen with you, cooking with you. Do you remember how much we laughed? And how everyone forgave you for your souffles falling because the cookies were perfect?"

"I suppose that's true." He reached over and touched a lock of her hair. "I want so much for you to be able to do what you really want to do. You were such a talented chef. I still can't get over that you quit."

"It wasn't fun anymore."

"Well, sure, but—"

"It wasn't fun because you weren't cooking with me. When we were in school and we had the space to mess up and experiment and learn, when you and I used to goof around in the test kitchen after hours, I felt so much joy in what I was doing. I loved cooking. But when you weren't in my life anymore, I just...

I didn't feel that joy anymore. And probably I shouldn't have let that get to me. No, I definitely shouldn't have. Because I blamed you for all of it without taking the time to reflect on what *I* had done wrong, and I realize now that I never let you in. I should have. I want to now. I want to fix what I did wrong before. I want to find that joy again, and I want us to cook together, and that's what I want our future to be."

Something in Brad broke then. "Linds…" But he didn't know what to say. God, he loved this woman. She hadn't said she loved him, too, but he knew she felt something. He leaned over, cupped her cheek, and kissed her, wanting to convey something but not sure what to say. She hooked a hand around his wrist and continued to kiss him.

She pulled away slightly. "It's just something I've been thinking about. You and me teaming up to take on the culinary world. Do you think… Do you think something like that is possible, or is it still a fantasy?"

"No. I think you and I could do anything if we teamed up."

She nodded.

She was saying all the things he wanted to hear, but this conversation had left him feeling uneasy. Why didn't he completely buy what she was selling him? Did he believe she changed? Could she make herself vulnerable for him? Could she take a big leap into the future like this without self-sabotaging again? He wasn't sure she could.

"I guess," Lindsay said, "back when we were dating, I didn't need to have our whole future planned, but I did need to know we had a future. And you seemed incapable of thinking farther than a week ahead, and I guess if we're really going to do this, I need to know not exactly what the future holds, just that we're thinking about it."

"We are. I am. And same. I just want you to be happy. For us to be happy."

She smiled. "Good."

That should have been satisfying, but Brad still felt unsettled. There was something here she wasn't saying. This job offer she was considering seemed odd, and she was only talking about it in the vaguest terms. Was it even real, or was she just trying to get him to react to something? "What aren't you telling me?" he asked.

"I'm not ready to talk about it yet. Let's just say, I have an opportunity, but I haven't made a decision about it just yet. I will tell you as soon as I do."

"Is it something I can help you decide?"

She gave him a long look. "No, I think I have to decide for myself."

For some reason that bothered Brad. He glanced at the clock. It was still pretty early, closing in on 7:00 a.m. Sunday morning. Brad wasn't working today, but he had errands to run and he was neglecting poor Hamilton. He'd called his neighbor and asked her to put some food out, but that poor cat had just been home alone for more than twenty-four hours.

He was curious about what she wasn't telling him, and a little miffed that she wasn't.

Brad got out of bed and started looking for his clothes, which were still strewn across the floor from the previous night. "You know, I meant to have a conversation with you about what we were to each other. Are we back together officially? Are you my girlfriend?"

"I thought we'd gotten past that."

"You're not answering the question."

"Yes, fine. We're back together. Why are you mad at me?"

Brad blew out a breath and pulled on his jeans. "I'm not mad. I'm...confused. It feels weird to me that you're not telling me about whatever this opportunity is."

"It's not something that has any bearing on you or us. It's just a decision I'm trying to make."

"Do you not trust me?"

"Of course I do! Can you please respect that I'm not ready to talk about it yet? I promise I'll explain everything in a couple of days, I just need some time to make sure I'm making the right decision for the right reasons."

"All right." Brad pulled on his shirt.

"You *are* mad."

"I just... I need some time to think, okay. I feel like we're still kind of talking past each other. And I really do have a lot to do today, so I have to go."

"All right." Lindsay climbed out of bed. Still completely naked, she walked over and put her arms around his shoulders. Then she kissed him. It was a long, lingering kiss, the sort of kiss that made his skin tingle and his toes curl, the kind of kiss that made him forget he was annoyed and instead prompted him to put his hands on her back and run his fingers over her smooth skin.

Because he was in love with her. He cherished Lindsay. He wanted them to just get past whatever this weird tension between them was so they could get to that future Lindsay kept talking about.

"I gotta go," he said.

"Okay. Are you working Monday?"

"Yes. Why?"

"I'll come by the café at the end of your shift. We can talk then."

"All right."

She pressed a kiss to his cheek. Then she stepped away and grabbed a robe off a hook on the back of her bedroom door. "I'll walk you out, I guess."

CHAPTER 24

MONDAY MORNING WAS AN AVALANCHE.

After she'd talked to Brad on Saturday, Lindsay was leaning toward the safe route. That restaurant still tempted her, but there'd be other restaurants. She could get back together with Brad now, keep her safe job, and then they could save money and build their own place in the future.

And then she got a phone call from Erica at the *Forum*.

"The meetings have wrapped and the board has made some decisions," said Erica. "The short version is that the new *Forum* management wants to go national and doesn't see much use in having a New York editor or a food section anymore. Well, the decision isn't final, but I understand that's the way the executive board is currently leaning. I just wanted to warn you, my job might be in jeopardy. Which means yours is."

And there it was. Lindsay couldn't stick with the safe option— the safe job wasn't safe. That was enough to convince Lindsay that waiting around to get laid off was stupid when she had this offer from Joey Maguire. She was still not sure she could run a whole restaurant, but it was like the universe was telling her she had to try. So as soon as she got off the phone with Erica, she called Joey.

"I'll take it," she told him. "On one condition."

"Oh, man. You're making my whole day, Lindsay. What's your condition?"

"I want you to hire Brad Marks as the executive pastry chef."

"Brad Marks? Why is that name familiar?"

After Lindsay explained—omitting the part where she and Brad were almost kind of a couple, maybe—Joey admitted he'd been reading all of her articles at the *Forum*, so he had of course read the profile of Brad. "But the cat treats guy? Really?" he'd said.

So Lindsay had laid out Brad's résumé.

Once Lindsay had her answer, she left her apartment. When she walked into the cat café, it wasn't even noon yet.

Paige was working at the counter with Monique, so Lindsay supposed the regular counter staff was still out sick. Paige said, "Hi!" brightly when Lindsay walked in.

"I need to talk to Brad about something. He's working today, right?"

"Yeah, he's in the kitchen. You want me to fetch him?"

"Could you?"

Paige finished plating two scones for a couple who was waiting near the register, and then she jogged to the door to the kitchen. Lindsay smiled at Monique and decided to wait. It occurred to her that she hadn't thought this through all the way. Brad was working. He was probably busy with something pastry-related in back. He might not appreciate the interruption or be able to step away from whatever he was doing without jeopardizing it.

Lindsay didn't bake much, but she knew sometimes that one extra minute in an oven could ruin a whole batch of cookies.

Paige emerged a moment later. "He said to tell you he's busy now but as soon as he finishes what he's working on, he'll meet you in the cat room. He said it should take another ten or fifteen minutes."

"Right. Of course. Then I'll just be…" Lindsay pointed to the cat room, then she walked through the door.

Brad had mentioned in passing during one of their recent conversations that the lunch crowd didn't tend to linger. The café sold a bunch of sandwiches to people who came in for takeout, but not always to people who sat down to eat. But there was a table of people in office clothes who were chatting over sandwiches and petting the cats. One woman had a minia-ture lint roller in her hand, probably to de-cat-hair herself once lunch was over.

Lauren and Evan were both sitting on one of the sofas, their laptops in their laps.

"Hey," said Lauren. "You working here today?"

"I came by to talk to Brad, but he's busy."

"Sure." Lauren glanced around the café. "He's probably finishing today's sandwiches."

Lindsay pulled over a chair. As soon as she sat, a little gray-striped cat hopped into her lap.

Lauren pointed to the cat. "That's one of Paige's kittens."

"Oh, wow. He grew fast."

"He'll get bigger still. Look how big his ears are. He's gotta grow into those."

The kitten did have big ears. Lindsay pet him, and he purred like he had a motor in his throat as he leaned into her hand.

"I hope it's okay for me to stop by," said Lindsay. "I wanted to tell Brad about what's going on at Pepper, and didn't think through the timing."

"Uh, didn't he go home with you the other night?" said Evan.

Lindsay felt heat flood her face. "Well, yeah, but I wasn't ready to talk about it yet. I hadn't made a decision."

"So what's your decision?" asked Lauren.

"Not yet. I'll tell you after I talk to Brad."

Lauren and Evan exchanged a look. Then Lauren said, "We're not that busy, so I don't mind you dropping by to talk to him, but maybe don't make a habit of it? I mean, you're back together now, right? It's okay if you come here to see him sometimes, but I kinda need him on pastry duty."

"Sure. That's fair."

Evan closed his laptop. "Unfortunately, I have to leave and will miss the fireworks. I have a client meeting down the street in half an hour. I don't know why I can't talk people into meeting me here."

"Some people have allergies," said Lauren.

"Yeah, yeah." Evan stood and slid his laptop into his bag. "I'm meeting the client at a coffee shop over by BAM. You guys make a better latte, though."

"I appreciate that," said Lauren. She closed her own laptop. "I gotta do payroll. I should probably go to the office for that. Can you entertain yourself for a bit, Linds?"

"I brought my computer," she said, patting her laptop bag.

"Cool. Come on back and let me know how it goes after you talk to Brad."

"Sure."

"I'd ask you to get a drink later, but Caleb's working the overnight tonight, so I have to go take care of our child. I bet they are both upstairs napping right now, so Hannah will be full of energy when I go home." Lauren let out a long-suffering sigh.

Evan laughed as he shouldered his bag. "Aw, sweetie. You have everything you always wanted. Your life is so hard."

Lauren rolled her eyes, but she smiled.

Lindsay figured she could kill some time by finishing up the last of her assignments before she quit her job, but instead of getting out her laptop, she opened the news app on her phone. As if to remind her that the job she'd had for all of two months was likely to end whether she had any say in it or not, there was a splashy headline on a New York media blog saying that the *Forum* was going national and would likely start phasing out its local reporting except for breaking news. Which meant fewer feature stories and restaurant reviews and the sorts of things people outside of the greater New York metropolitan area didn't care about.

The lull also gave Lindsay too much time to analyze what she planned to say to Brad when she finally talked to him.

He appeared about ten minutes later, looking a little frazzled. His hair was disheveled, and he had a bit of flour on his face. When he sat, she grabbed a napkin from the holder on the table and wiped at a floury thumbprint on his forehead.

"Rough day?" she asked.

Brad shrugged. "We were making cupcakes and one of my

assistants added flour to the stand mixer too fast and it went everywhere. It's fine, though. Let him learn things the hard way."

Lauren nodded. "I'm glad you could talk to me. I have something I want to discuss with you."

"Okay." Brad looked around. One of the kittens ran over and hopped up on the table, so Brad petted her. He pointed to the cat's purple collar. "This one is Shirley, and the gray kitten with the blue collar is Warren."

"Aha!" said Lindsay.

"Lauren doesn't usually put collars on the cats, but we couldn't tell them apart otherwise. They look completely identical." Brad put the kitten on his lap. "What did you need to talk to me about?"

"Well, I'll give you the abridged version. That day you ran into me in front of Pepper, I wasn't just there for an interview with Joey Maguire. Well, I was, or I thought I was when I walked in there, but after we criticized his old chef for a bit, he asked me to cook something for him. He liked what I did so much he offered me a job on the spot."

Brad stared at her for a long moment. "He... So, wait, is this the big opportunity you keep mentioning?"

"Yes. And I'm sorry I didn't bring it up sooner. I was certain I'd turn it down, and it didn't seem worth discussing."

Brad nodded slowly. "You've changed your mind."

"I did. I gave it a lot of thought. I realized I wanted to try working in a restaurant again. It's scary as hell, because I'm not at all sure I have what it takes to keep a restaurant in business, but it's exciting, too. The more I think about it, the more right it feels. And, well, my boss called me this morning to say she was likely getting laid off in the *Forum* reorganization, so I'll be in the market for a job soon anyway."

"Wait, *what*? He... Joey Maguire offered you a job."

"Yes. And it's a *huge* risk. I mean, I'll probably be unemployed three months from now. But I think it's time for me to take some risks. To really put myself out there and break out of my comfort zone and do what I really want instead of what's safe."

Brad stared at her. "So is that it? Are you going to take the job?"

"Yes. I talked to Joey Maguire right before I came over here. I accepted the job. And I want you to come with me."

"Come with you? What do you mean?"

"I mean, come be the executive pastry chef. Come run this restaurant with me. It can be everything we've talked about, but without the financial investment. Because Joey doesn't want to run a restaurant, he just wants to finance it. He'd give us complete creative control, with some occasional interventions. And...well, not all of his ideas are bad. He wants his grandmother's banana pudding on the dessert menu."

For the first time since they started talking, a laugh bubbled out of Brad. "Banana pudding?"

"I know. None of this is set in stone yet, but my thought was, if you're into this idea, we could have an eclectic menu to appeal to a wide audience, and there will be some homey, southern touches to make Joey happy, and we cater to families. Everything we've been talking about these last few weeks. I know it's a lot to process, but what do you say?"

Brad took a moment to contemplate what Lindsay was really asking him. They'd been talking about this fantasy of running a restaurant together a lot recently, and now she was telling him that fantasy could be a reality.

He wanted that reality so much he could taste it. But.

"Let me ask you a couple of questions," he said.

"Of course. Please do."

"You want us to be co-executive chefs at whatever Pepper becomes. That means you and I work together and make decisions for the restaurant together."

"Yes." She nodded vigorously. "I don't think I can do this alone. We can be partners in everything. And I do mean everything. In the restaurant. Romantically."

"Have you run this by Joey?"

Lindsay smiled. Brad was surprised to suddenly realize that she'd actually thought this all through pretty well. She'd probably been working on this deal for the better part of five days. He was still a little irked she hadn't spoken about it with him, especially since this now involved his career, too, but he saw that she had intended for this to be a surprise. It was almost like a marriage proposal.

And, well, if she'd brought this up sooner, he would have tried to talk her into it. But as was true for the two of them, this needed to be Lindsay's decision. She was right about that.

But this was a hell of a risk. It seemed out of character for Lindsay. But on the other hand, what she really seemed to be telling him was that she was ready to take a risk. On her job, on herself, on them. And hadn't that been what Brad had wanted all along?

He couldn't process all this, so he just stared at Lindsay.

"I told him I wanted him to hire you as executive pastry chef," Lindsay said, "and he was okay with it. But I don't want to pull you away from here if this is where you think you should be. It's your call, but the job is yours if you want it."

Brad took a moment to think about that. "I mean, my assistants here are nearly fully trained, today notwithstanding." He gestured to his face, which he was sure was still covered in flour. "I made a recipe book for the pastries that sell well here. So if future chefs follow those recipes, the café will be fine. Lauren might even be happy if I worked here less and she could cut my salary, since I'm more expensive than the assistants. In some ways, working across the street might be ideal, because I'd still be nearby to help out as needed."

"But?"

"Well, what about you? I don't want you to feel pressured to take this job because of this fantasy we cooked up together."

Lindsay surprised Brad by reaching across the table and taking his hands in hers. "You know what I really want? I want to build a future with you. I want the future we dreamed about. I want us to be together as romantic partners, and I want us to live together in an apartment with a big kitchen and our two cats, and I want to invent new dishes with you and run a restaurant with you. I want all of that. It's an incredible risk, but I think the reward will be worth it. And if it isn't, well, we'll still be together, we'll still come home to each other each night, and we'll dust ourselves off and move on to the next thing." Her eyes were big with excitement, showing Brad that she was being sincere. She smiled. "What do you say?"

It was everything Brad had most wanted to hear, which was maybe why he didn't completely trust it yet.

"You're serious about all of this," he said.

"I have a meeting with Joey in a couple of hours at the restaurant. You can come with me and talk to him if you want."

This was so surreal. "Oh-kay. We'd be working for an ex-boy-band guy who thinks he knows what southern cuisine is."

Lindsay laughed. "I know. It's very strange. But he's a nice guy. A little naive about the restaurant biz, but he seems to genuinely want the restaurant to succeed, and he seems to get what he did wrong the first time. Do I think I'm the right person to help him build a successful restaurant? No, not really, but he wants me, and it's a great opportunity."

Brad petted the kitten in his lap for a moment as he mulled all this over. It sounded too good to be true. Probably it was. Probably if he took this job, he'd have some kind of tiff with Joey Maguire. Brad could imagine coming up with some new spin on banana pudding—banana crème brûlée popped into his head suddenly—and Joey would push back. Probably Brad and Lindsay would have days when they fought more than they found harmony.

But Lindsay was right. This was an incredible opportunity.

He needed to know one thing, though.

"I feel," he said, "like we've spent these last weeks getting to know each other again, and like I told you the other night, I'm all in. You and me, Linds. I love you, I've always loved you, but I need to know that we're not in some kind of awkward, lopsided relationship like before, where we constantly worry we're about to lose each other. Running a new restaurant is going to be hard enough without worrying that our relationship is precarious."

Lindsay nodded and squeezed his hand. "I love you, too, Brad. You're the only person I would ever do something this insane with."

Brad believed her. The look in her eyes was open and earnest, but more than that, he knew she wouldn't lie to him.

He leaned across the table and kissed her.

He lingered at her lips for a long moment, slipping his lower lip between both of hers, getting a good taste of her, but he knew they were not alone.

The cat in his lap yelped and jumped off, which surprised Brad enough that he sat back.

"Sorry, buddy," he said to the cat.

"So?" Lindsay asked.

"All right. Let's do it."

"Are you sure?"

He laughed. "No, not at all. But if you're diving in headfirst, then I'll dive in with you. We'll do it together, yeah?"

Lindsay beamed at him. "Yes. Together. Let's do it."

EPILOGUE

THE CAT'S MEOW, THE FAMILY restaurant across the street from the Whitman Street Cat Café, had not been an instant success, but in the year since its opening, it had built a steadily growing, reliable base of regular customers.

A bead of sweat slid down the side of Lindsay's face as she ran a cloth along the edge of a plate to get rid of a wayward drop of sauce. One of the most popular dishes on the menu had been one of her inventions, a boneless fried chicken thigh that she served with creamy mashed potatoes and a bright, acidic arugula salad to cut the richness of the chicken. Brad had helped her with the chicken seasoning, and they'd made their own spice blend that they were thinking about bottling and selling at the restaurant.

Brad was right next to her, torching a banana crème brûlée. He shot her a quick glance as he shut off the torch and garnished the little ramekin of custard with a vanilla wafer and a sprig of mint. They put their plates up on the shelf above them and yelled "Order up!" simultaneously. Brad laughed.

Joey walked into the kitchen. "It's busy tonight! There are

six people waiting in the vestibule up front *and* all of the outdoor seating is taken."

"I know we're the only ones who care about the anniversary," said Brad, "but it's possible I told my friends to come tonight. They're at table eleven."

"Table seven is full of my friends," said Lindsay.

Joey laughed. "Well, you should go out there and tell them to hurry it up so that we can seat all the people waiting up front." He shook his head. "I'm only kind of kidding."

"I have a better idea," said Brad. "Come with me, Linds."

They walked out of the kitchen. Lindsay spotted her friends at table seven. Lauren and Caleb were there, with toddler Hannah in a high chair between them. Paige and Josh sat there, too; Paige had so much less stress in her life now that their wedding was behind them, and married life had seemed to be pretty good for them. Evan and Pablo were at that table, too, and *that* was a wild story, but Lindsay was just happy her friends were happy. It looked like they'd just been served dessert.

Aaron and Sam and their spouses were seated at table eleven, just as Brad had indicated. They looked to be about halfway through their entrées.

Brad snared a water glass from a busboy and banged a fork against it. All eyes in the restaurant turned toward them.

"Hi, everyone," Brad said.

Lindsay felt herself shrink in a little. She'd always been more comfortable behind the scenes. She didn't like that Brad was about to make a spectacle. But she figured if he just wanted to make a speech about how grateful he was that they'd made this restaurant last a whole year, she'd let him. They clearly looked like chefs now in their white coats with the Cat's Meow logo on them, so she figured everyone would know who they were.

The dining room was indeed packed. Lindsay craned her neck and saw a group of people waiting near the host stand. She'd never anticipated this kind of success, but apparently a creative restaurant welcome to families was exactly what the neighborhood needed.

"My name is Brad Marks, and I'm the executive pastry chef here. This here is Lindsay Somers. She's the executive chef. The two of us are mostly responsible for the meal you have before you. And tonight marks the one-year anniversary of our grand opening, so we wanted to thank you for dining with us tonight."

There was a smattering of applause, although some of the strangers probably thought this speechifying was a little weird.

But then Brad turned to Lindsay.

"As some of you know, Lindsay is my partner in both food and life, and I thought to use the occasion of the one-year anniversary of our running this place to ask an important question."

Lindsay realized what was happening with a start. She stared at Brad in disbelief as he reached into the pocket of his white chef's coat and started to lower himself into a kneel.

This was not happening. Was this really happening?

At her feet, Brad opened a ring box, revealing a perfect gold circle with a huge diamond.

"Lindsay Somers, will you marry me?"

Lindsay didn't want to cry in front of this big crowd, but she felt tears prick at her eyes anyway. Because of course she would marry him. She loved him. In the year that they had been working and cooking and living together, she'd grown to love him more each day.

"Yes," she said, though it came out sounding choked. So she cleared her throat and said, "Yes!" more forcefully.

Brad was on his feet and holding her in his arms before she knew what was happening. She laughed, caught up in his enthusiasm. Then he slipped the ring on her finger and held her hand in the air.

"In case you didn't hear that, she said yes!"

Everyone in the room applauded enthusiastically that time. Maybe people didn't care that a neighborhood restaurant had been open a year, but everyone was a sucker for a public marriage proposal.

Brad kissed Lindsay soundly and then turned back to the dining room. "All right, everyone. Thank you for indulging me. We gotta get back to the kitchen, and you deserve to finish your meal in peace. Also, if you're our friends, eat up and get out of here, because we've got people waiting to get in."

Lindsay's friends at least laughed at that.

When they were back in the kitchen a few minutes later, Lindsay kissed Brad and said, "I can't believe you did that."

"This is an important night for us professionally. I liked the symbolism of it."

Lindsay couldn't get over it. She admired the ring on her finger and thought about what a dream this was. All of it was a dream she never wanted to wake up from.

"Well," she said, shoving her hand in her pocket. "Tickets piled up while you pulled that stunt. Time to get back to work."

Brad grinned.

Acknowledgments

First and foremost, I want to thank my Writing Gals—Tere, Libby, Rayna, and Sabrina—for making me laugh and keeping me sane for the last two years.

Thanks to the Brooklyn Cat Café for being a source of inspiration and for all the amazing work rescuing and finding homes for cats.

She can't read this, but thanks to my cat, Sadie, for being such a big weirdo.

Thanks to my editor, Christa Désir, for helping to whip this book into shape.

Thanks to everyone who sent me photos of their pets after the first book came out. I love them all.

I wrote the book in lockdown, and it was a relief, in a way, to remember a magical New York where one could just go to restaurants and cafés without worrying about catching a virus. I hope we get there again soon. In the meantime, toss a few dollars to the animal rescue in your area, because there are a lot of animals who need good homes, and good people who need resources to take care of them.

About the Author

Kate McMurray writes smart, savvy romantic fiction. She likes creating stories that are brainy, funny, and of course sexy, with regular-guy characters and urban sensibilities. She advocates for romance stories by and for everyone. When she's not writing, Kate edits textbooks, watches baseball, plays violin, crafts things out of yarn, and wears a lot of cute dresses. Kate's gay romances have won or finaled several times in the Rainbow Awards for LGBT fiction and nonfiction. She also served in the leadership of Romance Writers of America. Kate lives in Brooklyn, NY, with two cats and too many books.

Website: katemcmurray.com
Facebook: facebook.com/katemcmurraywriter
Twitter: @katemcmwriter
Pinterest: pinterest.com/katem1738
Instagram: @katemcmurraygram